Stained glass
Monsters

by Andrea K Höst

Stained Glass Monsters
© 2011 Andrea K Höst. All rights reserved.
ISBN: 978-0-9808789-6-7
EBook ISBN: 978-0-9808789-7-4
www.andreakhost.com
Cover art by Julie Dillon

ONE

S hhooTHuMP!

The whole of the small shed which was Kendall Stockton's home shuddered, sending specks of grit pattering into her cropped blonde curls and sliding down the newssheet she held. The strange sound was gone as soon as she'd registered it, leaving all the geese and ducks and chickens which roamed the Back Green squawking their heads off.

Not able to guess what was happening, Kendall dashed outside. Nothing odd in the garden or around the blackened remains of Gran's house, so she ran round the other side of her shed, and stopped to stare. There was someone lying in the middle of the Green.

It was still well before evening, and the Green fell inside the village's circle, so Kendall felt safe taking a few halting steps closer. Lying there unmoving was a woman in a white dress, her arms stretched to either side, and her long pale hair fanned out around her.

"Are – are you hurt?"

There was no reply, only the retreating protest of fowl, and a shout from the Lippon house. Kendall hadn't been the only one in Falk to hear and feel...whatever had happened. Wanting to see more before the entire Lippon clan arrived, Kendall crossed to within a few feet of the strange figure.

The woman didn't move at all, just lay there in the grass. She was beautiful. Her long hair curled from a wide forehead, around her pointed face and all the way out to the very tips of her fingers. That hair wasn't much darker than her dress, and her skin was whiter than seemed possible. Though her eyes were shut, and Kendall could see no sign of movement, the woman didn't look dead. Her chin was up, and her head didn't sag to either side. Even her feet were neatly together.

"It's a lady!" The first of the Lippons had arrived. Fearless Jessamy, skidding to a halt just beside Kendall. "Ever so fine!"

True. The long, white dress shimmered in the sunlight, and the stitching was better than any fancywork Kendall had ever seen. Unlike Kendall, Jessamy didn't shy off taking the last few steps to the woman's side, but gasped and fell back, sitting down in a heap.

"What happened, Jessa?" asked Harry, the oldest of the Lippon boys, panting up at the head of the second wave of tow-headed Lippons.

"The – the air got heavy," Jessamy replied, sounding confused but not hurt.

"Heavy? What do you mean?" Harry moved beside his sister, and held forward a cautious hand. This didn't make him fall over, but Kendall saw sudden surprise on his face, and his hand trembled.

All the younger Lippons were crowding up now, fanning out in a circle behind Jessamy, while others from the village were appearing at the edges of the Green. Miller Best had brought his new musket, but lowered it after seeing the woman.

"Isn't she pretty?"

"Look at that dress!"

"Is she dead?"

"Where–?"

"How–?"

"Who–?"

As the crowd and the questions grew, Kendall edged around to one side, and held her hand toward the woman until she felt it go strange and heavy. It was possible to keep it there, but it was like holding a full bucket out at arm's-length. No wonder Jessamy had fallen, running right into this. Kendall's nose itched, and she backed away.

Then Mayor Dorstan arrived from the bakery, his arms still streaked with flour, though he'd left his apron behind.

"Stand back, the lot of you," he ordered impatiently. "Give the woman some air." He started to kneel beside the stranger, then grunted with sudden effort. The mayor was a big man, all muscle except in the gut, and they could see the struggle it was for him not to fall. But Mayor Dorstan was stubborn, too, and he continued slowly down on one knee and reached out to touch the woman's hand.

"My Lady?" he said. "Can you hear me?"

No response.

"She's warm." His fingers circled her wrist as if to lift it, but the only thing that happened was the muscles in his arms and shoulders stood out, and his face went slowly purple.

"What in Fel's name is this?" Mayor Dorstan muttered, then gave up and pushed himself to his feet, staggering away. Sweat dripped from his face, and he took quite a time to get his breath. The woman just lay there while more and more villagers gathered, and stared, and wondered.

"Did anyone see her arrive?" Mayor Dorstan asked finally, still huffing a little.

"No-one's come in since Cooper Robbins," said Kalan Huxtal. "I would have seen aught else. Sure as shine would have seen this'un."

"If you'd been using your eyes, maybe," Mayor Dorstan growled, glaring about him. He didn't like magic, wasn't even glad when the Circle-Turners arrived to make their rounds, and hated more anything that didn't make sense. "Someone must have seen her."

It was hard to imagine any lady, dressed beacon-white and with all that hair, getting even a step into Falk without half the village spotting her. But no-one had. She was just there, unmoving, and immovable.

CRSO

A morning in the sitting room had sent Rennyn Claire's eyes blurry. She'd been conscientiously transcribing one of the older books into neater, less faded script, adding commentary as she went. Surely she could allow herself an afternoon's work on the much-neglected garden until the world became less fogged.

She was passing by the Map Room when a muted THuNK froze her in place. Not quite believing, Rennyn stared through the doorway at the model of Tyrland. For the whole of her twenty-five years, and long before, a black spindle had been suspended above the map, swaying at the end of a single hair fixed to the ceiling. Now it was buried an inch deep in a flat patch near the city of Sark.

The Verisian clock's ticking caught her attention, as if it had deliberately grown louder to remind her that time was marching on.

"So." Rennyn couldn't think of anything less feeble to say, and went upstairs to pack. Sark was a day, a day and a half's ride away. Cuddy wouldn't appreciate the pace, and would make her regret not keeping the bay properly exercised, but it was better to ride than attract attention travelling more quickly.

"Ren! Ren!" Her brother came tearing up the stairs, only to notice her travelling gear. "Oh, you've seen."

She nodded, keeping herself cool for his sake. Sebastian was just sixteen, and most-ways sensible, but he fretted. "Can you start on the calculations while I'm gone, Seb?"

He tugged at his hair impatiently, eyes bright in his thin, clever face. "Yes. Yes, of course. You will – I'll have them done before you get back. Three days, right?"

"Thereabouts. Perhaps a little more, depending on what I find."

"Ren." He was thinking ahead now, concern edging through the excitement.

"This is the easy part, Seb," she said, touching his arm.

"Just – remember Great Grandfather."

That made her smile. "As if either of us ever forget."

After rechecking the location on the map, she paused in the hall and carefully tugged a comb through her hair, handing it to Seb when she was done. Turning her attention to arranging her hat, she frowned at the sight she presented. Cold determination had set her features into lines she barely recognised.

With some effort, she wiped any trace of her thoughts from her face, became the picture of a young countrywoman out for an afternoon's ride. All their lives, she and Seb had been preparing for that spindle to drop. She refused to falter at the first hurdle.

TWO

The village was called Falk, and lay just south of one of Tyrland's major cities, Sark. Rennyn was fairly certain Cuddy would never forgive her for riding till the very edge of night, then rising so early the next morning, but there was a time limit to what she had to do, and she needed to do it without being observed.

Somehow. Falk swarmed, as overrun as a harvest fair, and Rennyn shook her head at the mass of people buying, selling and gawping. It had been little more than a day: how had they assembled so quickly?

Attention was centred around a grassy area behind the main body of houses. It had been roped off, and was barely visible through the stalls and crowds lined up to pay for entry. This was not how Rennyn had pictured this day, but she decided that it was after all an advantage. Among so many, she was wholly unremarkable. It should be possible to hide her actions in plain sight.

Paying a coin, she left Cuddy to be watered and rubbed down while she waited in line. It was hot, a little past midday, and the press of folk made it seem hotter still. Rennyn adjusted her hat and gazed about at all the people come to see something strange and intriguing. Children who chattered or squabbled. Merchants bargaining over vegetables. Young couples, standing close together. A hired guard carefully cleaning his musket. She felt like she was on the other side of a pane of glass, as if she were in the world beside this one, and none of these people could see her.

Sternly, Rennyn forced herself to smile and look excited. Remember Great Grandfather, Seb had said. Remember the threat of violent death.

The people of Falk were charging a petthine to view their newly acquired curiosity, controlling the influx by only allowing groups of ten through at a time. Rennyn might have been annoyed by their greed if she did not have a reasonable idea of what the area would look like in a week's time. They would need more money than this soon enough, so she paid over her petthine ungrudgingly, and gazed across a sward of daisy-studded grass to the centre of her existence.

"So lovely," murmured one of the women in the new group of sightseers.

It was true. The figure on the ground was much younger than Rennyn had pictured, but a semblance of youth was common where mages and magic were concerned. The face reminded her faintly of a cat, with those very curved lips and large, wide-set eyes. A white cat, sleek and pleased with itself, somehow imperious lying in that fan of carefully arranged hair. Rennyn had known about the white hair, but was still puzzled by it. Had the bleaching occurred during the casting, or was it some by-product of the woman's long sojourn in the Eferum?

And so? Nearly sixty years of planning had led to this day. Niggling questions were no more useful than thinking too much about whether it was fear or anger knotting her stomach.

Her fellow sightseers were holding their hands into the circle of distortion, marvelling at the sudden weight. Rennyn tried it herself, recognising the sensation from her own transitions, though there was no true comparison. She glanced around at the crowds, the village beyond, relieved that there was sufficient space left empty, since there was no way to stop what would happen that night. What would she have done if the manifestation had been among the buildings? But – she forced herself to ignore all but the task. She had to focus on doing what she must.

Ignoring the others, she moved within reach of the woman's left hand. The smallest finger was missing its tip, severed cleanly at the upper joint, the injury long ago healed. Rennyn frowned at this tiny, vital thing, but didn't hesitate longer, curling her own finger to press against a pin threaded through her sleeve.

Dropping down to her heels, she held her hand into the circle again and allowed a bead of red to fall to that blunted tip. Then she waited, trembling with an effort of will. Blood to blood. They would call to each other. Almost anything else could not truly touch her, would be slowly shifted by the distortion to the edge of the circle. But – yes. This bright mote did not. With a sluggish shimmer it sank beneath flesh and was gone. Blood to blood.

Relieved beyond words, Rennyn stood away from the distortion, catching her breath. Done. Done without notice.

Businesslike, she moved to stand near the woman's head, and reached into the pocket of her skirt to close her hand around cold crystal. Her left hand she held against her chest, as if still catching her breath, pressing the familiar shape of her own focus against bare skin. A tingle ran over her, and all the hair on her arms and neck stood up.

She could taste it, could almost see the forces which warped the air in front of her, through the figure on the ground to a vast space beyond. She had to lock her knees or fall, for the weight of the distortion swayed briefly to envelop her, to press the stone in her pocket hard into the flesh of the hand which circled it. Her vision blurred, and for the barest moment most of her was standing in a dark place outside the world, with a sketch of a village in the distance and a blaze of white in the shape of a woman at her feet.

An eye-blink was all that was needed. Rennyn let go of both stones with a sigh, and looked away as if bored with Falk's new curiosity. Done. Done and done. It was time to head home.

"My eyes have come over queer, Danel," complained the man nearest her. "Let's have lunch now."

A good plan. But Rennyn paused, surveying the patch of green around her one last time. A fortunate location, not in the heart of the village. Hedge to the south, buildings to the north, a tree shading a puddle-pond far to the east. Closest were the back gardens of a number of houses slicing southwest, some with fences, some without. A girl had gone into a small shed at the near corner of one of the lots. Beyond, where the house should be, was a collapsed tangle of charred timber, the remains of an old fire surrounded by an extensive and well-tended vegetable garden.

Chewing her lip, Rennyn left the circle and counted steps to the rear wall of the shed. Too close.

She could hear movement inside, and circled the rough building to look in the open door. A narrow bed, a shelf, a brazier, pots, pans, clothing. It was surprisingly neat and clean, and barely large enough to accommodate the wary girl who had turned to look up at her. A delicate and pretty child of fourteen or so: blonde hair raggedly cropped to short curls, a sharp little chin and very blue eyes. The straight, dark brows lowering above them declared their determined rejection.

"Can I help you?" the girl asked, careful politeness underlain with hostility.

"I – was told you're available to run errands," Rennyn said, making some quick guesses. The child obviously lived here, and could probably use the coin.

"Sometimes," the girl said. She made a general gesture toward the busy crowds. "Not right now."

"Ah. Do you, then, know of anyone who would be available? It's important to me – I can pay a sennith for half a day's work."

That shifted her, rapid calculation flickering through blue eyes. However much money the village might be making at the moment, little of it would trickle down to the children set to handing out tickets or playing fetch and carry.

"What's it involve?"

Good question. "I was to meet a friend in...Morebly." Rennyn lowered her eyes demurely. "My father does not approve, and it has taken much to arrange. But my family's plans have changed, and, well – I must send word to him. The Gold Knight Hostelry. It just requires a note to be delivered before sunset, so he will not worry."

"Morebly," the girl said slowly. Two hours' walk away – easily done before dark, but not to return.

"I will add five petthine for your night's accommodation. Will you do it?"

"I – yes. All right."

Rennyn smiled, projecting relief. "Thank you. It's so important that he know where I've gone. You need only leave the note with the hosteller: he will ask if he has received any messages when he arrives. A moment."

She turned away, groping in the purse dangling from her wrist. There was a crumpled scrap of paper, fortunately. She had nothing prepared, but with her back turned she willed into existence a line of script, something suitably maudlin. It was even an advantage that the conjuring would fade in a day or two.

"My family simply won't understand," she added, handing over paper and coin. "You are doing me a great service."

"It's no problem, Miss," the girl replied, with just a hint of underlying scorn. Then she looked up, sniffing, frowning at the blameless blue sky.

Rennyn paused. "Tell me," she said, "Were you here when this...apparition arrived?"

"At this very spot," the girl replied readily, probably having fielded such questions all day.

"What was the weather like?"

"The weather? It wasn't raining, if that's what you mean. Smelled like it was going to storm, but it was clear like it is now." The girl sniffed again, looking puzzled.

Rennyn stole a hurried glance back toward the crowd. "Ah – I think that's my sister calling me. Thank you again."

"Good luck to you, Miss," the girl said, tucking the note away inside her skirt pocket.

Rennyn nodded, and took herself off. An unnecessary thing, but the idea of the girl sleeping the night in that shed would have haunted her. Mage-blood, too. It would have been a waste.

THREE

Romantic ninnies were profitable. A whole sennith, just for a couple of hours' walk. Even with the crowds come for the White Lady, Kendall wouldn't earn a quarter that in a week, which made it worth risking leaving her garden unguarded. And the hosteller hadn't charged her nearly five petthine to spend the night, either.

The only bad thing about the sudden trip to Morebly had been the arrival of a coach complete with outriders, which had passed Kendall just as she joined the drift of gawkers heading out of Falk. It had taken all her will to press on without waiting to see the new arrivals, or at least try and get a better look at the crest embossed on the door. But interesting strangers weren't worth the chance of not making Morebly before the sun set, and being outside a circle after dark.

She'd set out as early as she dared on the return trip, hoping the coach would still be around, but of course the sun was well up before the familiar roofs of home came into view. The crowds were already building, even so early. Kendall was just thinking about how the Mayor had said the White Lady was the best thing to happen to Falk when she realised something was wrong.

No chatter. Instead a low murmur tinged with shock, with the air of carnival totally gone. People weren't queued at the stalls, or waiting in line to enter the Green. They were crowded five-deep around the rope circle, staring at something to their right.

Wriggling through, Kendall caught her breath. The Back Green had sunk! And the trees on the far side had been knocked down. The White Lady was still there, not looking at all different except for being about a foot lower than she'd been yesterday. Kendall could see a line marking the circle where the heaviness above her had ended. But now – Kendall copied the person next to her and held out a hand. The weird force which pinned the White Lady to the Green had moved all the way out...here.

Kendall finally looked right, to the line of flattened plants, smashed fences, and splintered wood.

"No–!"

Forcing her way wildly through the crowd, she ran past strangers standing in familiar yards, and slammed straight into that invisible weight. She fell forward and lay there, a crushed, panting bug, staring at the trampled gardens, and flattened remains of a small garden shed which was everything she had in this world.

"Kendall!"

Harry Lippon. He pulled her backward out of heaviness and clutched at her, face all eyes. "You weren't – you're – you're... Where have you *been*, Kendall?"

But Kendall had no time for Harry Lippon. Jerking away, she surveyed the remains of her home. It was only a few feet in, the wreckage fanned out in a spray toward the outside of the circle. There were people standing in her gardens, but she didn't see that she'd be able to get them out.

"I've got to get my stuff," she said, determinedly.

"Stubborn brat," said a hoarse voice. Ma Lippon, arms folded across her massive chest. "Should have known you'd turn up in one piece."

Kendall lifted her chin mutinously. She wasn't going to let Ma Lippon get her claws in her, just because – just because...

"Ay-eh, and here I was thinking I'd never enjoy that black glare again." Ma Lippon reached out and tousled Kendall's hair in the way Kendall particularly hated. As if she was some toothless babe, some puppy too stupid to take care of itself.

"When did it happen?" Kendall asked, stepping out of reach.

"Just on dawn. Where were you, girl? One of the Sentene went in and checked for your body, and no-one knew what to make of it when he couldn't find you. Thought you'd been swallowed up by the Devourer himself."

"Morebly. Just a delivery." Kendall shrugged irritably, trying to think what she could do now. Get her stuff, yes, but what then? She wouldn't let Ma Lippon take her over, like she'd been itching to do these past two years. She– "Did you say Sentene?"

"Three of them," Harry said, with a glance at the crowd gathering around his mother. "They arrived yesterday afternoon."

That must have been who was in the coach. Sentene were monster hunters, special soldiers whose job it was to get rid of the nastiest of the Night Roamers. They were said to be all mages or sword-masters or both, and for three of them to come see the White Lady meant she must be particularly – what? A monster?

Kendall glared at the centre of the Green. Nothing good, anyway. Not from where Kendall was standing. Snorting, she went as close as she could to the remains of her shed. Her savings were hidden by the remains of Gran's house, but she wanted her clothes, and the few precious things she'd salvaged from the fire.

It wasn't an easy thing. Even taking one step into the heaviness was enough to put Kendall on her knees, and holding out a rake to try and claw some of the debris out of the circle was even harder. But she found herself with many helpers, and it turned into a competition between the strongest men of the village and the visitors to see who could cross a few feet of wood-spattered grass and pick up a piece of clothing. Showing off, but she had to be glad of them.

Soon enough she had a battered collection, and retreated away from the crowds to the back wall of Gran's ruined house to sort out what was still of any use. She set herself right next to a certain brick and, double-checking that no-one was near, dug in the dirt beneath until she found a small tin. Normally she wouldn't risk carrying her savings about, but things were too strange right now, so she quickly stuffed the tin into her big carry-bag.

Kendall had just picked up the tattered remains of her favourite shirt when a step right behind her made her start. Someone had been watching–? She turned hurriedly and found herself eye-to-eye with the hem of a long black coat. Staring upwards, her eyes widened as she found curling lines of red and gold tracing their way up to the instantly recognisable image of a golden bird, small and elegant, head looking back over its shoulder at the great flaming tail pouring down the coat's front. The Phoenix of the Montjustes, the symbol only worn by the Queens' men.

There wasn't much else she could see. The coat was all-enveloping, covering even the hands, with an outsized round collar so high and wide Kendall couldn't even glimpse the face from this angle. It was like the coat itself had walked up behind her.

"Do you have time for a few words?"

The voice was a woman's, reassuringly ordinary, and Kendall nodded, feeling a little less like she was about to be turned into a frog or something. When the Sentene turned and walked away it took her a moment to realise she was expected to follow. Pausing to grab up her bag left Kendall far enough behind so that she could see the top of the woman's head. Carroty-red hair, not at all the proper colour for a soldier who hunted Night Roamers.

Conscious of the interest of the crowds, Kendall trailed the Sentene to Micajah's Hostelry. The coach she'd seen the previous evening was sitting out front, and one of the outriders, dressed in dark brown and burnt orange, stood by the door so that everyone would know who was inside.

The Hostelry had been full to overflowing the previous day, but it seemed the Sentene had turned everyone out. Kendall followed the woman through the silent entry-hall into the taproom to the right, eyes widening in awed interest. All the tables had been drawn back to the walls and a woman in a dark travelling dress was kneeling in the middle of a complex circle of weird writing chalked on the well-swept floor. Magic. The very idea made Kendall's nose itch.

"Here's your stray, Captain," said the Sentene woman, as Kendall belatedly noticed there was a third person in the room, standing near the far door. A man this time, lost in the gloom so that only the Phoenix was properly visible.

"Put her in the corner for now," the man said, and Kendall shivered. His voice was strange, whispery and thinned out. Definitely creepy.

What did they mean by 'your stray'? What had she done that Sentene wanted to talk to her about anyway? But still, this was ten times more interesting than anything she'd read in the newssheets, so Kendall obediently took herself to a chair in the corner and joined the other two in watching the woman kneeling in the circle.

She looked totally out of place on Micajah's floor. Her dress wasn't fancy but it was quality, and her iron-shot black hair was braided up in a way that Kendall couldn't imagine spending the time over. She wasn't doing anything much, just kneeling there with her eyes closed and her hands held loosely at her sides. But the air felt thick, and made Kendall want to sneeze. It was a disappointment when, after a long while where exactly nothing happened, the woman just opened her eyes and let out her breath.

"Any result, M'Lady?" asked the female Sentene.

"There's no sign of an origin point in the near area." The older woman rose stiffly. "Nor does this show any sign of waning."

"Not what you expected?"

"Far from it. The White Ladies are rare, but a known phenomenon, occurring only once or twice a century. They invariably vanish within a day or two of their manifestation. Nowhere in my records is there an instance of one persisting so long, or producing an Efera expansion. This is something new. It is –" She paused. "It may be very serious. I will attempt another divination shortly."

Turning, she noticed Kendall. "What is this?"

"The missing resident of that shed. Captain Faille wanted to interview her."

"Oh?" There was tolerant amusement in the word. "This is your great disbelief in coincidence at work again, Faille?"

"It is too convenient," the male Sentene said, leaving his corner. "You were in the next town?"

Kendall was disappointed. This was all they wanted with her? "It was just a delivery, a note," she explained. "The Hosteller will vouch for me."

"I don't doubt that." He was a tall man, and she saw that his hair was a bleached grey, though his face – the top half of it at least – didn't look so very old. His eyes were faded grey too, and uncomfortably direct. "Who sent you?"

"One of the gawkers come to see the White Lady. It was just some silly woman sending word to her boyfriend," Kendall explained. "Father didn't approve, that kind of thing. Nothing strange."

"She couldn't use the post?" the female Sentene asked, taking a sceptical interest.

"It was urgent." Kendall tried to picture the woman being involved in some kind of plot. "Supposed to meet him that night, but her father was dragging her off to Sark instead. Easiest sennith I've ever made, and she paid for the night's lodging." Which was...convenient? That woman had saved her life, whether or not she'd meant to.

"Did she speak of the White Lady at all?"

"No. Asked me what the weather was like, when the White Lady first arrived, but didn't seem to care much. Called her 'this apparition', if that helps."

"The weather?" The older woman leaned forward, studying Kendall narrowly. "And what was the weather like, when she arrived? You would have been close."

"Exactly like it is today," Kendall said. "Sunny and cloudless."

"And what did it smell like?"

Perplexed by this interest in minor details, Kendall shrugged. "It did smell like it was going to storm, but nothing came of it."

"Ha." The woman smiled with strange approval at the one called Captain Faille. "Your instinct, as ever. I suppose, girl, that it smells like it's going to storm now, as well?"

"A bit, I guess." Kendall sniffed. "It's not the same."

"It wouldn't be. And did it smell like it was going to storm when you were speaking to this woman?"

"...yes."

"Ha."

"What did the note say?" Captain Faille asked.

Kendall, about to deny reading it, faltered under the man's steady gaze. She had, of course. It hadn't been sealed.

"It was addressed to Joshua Goodwin," she said slowly. "I'm sorry. Papa insists we go directly to Sark. He suspects, I am sure. I have not changed my mind. Please – come for me.'" If there was some hidden meaning in that, Kendall couldn't guess it.

"Send Ricaden to see if anyone collected it," Captain Faille told the other Sentene.

"And bring it back," added the older woman. "We may be able to use it as a trace."

"Describe her," Captain Faille commanded.

More interested in why the weather was so important, Kendall thought back to that brief encounter. "She was, um, about as tall as this lady here," she said, indicating the older woman. Higher than average. "Her hair was black, and long, mostly straight, with just a bit of a curl at the very end. Worn loose at the back, but the sides were caught up. She was over twenty, I guess, but not thirty yet. Dark eyes, slim, pretty but not really beautiful. Sounded like she came from the north, not Sark. She wore a hat with a couple of black ribbons trailing off the back. Good clothes, not cheap but not showy. Fitted jacket, split skirt with riding breeches beneath. Old boots, nice ones. No jewellery. Clean hands."

"Well observed," said the lady, sounding approving. "I needn't ask if you would recognise her again."

Kendall nodded, then asked cautiously: "Why does it matter if it was going to storm?"

"It mattered because that scent, scents like lightning, or dust driven by oncoming rain, that is given off by raw Efera, by unshaped power or loosely worked magic. This person was a mage, and she had just been casting. I imagine you looked at the sky, reacted to the scent. She saw that, and asked if you had smelled anything when the White Lady arrived."

"You can smell magic?" Kendall asked, astonished.

"*You* can smell magic," the lady replied, with gentle emphasis, then turned away as the other Sentene returned. "Lieutenant, this girl needs some basic instruction in magecraft. We will take her with us."

"Yes, M'Lady," said the Sentene, as if this was the most natural thing in the world. "Are we to leave soon?"

"That will depend on the result of my next divination," the woman replied. "I fear we may have little choice on the matter."

The Lieutenant bowed, then came sit beside Kendall.

"So what's your name?" she asked, unfastening the collar of her coat so that it flopped down. She had a round face, spattered with orange freckles to match her tightly-braided hair. Not scary at all.

"Kendall Stockton."

"I'm Jolien Danress. That's the Grand Magister, Lady Weston, who has charge of the Sentene. And my Captain, Illidian Faille."

Kendall supposed her eyes had gone very round. The Grand Magister, here in Falk. It hardly seemed possible. She stared at the woman settling back onto the floor of Micajah's taproom. "Why–?" She paused, wondering what to say.

"Why are we here, or why are we taking you with us?" The corners of Lieutenant Danress' light blue eyes crinkled with sympathy. "You because you're our only link to a woman we've reason to trace. You're the only one who can positively identify her. And, well, you're a homeless orphan able to sense magic, and Lady Weston would no more leave a potential mage undeveloped than pass up a chance to investigate interesting magical phenomena, which is the reason we came here. We weren't expecting this morning's drama." She frowned, then shrugged. "It could still come to nothing."

"I'm a mage?"

"You could become one. Not such a bad thing to be. I've always liked it, anyway, and I would have killed to have Lady Weston taking an interest in me when I started out."

Taking her over. Kendall stared from Lieutenant Danress' face to the woman kneeling on the floor. Taking her over, just like Ma Lippon had been itching to do for years. And a damn sight harder to escape from.

Could she say no, and leave? And did she want to? Magister Kendall Stockton. That sounded strange, unlikely. But it meant money, the one thing that had been so central since the fire had taken Gran away. Mages were important, even shoddy ones, so long as they could manage a shield circle. Every farmhouse, every village and town, they all needed circles to keep Night Roamers like Life Stealers out. If she could just learn to do that, she'd be set.

Anyway, she needed somewhere to go, now that the shed had been destroyed. She'd probably get to see the capital. And Lady Weston was surely a busy person, who'd get caught up in other matters once this thing with the mystery woman was cleared up. Nor could she make Kendall stay, or try to hold some kind of debt over her. Kendall was the one who decided what happened to Kendall. No-one else.

She'd just settled this to her satisfaction when she noticed that Lady Weston had opened her eyes again. Her mouth, usually full and generous, was set in a thin line.

"Faille," she said, her voice lacking any note of humour. "Send to Sark for troops. We need to evacuate this village."

Even the grim Captain straightened in surprise at that. "M'Lady—?"

"It's worse than I thought. Unless I'm sorely mistaken, some fool is trying to repeat the madness of Queen Solace."

"What?" Lieutenant Danress shot to her feet, face incredulous. "The Black Queen's Summoning? It's not possible."

"So we thought." Lady Weston brushed dust from the skirts of her dress. "All the same, I cannot see any other explanation. The apparition out there is the first expression of a Grand Summoning, and this village will shortly be destroyed."

FOUR

R ennyn found Sebastian sleeping on the window-seat in the Map Room. There were black circles under his eyes, ink smudges on face and fingers, and his hair stood out in spikes where he'd pulled on it. She touched his forehead, which was damp but not feverish, then stroked his cheek gently.

"You didn't have to do them all," she murmured. He'd make himself sick, if she didn't watch him. "You're just like I was, little brother. And Father not here to teach you when to stop to take a breath." She'd been Seb's only family for five years now, and found it hard to be glad he was as consumed by their task as she'd ever been.

Turning to the map of Tyrland, she studied the scattering of thumbtacks Seb had added, each carefully numbered and bound to the spindle which marked Falk by a long strand of black hair. Most of them were close to the capital, as expected, but she had to shake her head at the location of the tack painted with a minute white '1'.

"Almost all the way back along the road just travelled," she murmured. "I think I'll take a carriage this time." She'd more than enough chafing from the first trip.

Seb had chalked rows of sigils on the wall, the core structure of the spell they'd been training all their life to cast, unchanged since their Great Grandmother had devised it. Rennyn reviewed the transcription for accuracy, then left to wander about Little Mutching cancelling milk and meat deliveries, selling her horse, arranging for a carriage and a cart, for boxes, for people to lift them. She stopped for spiced tea at Miss Cavendish's shop and made sure the biggest gossips in the town heard all about how the two they knew as Taren and Severian Justane were off to stay with their Aunt Letitia in Braidford.

Only then did she return to check the map location calculations, which took her well into the afternoon. At least it was easier to confirm the math than it was to work it out in the first place. Seb woke while she was carefully dabbing every tack with a drop of her blood, and drawing her finger along each taut hair. She worked in reverse order, finishing with the spindle, then looked at her gloomily silent brother across the wide expanse of the map.

"Ready?"

He pulled a face. "As I'll ever be."

Rennyn smiled, and stood still as he pricked his own finger and pressed it between her brows. She didn't watch the sigils light with power, but instead closed her eyes and thought of a white-haired woman lying in grass. A beautiful face.

Around her the air grew heavy, and she lifted her eyelids enough to watch each thumbtack sink heavily into the map. The spindle followed suit, descending with a crushing weight improbable for such a small object, until the model of Tyrland buckled and cracked all around it.

One of the tacks competing for space in Asentyr began to glow, the light spreading through the fine black web to each of the surrounding points. In response, Rennyn's hair gently lifted away from her head, each strand surrounded by a blue-white nimbus. The ground seemed far away and uncertain, and she had to steady herself with the table edge and concentrate on breathing, proud of Seb because he was not looking at her, was glowering at the wall with a fixity of purpose, with the determination he needed to finish the casting cleanly.

Then it was over, the thumbtacks just bits of metal with a few melted wisps attached, the weight gone. The spindle had been driven so deeply into the map and the table beneath that only its tip remained visible. Seb dropped to the ground beside her, panting and white.

"Well done."

"Was it?" His eyes were dark. "Why was it leaking on to you?"

"I think that might be inevitable. To be a conduit for this thing, and expect no physical side-effect, is asking too much."

"But this is it in small scale, Ren. What happens to you when the whole weight of the Grand Summoning is behind it?"

Rennyn stood looking down at him, then reached out to haul him to his feet. "When that happens, side-effects will probably be the least of my worries." She switched determinedly to practicalities. It was so much simpler to just do the things they had to do. "Can you feel any residue?"

"N-no."

"Good. That's two steps taken. Let's go have something to eat and get started. We've a lot of packing to do. I've booked us on the mail carriage in the morning, and we need the luggage for the cart ready before then. Worry about that now."

⋘⋙

Falk was home to one hundred and thirty-seven people, too many fowl, dogs, goats, five horses, several cows and somewhere in the order of fifty dozen cats. A troop of militia from Sark had been given charge of removing everything that could possibly be moved and transporting it to neighbouring villages, or back to Sark. And that was only the beginning, for Lady Weston had spoken of evacuating other villages.

A lot of people simply didn't believe. Even the Troop Captain didn't act like he really believed it, though that hadn't stopped him from emptying Falk in less than a day. Only a few had resisted, most not willing to say boo to the Queen's troops. Some had refused to go further than the cordon which had been set up well beyond Falk's circle, even though the sun was setting and they'd be unprotected from Night Roamers. In such numbers they'd probably not be at risk unless they slept, but the ban against being outside a circle after dark was so strong that even the presence of two Sentene and the Grand Magister couldn't stop Kendall from watching the slowly bleaching horizon as much as the silent village.

She almost missed it, would have if she hadn't caught the scent of a storm and realised what it meant just in time to turn her eyes back.

ShhooTHuMP!

Falk exploded. Not in flames, but into splinters. The outer buildings were shredded by fragments of the houses that were closest to the White Lady, only a few remaining upright. Pieces of wood flew well beyond the village's circle, spearing into the ground after crossing more than half the distance to the cordon. The first wave of destruction passed in a moment, but among the buildings which hadn't been completely destroyed there followed a series of sliding crashes, as walls collapsed and settled.

"Stronger than the last," said Captain Faille, as if he watched homes being shattered every day.

"Yes." Lady Weston shaded her eyes to peer through the night, ignoring the cries of astonishment and dismay all around. "Danress, prepare the same divination at its edge please."

"Yes, M'Lady." Lieutenant Danress took two of the outriders and headed into the edges of Falk's ruin as both the Troop Captain and Mayor Dorstan approached the Grand Magister's carriage.

"Captain Vesan, I will perform some further divinations here before heading into Sark. One of the Queen's Hands will reach here from Asentyr by morning, and will take charge." Lady Weston nodded at the militia-man, then turned a softer look on Mayor Dorstan. "I'm sorry for your loss, Sir. I wish I had been able to prevent this."

Mayor Dorstan was a ghost of himself, hollow and without his usual force. He touched his hand to his forehead, and muttered something, then added: "We're all whole, M'Lady. That's as much as any man can hope for, when such a thing's visited on him. It will – you say it will keep expanding? Could you reckon how far? There's some who are fixing to set themselves up in Morebly, and I mislike uprooting them twice."

"The size will depend on the quality of the caster. The first Grand Summoning, that of Queen Solace, formed the basin of Lake Surclere. I would not depend on Morebly."

The Mayor took a step backward, then bowed and faded into the twilight. Kendall didn't know how big Lake Surclere was, but she did know that there used to be a town there, one which had had thousands of people living in it. And three hundred years ago the Black Queen had cast the Grand Summoning, trying to increase her power. The spell had let all kind of monsters loose on Tyrland and, the stories said, the town and all the countryside around it had been sucked down into a pit, into the Hells outside the world where the Life Stealers lived.

Examining this idea, Kendall followed Lady Weston and Captain Faille to the new edge of the heaviness, where Lieutenant Danress had cleared and compressed a section of dirt, and marked out a circle of magic writing among the ruins of Falk. It was easy to tell where the heaviness started, because that was where the ground began to slope downward. The gleaming white figure was now about three feet below them, in the centre of a rubble-strewn cone sunk into the earth.

"Guess we should have slit her throat while we had the chance," Kendall said to Lieutenant Danress, as Lady Weston once again began to cast. "Could we have stopped her from finishing her spell if we'd understood sooner? And why did she decide to do her spell in the middle of Falk instead of somewhere people didn't live?"

"It's a little complicated." Danress glanced at the shadowy stillness which was her senior officer, then moved a few feet away. "Before the expansion, Lady Weston thoroughly examined the White Lady and found little in the way of a physical element, for all she appears to be directly in front of us. That may be what the caster looks like, but she isn't really here. The apparition is a distortion out of the Eferum, and no weapon would have been able to even scratch her."

"She's in the Hells?"

"If you want to call it that. The proper name for the world surrounding this one is the Eferum. While Efera flows from there to here constantly, like water through a sieve, magi risk their lives to enter the Eferum to Summon their focus stones, to increase the amount of power they can call upon. It's only possible to stay there for a short time, and it's dangerous. Queen Solace – the Surcleres were pre-eminent experts on the Eferum, and the Queen discovered a way to prolong the amount of time she could endure in the Eferum, immensely increasing the strength of the focus stone she would be able to summon. But the Grand Summoning, as well as the obvious destruction, caused the barrier between the Eferum and this world to weaken, and there were a great many incursions.

Most natural breaches aren't open wide or long enough for many Eferum-Get – what you'd call Night Roamers – to get through, but the Grand Summoning created rifts of dangerous length."

"Night Roamers are going to come out of Falk?"

"No. This projection is something unique to the Grand Summoning, a physical manifestation of the spell, of the amount of power the caster is drawing to bear. What you can feel when you come into its range is the weight of the Efera itself. It is...the strength of it will dwarf all of Tyrland's mages, make us into ants. Whoever is casting this will be like a god to us if they complete the Summoning."

"How do we stop it then?" Kendall asked practically. "Prince Tiandel stopped Queen Solace didn't he?"

"Prince Tiandel knew the precise construction of the Grand Summoning, witnessed its casting, and had been entrusted with Queen Solace's younger focuses, which he used as a tool against her. He would not share the knowledge after; we don't even know precisely what he did to kill her beyond disrupting the Summoning with the focuses. Then – there was a great backlash against the Surclere line after Queen Solace's death, and Tiandel Montjuste-Surclere renounced claim to the throne and withdrew from society. Hero and villain. It was Tiandel who assisted her, Tiandel who helped prepare the spell, who had custody of her library, all her researches. There were frequent attacks against him, calls from the Court to have him brought to account, many stories that he intended to attempt the Grand Summoning himself. Yet it is believed that it was actually loyalists of the Black Queen who set fire to his home. The entire Montjuste-Surclere family were killed, and that library, all the primary records of the Black Queen's researches – gone."

"Oh." Kendall stared through the increasing gloom at the White Lady. "So what can we do? Just wait till whoever she is finishes and hope she's nice?"

"It may amount to that," Danress muttered. "Of course, there is this mess, and there will be the incursions to deal with. Beyond that – you realise how important it is to find that woman, don't you? She knew, before any of us, that the Distortion circle would expand, that this was a Grand Summoning. She must know the caster, probably knows the initiating point. If we're to do anything at all, we need to find that place, and be ready for the caster's return from the Eferum."

"I guess," Kendall said unenthusiastically. She hadn't been entirely convinced that silly woman was really involved at all until one of the Ferumguard – the Sentene's outriders – had returned from Morebly with a blank scrap of paper. Lady Weston said the writing must have been conjured, so it couldn't be used to trace her, even if she was close enough to trace. "I don't see how we're going to find her, though. She's long gone. Are you going to collect all the black-haired girls in Tyrland for me to look at?"

"Not that improbable an idea," Danress replied. "All the black-haired mages, at least. We will certainly be combing the Register for anyone who fits the description you gave."

"What about the White Lady? You saw her up close, didn't you? Lady Weston didn't recognise her?"

"No. And she's certainly distinctive. An outland mage, perhaps? It's more than confusing, because the White Lady sightings have been occurring for centuries. The most recent was in Loise, almost sixty years ago, but there was no expansion in any of the previous cases. It's a greatly confusing thing to discover this White Lady is related to the Grand Summoning – they've been occurring innocuously for so long that we have no explanation as yet."

Lieutenant Danress sighed, then moved back to watch Lady Weston doing nothing visible. It was almost full dark now, the moon not yet risen, and the night broken only by the lanterns held by the militia and Ferumguard. Kendall shook her head, tried not to think about Night Roamers, and went to sit in Lady Weston's carriage.

She didn't want any part of this, and maybe would have taken the chance of ditching the Sentene once they reached Sark if not for the memory of Ma Lippon's face as she herded her brood down the road toward Morebly. Lippons had been living in Falk since forever, just like the Stocktons. Ma Lippon might've been bossier than anyone could care for, so sure she knew what was right. But

Kendall would no more have seen her turned out of her home than she would have struck the sun from the sky. Ma Lippon belonged in Falk, and Falk wasn't there any more.

Kendall made a practice of looking after herself, of not poking her nose into other people's doings. This wasn't her business. Not her job to fix wrongs or try and protect kingdoms. Not her problem if the Lippons no longer had a home to go to.

But if she had the chance she'd point out the woman who knew about the Grand Summoning, all the same.

FIVE

There was something more than strange about Captain Faille. Kendall hadn't noticed anything except his weird voice during the fuss and turmoil of evacuating Falk, but this morning in Sark she'd seen that his hair was blond not grey; a pale, clear yellow like wine. Or so she'd thought, but inside the carriage it had looked grey again, transparent and faded. It was very fine, reminding Kendall a little of feathers: short, soft and following the shape of his skull. When they had the door closed and no handy magelight uncovered so that it was all gloom inside, it had been hard to see him at all. Unlike Danress with her bright hair, he faded most completely into his corner, till only the Montjuste Phoenix reminded Kendall anyone was there at all.

Kendall had been debating whether it was only imagination when one of the Ferumguard knocked on the outside of the carriage, and the driver drew them up. Both Sentene got out to see what was going on, and Captain Faille paused a moment just outside the door to say something to Lady Weston. Kendall could only stare, for his hair was most definitely blond now, sunshine gold, and his eyes were yellow disks, the pupil drowned. Lit from within, like there was a candle inside him.

That certainly wasn't imagination, though Kendall rubbed at her own eyes as if that would change what she'd seen. She glanced surreptitiously at the Grand Magister, who had been busy making notes in a journal, but must surely have seen it as well.

"Lady Weston?"

"Yes, child?"

"Why does Captain Faille keep changing colours?"

The Grand Magister hesitated, though she didn't seem surprised. "Faille has, quite a number of the Sentene have non-human ancestry. Have you heard of the Kellian?"

The word was vaguely familiar. "Wasn't that the name of the Black Queen's bodyguards?"

"Just so. They were a magical construct, a variation of a flesh golem. Their descendents are rather more human, but retain many of the properties of the Kellian. It makes them ideal for dealing with strays from the Eferum, for those creatures are difficult to find or combat without the ability to sense Efera in some form. Others among the Sentene are descended from higher Eferum-Get."

Kendall was incredulous. "Stalkers can have children? With people?"

"Not those particularly. Most Eferum-Get have little intelligence, and the Life Stealers don't even have any substance. Stalkers are monstrous animals. But occasionally something different emerges into our world. These are not unlike humans. Travellers, they're known as. They appear in our world for only a few days, and have a tendency to take an interest in, ah, willing females. Danress is a grandchild of one such as this."

"Really?" This was the last thing Kendall would have expected of the freckled and carrot-topped Danress.

Lady Weston laughed at her. "Truly. Indeed, some argue that all with mage talent could unearth Eferum-Get in their family tree, if only they looked back far enough. For Danress, it is merely fewer generations."

The carriage door opened again, and Lieutenant Danress climbed in, looking entirely human even in her impressive uniform. Captain Faille remained standing outside, his eyes small suns.

"A messenger sent to intercept us, M'Lady. There's a sighting outside a town east of here. At least two Escaton-types."

"We'll divert," Lady Weston said immediately.

Captain Faille nodded, and closed the door again. The carriage shook as he climbed up with the driver, and then they started off again.

"The first incursion brought on by the Summoning?" Lieutenant Danress asked.

"Very likely. Prepare yourself, Jolien. Escaton are not to be taken lightly."

The Lieutenant nodded, then drew a hinged book of slates out of her coat and opened it. She spent the rest of the journey drawing chalk symbols and making them glow. Lady Weston took another slate-book out of her bag and filled it with tiny, precise writing but not making it glow. Kendall sat taking up seat-space, wondering if Escatons were something other than Night Roamers, since Night Roamers just didn't come out except at night, and trying to decide whether she could really herself be just a little bit not human. It would be interesting to be a person who messengers rode furiously to fetch. How good a mage would she have to be, to become a Sentene? And how silly would she look in that coat?

It had grown overcast by the time the carriage drew to a halt, and a fine misting rain was keeping everything in whatever town this was damp. A far bigger place than Falk, with a lot of dark stone crawled over with ivy. The carriage had drawn up in the centre of a cobbled, lichen-spattered square and when Kendall jumped down she could see the main part of the town to the right, and to the left a hedge-lined road. Straight ahead was a stone wall topped with a spiked fence, along which stood a row of musket-men with their guns trained on the fields. Guns, even magicked ones, were said to be not very effective against Night Roamers, but a whole row of them might be worth trying. A great heap of other people were confident enough to crowd to either side of them, peering through the fence.

"Thank you for coming," said a round, elderly woman, moving toward them among a group of town guard. "They were sighted several hours ago, and went to ground almost immediately. One we inadvertently flushed while putting up a cordon, but we did not pursue and have not seen it since, so we do not think it moved far."

"Fortunate that we reached here before nightfall," Lady Weston commented, inclining her head to the townswoman. "If you will tell us the layout of the area infested, we will decide our approach."

While the old lady proceeded to use a lot of words to say there were a few fields criss-crossed by hedges and the occasional line of trees, Kendall watched Captain Faille do his own bit of preparation. First he took off the coat, revealing a uniform fashioned of heavy black cloth reinforced with dark leather. Much more practical for fighting. Then he slid a long, thin sword from beneath one of the seats and strapped it to his back. His hair and eyes had gone grey again, and the fine rain spun about him and turned him into an insubstantial thing, a man of mist wearing night.

It was the first time Kendall had even seen the whole of the Captain's face. He was more fine-boned than she'd expected, the jaw almost delicate, but his mouth was a thin, harsh stroke bracketed by bitter lines. There was something about his proportions, a stretching that went beyond long-limbed. He was very tall, and whip-cord muscular and...wrong to look at. Best of all, he had claws. Or, at least, nails which projected past the fingertip and finished in a point which looked sharp enough to cut. He, far more than Lieutenant Danress, really did look like he'd been fathered by something out of the Hells.

Not wanting to be caught staring, Kendall looked away, and felt her jaw sag. A woman had walked up the hedge-lined road, and had that moment reached the point where it opened up into the square. She was dressed for riding. Her hair was long and black and she wore a hat with ribbons trailing off the back. She saw Kendall staring at her and went still, then turned her head to one side as if considering a sudden retreat.

Captain Faille had caught Kendall's change of expression. He pivoted on his heel, gazed at the only person standing in that direction, and said "M'Lady" in a warning tone, so that the Grand Magister and Lieutenant Danress turned. Kendall was very surprised when, after another moment's hesitation, the black-haired woman began walking toward them.

"Child, is this–?" Lady Weston began, and Kendall nodded. "No coincidence at all, then." Lady Weston sounded dangerously pleased. After staving off the townswoman with a word, she went to meet the person who'd saved them all the trouble of hunting her down, Kendall and the Sentene in train.

"It seems the adage about no good deed going unpunished is a true one," the woman said when they were in earshot. The quizzical look she added sent a sudden rush of heat over Kendall's face and throat. She hadn't thought about it properly, but this woman had saved her life. She hadn't gained anything out of that, had just done it for no reason that Kendall could see. In return, Kendall had put the Sentene on her trail.

That's what you got for not minding your own business.

Still, she didn't look too terribly upset, and was eyeing Lady Weston without any sign of dismay. "You have something to say to me?"

"I have a great many things to ask you, young woman," Lady Weston said, and Kendall blinked at the ice in her voice. "You will not deny foreknowledge of these events, I presume?"

"No."

"I wonder that you can admit it so calmly." Lady Weston did not at all resemble the relaxed gentlewoman Kendall had spent a day watching. Instead, holding herself very erect, each word clear and clipped, she was truly the Grand Magister, commander of Tyrland's magical defences, and very angry indeed. She lifted a hand and one of her bracelets began to glow. As the air filled with a scent like overheated metal, Kendall saw there were sigils etched around the circle of silver. A hot wind swirled around the black-haired woman, who frowned and held on to her hat, looking none too pleased herself.

"Now," Lady Weston said grimly. "You will tell me who it is who has cast this Grand Summoning, where they cast it from, and how they reconstructed the spell."

The woman didn't respond immediately, her dark eyes narrowed and her mouth turned down. Kendall could see the faint mist of raindrops turning to a haze of steam as they came close to her, and tried to guess at what exactly the spell did. Then the stranger let out a little 'tuh' of breath.

"Solace Ariendal Montjuste-Surclere cast it," she said, her voice underlaid with irritation. "She cast it from the Summoning Hall, at the palace in Asentyr. As for reconstruction—"

She looked at the ground, and Kendall gasped, rocked back on her heels by a boiling gale which blasted out from the woman all the way across the square. Suddenly the horses were snorting and backing, the crowd was gawping inward instead of outward, and Captain Faille had somehow drawn his sword and had it at the woman's throat.

The stranger shifted her eyes to him briefly, but remained facing Lady Weston. "You are over-hasty," she said. "And are asking questions to which you should already know the answers. This is no recreation. It is the first, the only Grand Summoning."

"But Queen Solace was killed," Kendall protested, when it seemed no-one else would speak. "The Prince killed her."

"Tiandel pushed her deep into the Eferum. That could have killed her, but it seems not, since she keeps coming back."

"Keeps–?" Lady Weston began, then stopped, and gestured for Captain Faille to move away his sword. "The White Lady phenomenon has each time been an expression of Queen Solace's Grand Summoning?"

"At the earliest stage."

"The Summoning starts over?" Lieutenant Danress asked. "But, then, why has it not gone further until now? What's different about this time?"

"It's more what was different about last time," the woman replied, then glanced toward the fascinated audience along the fence. "You do know there's a Kentatsuki roaming around over there?"

Both Sentene stiffened, their attention shifting firmly to the fields beyond the town.

"The breach here was larger than I was expecting, though only a few Eferum-Get passed through it," continued the woman steadily. "The next major one will be in Asentyr, the Temple District near the Devourer's Shrine. Close to midnight, the third night from now." She turned, obviously intending to just walk away.

"Wait." Lady Weston was no longer angry, but there remained a great deal of command in her voice. "You haven't told us what your involvement in this is. How do you know these things? What are you planning?"

"I plan to stop her, of course." The woman gave the faintest smile, as if she knew how unlikely that sounded, then added: "I'd appreciate you not interfering."

"Inter–" Lady Weston's head came up, a combination of affront and amusement. "Where is your sense? If you speak the truth, then the best course is for us to join forces."

The woman shook her head, and started off. "All that would achieve would be to expose myself to attack," she said over her shoulder. "I can't risk being too easy to find."

"M'Lady?" asked Captain Faille softly.

"Let her be." Lady Weston looked down at her hand, and Kendall saw there was a fresh burn mark around her wrist. The bracelet was gone. "Set one of the Ferumguard to follow her, though I doubt that will serve much purpose. She spoke the truth before she broke my injunction, so we have the information we needed, for what little good it does us. Nor can we neglect a Kentatsuki for a moment longer than strictly necessary. Go."

The Sentene strode off, and Lady Weston returned to the townswoman, rattling off a string of orders. Kendall, well aware that she'd ceased to be important as soon as she'd identified the black-haired woman, returned to the coach.

For some reason she didn't want to watch, didn't want to try and catch a glimpse of whatever was roaming around out there. All her life she'd been warned about Stalkers and Life Stealers, heard tales of Night Roamers rarer and more powerful, but she'd never seen any. She didn't want to start.

Now what? Kendall had few illusions about how much she'd be involved after they'd reached Asentyr. Even if she was able to learn to be a mage, all that meant was that she'd be shuffled off to some school. Would Lady Weston pay for that? Or would Kendall be expected to work off some debt, once she had the means? That was the trap you fell into when you started letting people do things for you. They always expected something in return.

Not that she could go home. Falk was kindling, and none of the surrounding towns were a good idea. None of Tyrland was a good idea.

Threats to the kingdom, magic and monsters; it was all completely beyond the day-to-day worry about food and savings which had been Kendall's world since Gran died. What would it be like to be that woman? To be so powerful, to know what was going on, to be in control. What kind of person could stare down the Grand Magister, ignore a sword at her throat, dare even to say they were going to stop Black Queen Solace?

It seemed to Kendall that if that was what a mage could be, she would certainly have to try it.

SIX

"Y ou're going to give that to them?"

Rennyn glanced up at Seb, then finished drawing an anti-trace casting in a circle around the list she'd made. "I'm worried about the duration of the first breach."

"The Sentene exist to deal with these kind of things."

"True."

She could practically hear him deciding what to say next.

"Planning to just walk up and hand it to them?"

"I was toying with the idea of sending it to the Grand Magister in the mail. It's a difficult one. Perhaps it was always too much to hope to have nothing to do with the Sentene until the last couple of incursions. They know my face now, and the more I avoid them, the more they'll come after me. This is a compromise – hopefully it will distract them."

"Likely?"

"Not at all."

She finished her casting and went to the kitchen, but was not surprised when he followed her. He was trying so hard not to criticise, but couldn't quite let it alone.

"How can we justify it?" he asked, worrying at the point which bothered him most. "Yes, I – I guess that villager would probably have died if you hadn't sent her off. How many will die if we fail? We have a duty to see this through. And to do that we have to stay alive, keep ourselves safe. Now, for the sake of some random village girl, you're exposed."

"Would you have left her to be crushed by the expansion, then?"

He flushed and looked down, chewing his lower lip. "If it put what we had to do at risk. I suppose it must have seemed unlikely they'd work it out, though," he conceded. "But you know that eventually—"

"I know." She sighed. "People may have to die. But she didn't. Yes, just some random villager, but even knowing it would mark me, I'd probably do it again. I don't want to be a person who stands and watches. And she at least taught me not to underestimate the Sentene. Or pure bad luck. Besides, all it's done is throw off our timing. No-one cut my throat."

For all one had had ample opportunity. Her great-grandmother had loathed the Kellian, had called them stained glass monsters, but it was not the right term for the man of mist and flint she'd met. A creature born of cobweb, dew and dawn light. And flesh. The cobweb had given strength, the dew an unusual relationship with light, and dawn brought speed. Who, after all, could outrun the dawn? The Kellian were a triumph of Symbolic magic, and immensely dangerous. The originals had all been women, voiceless and deadly. Bodyguards who would never betray their Queen. It had been such a gamble, to walk up to a descendent of one, to trust to her defences. And for all she knew about Kellian speed, she hadn't quite been able to believe how quickly he'd drawn that sword.

"Telling the Sentene where the incursions will take place will make meeting with them more likely, but I'll accept that if it means not having things like Kentatsuki loose any longer than necessary. Even with them on the scene, it's easy to avoid encounters so long as I'm prepared. To which point—"

Slipping into her jacket, she began checking the contents of her skirt pockets, making certain she had all that was necessary before picking up a sturdy stoneware jar filled with water, which she concealed by draping a coat over her arm. If she made her move while it was still the middle of the day, she'd have a better chance of avoiding any watch the Sentene may have set for her.

"I'll have a hot dinner waiting for you." There was a hint of apology in Seb's voice, underlying the worry and frustration he felt having to continually see her off into possible danger.

"And something sugary for afters?"

"You and your cakes. I'll find something. Come back as soon as you can, Ren."

She smiled and snapped him a salute, then walked through the wards to the landing. A quick clatter down the stair and she was out into the noisy streets of Asentyr.

The capital of Tyrland was a sprawling city, cramped only in a few places. The palace stood on a hill and looked down over the Temple District to the Docks and the river which cut through marshes to the west toward the sea. The bulk of the city spread east, rolling over a series of smaller hills which gradually petered out into fields and fields and fields punctuated by smaller towns and villages.

There were three Claire properties in Asentyr. The neat and compact apartment on the northern edge of the Temple District would be home until the Grand Summoning was complete. There was also a basement storehouse close to the docks, which held a great deal of old Surclere junk and copies of the most important books. On the far side of Aliace Hill, on the outskirts of the city proper, was a dusty house surrounded by a high wall. Seb had checked it once to ensure it was intact, and they would only go there again if they were desperate for shelter.

The northern edge of the Temple District held the city's busiest streets. Tall houses were jammed together, crammed with people, and a dozen play-houses stood out among the narrow buildings, queens each with a little court of taverns. The area was called Crossways, and it seemed to Rennyn as if the entire population of Tyrland passed through it three times daily. A useful thing. She lost herself in the crowd, letting it carry her down the largest of the roads toward the river.

They'd started setting up the blockade already, though people would be allowed through until sunset, and then a curfew would be enforced over the entire Temple District. A dramatic move, but a sensible one. It would be night, and even warned and waiting the Sentene might not be able to intercept a major creature immediately. Keeping the area as free from unnecessary wanderers as possible would prevent deaths.

People weren't afraid yet. This blockade had been announced as a precaution for a suspected outbreak, and the destruction of Falk was the centre of gossip as an ongoing magical disaster, but they'd not announced the Grand Summoning for what it was. Rennyn had no doubt it had been discussed in Private Council, and it was sure to eventually become obvious to anyone who had read a history book, but for now Tyrland went about its business much as usual.

Sliding her free hand into her pocket, Rennyn carefully slipped a ring onto her middle finger, and lifted up the egg-sized stone attached to it by a sturdy chain. Solace Montjuste-Surclere. She'd been a strong ruler, occasionally harsh, but not unusually so. Until the Grand Summoning, she'd not done anything to make herself reviled. But her rule had been threatened. Internally by a cousin who claimed a truer right to the throne. Externally by a foreign empire greedy for expansion. Her response was called the Madness of Queen Solace now, but it seemed to Rennyn a coldly calculated and conscienceless move. The Grand Summoning. It would make Tyrland almost impossible to attack, and consolidate the Montjuste-Surclere rule. What were a few innocent lives compared to that cause?

Rennyn let go the stone, so it swung below her hand. The Grand Summoning had destroyed the town of Eberhart, the first expansion killing at least a hundred. The half-dozen incursion points that opened over Tyrland had released Eferum-Get which had killed many more. Sacrifices to a cause. How many did you have to make, before they called you evil?

The stone swung forward, tugging at the ring. Rennyn followed its pull, and was not surprised to be led along the street until she was directly in front of the Devourer's Temple. She stopped, ignoring the swirl of the crowd, and gazed up the broad flight of steps to the huge cowled statues, each with most of the face hidden, but for an overlong mouth which curled up too far. Patient, smirking Death, greedy and complacent.

Turning in a circle, Rennyn decided on the building opposite the Devourer's, which was three stories high and flat-roofed. It housed some kind of private and irreverently-named club, and there was not a great deal of traffic moving in and out. Rennyn followed an alleyway alongside it, and found herself among neatly-kept trash bins outside a busy kitchen.

There were wards on the doors and windows, but nothing which would notice her lifting herself onto the roof. There she found pigeon-cotes and gently smoking chimneys and a nice clear space at the front.

Setting down the jar, she took a paintbrush from her pocket and began marking a circle of sigils on the dark stone. It was necessary to work quickly, before any part dried, but was a simple method of ensuring that any sign of her casting would evaporate soon after she'd gone through. The jar sitting quietly in the corner of the roof would be much less obvious than the usual chalk sigils. Satisfied that she'd drawn the circle correctly, Rennyn absently murmured the names of the sigils as she pushed power into them, and watched the world fade about her.

Last time, at the town north-east of Sark – Finton it had been called – she had arrived close on the incursion. Starting a full twelve hours beforehand in Asentyr meant she had time to pause in the cool of the Eferum, to close her eyes and allow the power to tingle through her, enjoying the conflicting sensation of floating and being crushed. This, she'd often thought, must be what it was like in the very depths of the ocean. Nothing all around but cold blackness, supported by the water, wrenched at by the tides.

Since she wasn't here to summon, Rennyn made no attempt to hold off the great force of power, but simply let it flow through her, stealing warmth and teasing her thoughts out in streamers which swept away and were lost on the currents. She often used black ribbons in her casting purely because she'd spent so much time in the Eferum it felt as if half her mind was out there, spun into lost threads of thought.

Turning, Rennyn oriented on the point where the incursion would take place, allowing herself to see the outline of the buildings and road and the fantastical trailing pinpricks of light which were people. Already hours must have passed. The trails of light died away of a sudden, until only the occasional mote zoomed by. The curfew was in place. Soon, soon now.

She clasped the stone, making certain the ring was firmly in place. It was coming, changing the tides around her. A great wave of power, distorting the normal flows, bellying out to touch the world beyond. Rennyn tightened her hand and felt the stone slip and tug, vibrating with the force of the Grand Summoning. She had—

Rennyn gasped, a futile thing in a place without breath, serving only to chill her lungs. Outside Finton she had seen the three Eferum-Get as they escaped into the world. The breach from the Eferum had been a sizeable width, increasing the likelihood that something would be near enough to slip through. This one was not much larger, but – no, the shadows which were momentarily outlined by the breach hadn't been nearby. They'd been brought to this point – pushed by – riding? – the wave of power itself. And there were so many.

Astonished and dismayed, Rennyn spoke the trigger which would shift her to the far side of the veil. She'd delayed last time, measuring the flow of the Eferum, and come out many hours after the incursion. Even now, she would be returned well after the moment of incursion, but she had to – had to—

Coughing, skin goose-nabbed and jittering, Rennyn staggered the few steps to the small wall which edged the roof and looked out at the city. She could hear screaming. Shouts. Something breaking. The third building down to the right was in flames. A clutch of people stood before it, black shapes dominated by the glimmer of the Montjuste Phoenix. And everywhere moving shadows. Shadows with claws.

Even these Summoning-produced incursions should not involve more than a handful of Eferum-Get. They were problematic because the breaches were large enough to allow through other types of Eferum-Get than the more common Night Stalkers and Life Stealers, those which excelled at slipping through the smaller, natural breaches. This – this had been dozens, perhaps even *hundreds*, cramming through in one concerted rush.

Leaning out, Rennyn strained to see the blockade at the head of the street. Movement: fire, flickering shadows, the occasional flash which told her mages were at work. Most of the Eferum-Get would not have engaged directly, but simply run. They would burrow into Asentyr, away from the people with blades and flame, and then they would hunt. They—

Rennyn gasped again, and broke into another fit of coughing, the price to be paid for taking a breath in the Eferum. The group in front of the burning building were mostly Sentene, but there was a small collection of more ordinary folk in their centre, clinging to each other protectively. At their fore was a dark-haired youth clutching his abdomen, the focus of all their attention. Rennyn shook her head in utter disbelief, then twisted shadows into a pocket and took herself below.

"Seb."

"Ren!"

Seb was used to Rennyn's favourite castings and simply sagged with relief when she appeared before him. The woman behind him screamed, and there was a brief flurry of movement from the Sentene which Rennyn ignored, staring at the dark blood leaking around the pad of cloth her brother was clutching to his stomach.

"What was it?" she asked.

"Irisian, I think," he said, voice shaking. His eyes were wide and agonised, not only with pain, but with the magnitude of disaster. And the effects of the poison an Irisian would have left in him.

"And you are here why?"

"There was a girl. I know I – you were right. About watching people. I – Ren–"

"Enough. I understand." She squeezed his shoulder. "You're still alive, Seb. Anything else is secondary." And, in truth, their long-term goals weren't even an issue at the moment. To which point she turned to the Sentene watching her and asked: "Which of you is in charge?"

"I am." One of the Kellian, a woman wearing a sword but carrying the slate which was the classic symbol of a mage. Rennyn had known there was a Kellian mage, but if she posed an added danger it didn't seem to be immediate.

"If I draw them to me, can you stand against so many?"

"Draw–?!" someone behind her began, but broke off.

The Kellian in charge weighed the question, her reactions hidden by the all-enveloping uniform. "Suitably prepared, yes. Where will you cast?"

"The centre-point of the breach."

"We will need to reinforce our numbers." The woman turned away, and began relaying orders in a voice notable for a thready, reedy quality. "Essan, Steen, take these out of here, and inform Lady Weston. Bring back the second squad, and the Hands." She paused as one of the shadows clinging to the wall opposite the fire made a sudden movement, then added: "See the boy gets treatment."

An Irisian's poison wasn't immediately fatal, but it would be a battle to keep Seb alive through the night. Rennyn nodded to acknowledge that addition, then leaned down to press her cheek against her brother's, murmuring: "Stay alive, stay quiet. We'll get through this."

"I'm sorry, Ren."

"I'll only be angry if you die on me, little brother."

She let him go, carried easily by one of the Kellian while the other herded the civilians and watched for attack. Rennyn strode in the opposite direction, immediately flanked by four Sentene. Her mind was reeling through consequences, incredulous at the sheer numbers of the incursion, shrinking from the possibility of Seb dying, and the sudden unravelling of a sixty-year plan. But reaching the breach point, she made herself stop thinking of anything but the now, taking her box of chalk from her skirt pocket and rapidly sketching out the kind of circle she'd need onto the road's slabs of stone. At least the Temple District wasn't cobbled.

Three concentric rings of sigils. Not a quick task, but that allowed the reinforcements time to arrive, and they had their own preparations to make. When she looked up, she found herself surrounded by mages holding closely-written slates and standing in protective circles. The Sentene usually worked in pairs: a mage and a weapons-expert. Those with weapons, almost all Kellian, had positioned themselves in alternating places between their mages. Slightly closer were the Hands: more senior mages responsible for unpicking complex castings and investigating violations of the laws constraining mages.

Almost fifty people, which must be at least half of Tyrland's Sentene and Hands. They'd been diverted from the urgent pursuit of Eferum-Get to form a wall around her, which said something for the weight placed on the judgment of the Kellian mage who'd made this decision. Rennyn wondered if it would be enough and, looking around, spotted the woman she'd met in Finton, Lady Weston.

"I'll not be able to defend myself while this goes on," she said. "They'll disperse again if I'm interrupted."

"My dear, if you can truly bring them, be assured we will not be lax concerning their despatch."

Rennyn nodded, and with a glance up at the unsettling shadows lurking in the portico of the Devourer's Temple, began casting. This was a spell of many phases, represented by her three circles. The inner was similar to the gate she had cast previously, but this time she didn't intend stepping into the Eferum, but looking into it; to thin the veil between worlds so that it became a window.

The flags of the street faded to soot, leaving the sigils forming the inner circle glowing white against nothing. The second circle flared brightly as the dark flowed past it, not stopping the tide but anchoring it so that it would not extend beyond the borders of the original breach. A wave of cold followed behind and Rennyn's breath puffed mist as she waited for the full breach to be outlined. Even firmly anchored, almost the entire width of the street was engulfed, with all but a few of her defenders standing on the surface of a black lake.

The Hand members were watching her with open fascination, but not a single Sentene faced inward. They would not turn their backs on Eferum-Get. That unity made Rennyn a little more confident about survival, and she set her jaw to stop her teeth from chattering as she activated the outer circle. Dark lines began lifting from the surface of the lake, slowly at first, then streaking upward and outward like a tarry sunburst. One, two, three darted directly into the furthest recesses of the Devourer's portico, but most spread far out into the city.

They'd all passed through this point, all the Eferum-Get loose in Asentyr. That was the connection she exploited, making tangible the fact of their passage, turning it into a visible trail.

"Be ready," she said, lowering herself to her knees then resting back on her heels. One hand she lifted to press against her focus against her chest, warm with her body's heat. The other she held above the surface of the dark beneath her. Then, closing her eyes, she made a scooping, gathering motion, as if collecting a tangle of black ribbons floating beneath the surface. The trail became a thread, a link, a chain. And she hauled on it.

"Above!"

Rennyn firmed her grip as whatever had been lurking in the portico leapt straight at her. There was a brief warmth as someone loosed a casting, then heavy meaty noises. The noises were harder to block out, but she tried, hauling on the icy, slippery tangle which joined the Eferum-Get to the breach between the worlds. Hand over hand, dragging them back, her fingers turning to sharp spikes of pain, then losing feeling.

Sounds kept breaking through. Sharp commands, the ring of steel on...something, bursts and whumps of offensive casting. The staccato of hasty sigil writing. Her throat and chest started to hurt, and it became as hard to breathe as it was to hold on to the tangled, thinning rope, and that was very hard indeed when only the effort it took to pull told her she still had it.

The thinner it grew, the heavier it seemed, until she finally realised that she wasn't able to pull the last strand any further. Telling her fingers to tighten, she wound it around and around her hands so it wouldn't slip, and opened her eyes.

Pieces of monster were everywhere, scattered across a street slick with blood and ash. The neat formation of mages had broken, and beside her was a little cluster of people working over two fallen defenders. Everyone else, all of them, were arrayed to her right, toward the Docks District. She couldn't see what they faced, but she could feel it. An intensity, a swell of power which left her head throbbing, like a sound too low to hear.

The urgent discussions among the Sentene on what to do next gave her a name. Azrenel-type. Possibly the most powerful of the

Eferum-Get. They were intelligent with little physical presence, similar to the Life Stealers though fortunately far rarer. Only two had been encountered in recorded history. Rennyn looked down at her hands, at the black line cutting into numb, blue skin. This fragile thread stretched between her and a thing that unchecked could lay waste to the entire kingdom in a matter of weeks. She'd been dragging it up the street.

There was a strange noise, high and harsh, and she realised it was her breath, tearing in her throat. She'd done too much, was exhausting her physical as well as casting strength. The sixty-year plan, the entire purpose of her family, had been suddenly side-lined, leaving only that thread. She would hold it till all her strength was gone. Then she would sleep, if her heart did not stop, and the Azrenel would no longer be pinned.

What was worse? To let go, to let this creature run loose so she could continue on the task she'd been raised to carry out? Or to turn away from stopping Solace? The Grand Summoning seemed diminished by comparison. And yet, wasn't this an effect of the Summoning, on a vastly larger than expected scale? There would be five more incursions.

Overwhelmed, Rennyn leaned forward, curling over her bound hands. She couldn't think of it. Better just to close her eyes again, and remember to breathe.

SEVEN

unlight. The smell of medicine and recently-laundered linen. A bed, over-firm, though the pillow was nice. She was lying on her back, and her arms ached, and her hands were stiff. Her chest felt like she'd been breathing knives. Rennyn flexed fingers cautiously, and found they were bandaged but seemed to be all there, so she opened her eyes.

There was a Kellian watching her from the doorway. Two Kellian, and a red-haired woman. Rennyn lifted her head to look at them properly, then lay back and laughed. Not dead after all.

Ignoring her audience, she looked around more of the room. Four beds, and Seb on the one beside hers. Pale and lying very still, but he breathed.

"How is he?" she asked the small, elderly woman sitting on the far side of his bed.

"Out of the woods. He'll be sitting up in a day or two. It will take several weeks of treatment before muscle function is fully restored, though."

Irisian poison paralysed before death. But still, he would recover, and in time. Not much else was going according to plan, but she would at least have her brother.

"Is it still the same day?" she asked, suddenly worried.

"The same." The woman was watching her with an air of entertainment which Rennyn definitely didn't appreciate. "You'll be hungry, I expect."

More than. Moving cautiously, Rennyn sat up. She was wearing some kind of shift, and her focus stone was missing. Both of them. The sense of unreality was fading, leaving her feeling less than pleased with herself. Events had spiralled out of her control.

"What is this place? Sentene headquarters?"

A third Kellian had appeared in the doorway, and this one Rennyn recognised. "The infirmary of the Houses of Magic in Villemar Palace," the Kellian mage said. "The Sentene occupy one branch of the Houses. The Grand Magister asks if you feel able to meet with her after lunch."

Time for interrogation. Rennyn supposed there was no escaping that. "Provided my clothes can be found," she said, which proved an effective Sentene-banishing charm. They withdrew to other parts of the infirmary while the old woman produced her clothing, recently laundered, and directed her to a small side-room where she could change and clean up.

Her clothes, but not her other belongings. It would be inconvenient if they tried to keep the focuses. Rennyn took her time dressing, weighing options: how much to tell them, what to keep back, and when to lie. Associating with the Sentene now changed the timing but not the main features of the plan. Since she'd survived the night she would make the assumption that she wasn't under imminent threat from within their ranks. Besides, after last night she had to shift her priorities, due to both the strength of the incursions, and Seb's injuries. She couldn't care for him and go racketing about the country, which left her with absolutely no choice in the matter.

"You've some minor frost bite on your hands," said the old woman, when she emerged. "The severe chill was the more serious matter. Exhausted as you were, you're at a high risk for lung infection. I boosted your defences as best I could, but you'd be well advised to keep warm and take a few days' rest."

That sounded nice. Rennyn put it on her list of things to do, and turned to the tray of food which had been brought in her absence, concentrating on filling the aching pit in her stomach. A cup of spiced tea with half a pot of honey dumped into it raised her spirits enormously.

"Thank you for looking after my brother," she said, when she rose to depart. "I mightn't be here when he wakes, so can you tell him that before I get back he needs to produce a highly imaginative and original explanation of just what exactly he was doing anywhere near that incursion?"

There was only one Sentene outside the door now, the red-headed woman she'd seen in Finton, who said: "The Grand Magister's Chambers are upstairs," and led her past a number of empty rooms to curving corridors and then up stairs which wound inside a circular tower. They stopped at a well-lit room dominated by a long table.

The Grand Magister was standing with a group of people on the far side of the table, but turned and nodded her welcome when Rennyn came in. "I am glad to see you recovered, young lady," she said. "Please, sit."

The missing contents of her pockets were lined along one end of the table, so Rennyn sat down before them. Both focuses were there, two innocuous round globes, one less than half the size of the other. The larger was clear, with only a few faint traces to show how it had grown, while her own was pitch black. She fastened it around her neck.

"How many died last night?" she asked, as the others settled around the table.

"We don't have a final tally," Lady Weston replied, lines momentarily etching themselves between her brows. "It may be days before we uncover all the bodies. The Docks are the worst hit. Households, ships, even an entire street with nothing but dead. Over a thousand."

It could not have been more than an hour between the breach and Rennyn's casting. A thousand dead in an hour. Rennyn stared down at her bandaged hands, and wondered if there was any way she could have prevented this.

"No injunction this time?" she asked, rather than prod that sore.

"My dear child, I'm not altogether sure I would dare," Lady Weston said, with a serious edge beneath the light words. "You are quite the strongest mage I've ever encountered. Besides, it was rude of me. Can we begin again, with some introductions? You probably know that I am Honoria Weston. This is Councillor Vargas, High Magister Fennis, Senior Captain Illuma, Senior Captain Faille and Senior Captain Lamprey."

Vargas, an ageing but still handsome blond man, was the Queen's closest advisor, and the only one looking at Rennyn as if he thought her liable to bite. The Sentene, though they'd unfastened their uniform collars enough for her to see their faces, were expressionless. Magister Fennis, balding and pink-skinned, showed every sign of someone in for a rare treat.

She'd paused overlong without responding, and her reply felt strange in its honesty. "Rennyn Montjuste-Surclere."

"Ah." Her answer hadn't been a surprise. The Grand Magister had been doing some thinking since their last encounter. "So there was a survivor of that fire. One of Prince Tiandel's sons?"

Rennyn leaned her chin on one hand. "The whole family, actually, since Tiandel was expecting the assault. Feeling was very high against him, and there'd been other attempts. By then he'd realised that he'd only succeeded in interrupting the Grand Summoning, not halting it permanently, and thought it best to remove himself from sight and prepare for Queen Solace's return."

Magister Fennis leaned forward, eyes widening to comical effect. "He *chose* to disappear? But then – Queen Solace's library? Her researches?"

"Moved to safety well beforehand," Rennyn said. This was a question she'd been expecting. "Yes, most of it still exists. Yes, I have it. Perhaps, if this current mess can be resolved, I'll present it to the kingdom or something. But not until then."

"But, don't you understand?" Fennis asked, sounding straightforwardly astonished. "With access to that library, to the original documentation, we may be able to discover a way to break the Grand Summoning."

"Perhaps you could," Rennyn said. "The Montjuste-Surcleres have been researching that very problem for the past three hundred years, but I suppose it's within the bounds of possibility that you could succeed in the bare month you have before the Summoning is complete. I'll certainly give that idea some thought, and let you know my decision."

His face stiffened, and he looked so like a disappointed child she had to smile apologetically at him. "I suppose this will go quicker, and I might manage to be marginally less offensive, if I just

51

gave a précis of the situation, rather than go back and forth with questions and answers."

"Please do," said Lady Weston, with a quelling hand touching Fennis' elbow.

Rennyn glanced at Councillor Vargas, least likely to understand. "When a mage enters the Eferum to summon a focus stone, they are limited by their inborn strength, plus the strength of their previous summoned focuses. It's rare to make the attempt more than three or four times because the risks – exhaustion, cold, and Eferum-Get – increase along with the amount of power summoned.

"The Grand Summoning abandons the normal progression entirely. Queen Solace didn't even take her younger focuses into the Eferum with her, but commenced the Summoning with her own raw ability. And instead of drawing as much power as she could and immediately compressing it, she is using it to – this is hard to express. If you have a large bowl of water, and swirl a spoon around in the middle, it sets up a current which brushes the edges of the bowl, even though the spoon never passes there. The Grand Summoning uses the caster's own strength to set up a motion, and then structures that motion so that it continues to increase. When each cycle completes, it begins again, drawing on the power produced in the last cycle. Because the power involved is mainly raw Efera, not the caster's strength, energy can be diverted to surviving the dangers of the environment, and there is not the problem of exhaustion."

She reached out and picked up the clear focus. "These are Solace Montjuste-Surclere's younger focuses." Holding it up, she could see the faintest of outlines of three further spheres inside the outer. "She left them with Tiandel both because they worked at a slight cross-purpose to the Summoning she was attempting, and because they offered a solution to a practical difficulty."

"Which was?"

Slipping the focus into her skirt pocket, Rennyn made an expansive gesture. "A focus the size of this room. Focus stones operate when in contact with their owner. It's a little hard to estimate just how large the result of the Grand Summoning will be, but I'm fairly certain it won't, well, fit through doors, for a start.

"Tiandel's role was to attune the younger focus to the Grand Summoning. He could do this by touching the edges of the power she was summoning, using the breaches the power was causing. This would allow her to use the new focus even at a distance. Unfortunately for Solace, it also gave Tiandel the perfect tool. Just as the casting completed the final phase, but before the compressing power could solidify into a focus, he used the power to push his mother deep into the Eferum."

Rennyn began collecting the other items lined up on the table: the half-empty box of chalk, her apartment key, a small purse of money, the paintbrush. She left the note.

"Solace did not die, but it was ten years before she returned, and as soon as she reached the correct point in the Eferum, the Grand Summoning commenced again. Probably she would be drawn back to that point no matter what her wishes, for she is trapped in the spell, still constrained by the Sigillic casting she established in the Hall of Summoning here."

Rennyn had to repress a shudder. Her family pushed Solace back for good reason, but it was a cruel task. The whole conversation was trying her nerves, but she went on as dispassionately as she was able. These people had not grown up reading Solace's working diaries, appreciating the mind if not the person, and wouldn't share any sympathy at all for the Black Queen.

"The White Ladies are a side-effect, a manifestation of the uncompressed power the spell generates. They have just enough substance, just enough connection to the actual person, that she can be touched through them, and pushed back at the beginning of the Summoning rather than at its conclusion. Each time since, it has taken slightly longer for her to return, and each time a Montjuste-Surclere has used the attuned focus to push her back into the Eferum almost as soon as the spell began to manifest."

"Until Loise."

It was the Kellian called Faille who had spoken: the singularly humourless-looking man who had been so quick with his sword.

"Yes. Until Loise, when someone killed my great-grandfather just as Solace was pushed back. The – part of the attunement was in a structure built around the focus, and that was shattered. I don't know if this was deliberate, but it means that we now merely have her younger focuses, not attuned to the Grand Summoning. This time when she manifested there was nothing we could do to push her back. So I'm reconstructing Tiandel's steps, attuning the focus again so that she can be stopped at the final moment rather than the first."

Councillor Vargas cleared his throat. His colour had risen, turning him an interesting plummy shade, though he showed no other sign of what she guessed to be highly outraged indignation. "Would it not have been more responsible – indeed, was it not your duty – to bring this to Council, to turn over this focus and allow the matter to be properly dealt with? How many died last night because we were not prepared?"

Rennyn blinked, but answered the first point without rancour. "I wasn't clear. Tiandel could attune the younger focus because he had a blood link to Queen Solace. Because he was a Montjuste-Surclere, because he was her direct heir. Currently, there are two Montjuste-Surcleres, one of whom is lying in your infirmary after suffering a fit of heroics. And sixty years ago, someone killed my great-grandfather.

"Hard as it is to credit the idea of a kind of counterpart to my family, working toward Queen Solace's return, I have to anticipate the same kind of attack. If Sebastian – my brother – and I are killed, then the younger focuses cannot be attuned, let alone used against Solace."

She picked up the note she had so carefully prepared yesterday. "My task is set: to repeat Tiandel's steps. It's not a difficult thing, but requires being in certain places at certain times, and to not have someone kill me. The best chance for success is to avoid notice, not allow people to know where I am, and not involve myself in anything else. I only warned of the incursion in Asentyr because it was inside the city's protective circles, and I may not have done that if the Sentene had not already become aware of my existence. I was weighing up what additional harm there would be in providing a list of the incursion locations, given that it is basically a map of where

I'll be going." She put the piece of paper down. "Last night changed everything."

"That is something of an understatement." Lady Weston rubbed her eyes, and Rennyn realised the woman probably hadn't slept. "You were in the Eferum during the incursion?"

"Yes. It's the only way to continue the attunement. During the first incursion, I noticed that the breach was very large and stayed open for a longer period than those recorded by Tiandel. Last night – the breach was a similar size and duration to the first, but the Eferum-Get – I could not tell if they had been swept together by the force of the Summoning, or if they had deliberately gathered to wait for it. Neither possibility is pleasant."

"The Eferum-Get organising to exploit the breaches, or Queen Solace deliberately thrusting them into Tyrland." The Kellian mage, Illuma, was as expressionless as ever, but had curled her hands into fists. She seemed to realise it, and opened them, palm-up. She'd trimmed the dagger-points of her nails on one hand, but the other palm was lightly cut. "Either way, a war."

"Do you really believe that?" Councillor Vargas asked, looking from Illuma to Lady Weston to Rennyn. "That the Black Queen would go so far?"

"She has been in the Eferum an unbearably long time," Lady Weston replied. "She may be mad, she may be vengeful: we can do no more than speculate. Enough that we could face the same number of Eferum-Get, or more, during the coming breaches. You will work with us in combating this?"

Rennyn nodded. "The locations I presume you read. The younger focuses can be used to identify the exact point of an upcoming breach."

"And that makes a very large difference indeed," Lady Weston said. "To know exactly when and where an incursion will occur makes it possible to contain it. We will trap the Eferum-Get even as they emerge. Am I right in believing that there will be an increase in natural breaches during the Summoning?"

"Yes. The effect of the casting is much like a storm in the Eferum – it places strain on the boundaries between the worlds."

"We must divide our resources. Lamprey, you will have charge of the second and third squads, deployed to the Sentene's regular duties. Illuma, Faille, the Hand will support your squads in dealing with the major incursions and ensuring the safety of the Montjuste-Surcleres. Fennis, I want you to revisit the Loise investigation, and more generally try to uncover any hint of who was behind the attack. Is there more you can tell us there, Lady Montjuste-Surclere?"

"We abandoned the title. As for Loise – my great-grandparents travelled there together, and arrived late in the night. My great-grandmother had stayed with the horses, and heard a cry, then the sound of someone running. She found her husband and the focus' vessel in pieces. And yet, the focus was still there. The locals camped near the site were attracted by the light she conjured, and so she had to leave him. She became...very determined to find a way to stop the Grand Summoning after that." Rennyn looked down at her bandaged hands, and thought of all the chances she'd had last night to die. "You see where the strategy of keeping ourselves invisible comes from? If we can be found, we can be killed. And the first expression was a place we were certain to be."

"You will be well-guarded here," Lady Weston began, but Rennyn shook her head.

"Guard my brother, by all means. I'll limit my exposure to the actual periods of the incursions."

For the first time Lady Weston showed a hint of frustration. "That may not be the wisest course," she said.

"But it is the one I will take."

"Having demonstrated how capable you are of hiding yourself," said Captain Faille.

This made Rennyn smile. "A fair point. Still, it makes more sense for Seb and I not to be handily in the same place."

"You don't trust us." The third of the Sentene captains, Lamprey, was a human man with dark skin. Outrage had broken through the professional mask. "You're not concerned about our ability to protect you, but our opportunity to attack you."

She hadn't realised she'd shown that, and said carefully: "I'm tolerably certain that I wouldn't have survived the night if I'd come close to anyone who wanted to kill me. In this, it is simply as I said: staying here makes me too easy to find. It's almost a moot point, since I'll be spending so much time roaming about the countryside. And on that subject – the next incursion is in three days, and not far from Asentyr, but there is a stage of the attunement I must perform immediately after that. The vessel for the focus needs to be constructed, and to do that I must also visit the places Queen Solace summoned her younger focuses. These– " She frowned. "These should not be incursion points. No breach was recorded in the previous iteration, but like the first expression, they are known places that I must visit."

"A place to expect attacks? Where are they?"

"The first is her home. Surclere Manor, or what little remains of it. The second is the palace's Hall of Summoning, which at least is conveniently close." Rennyn stood up. "I presume you want to establish at the next incursion site well beforehand. I'll return the day after tomorrow, near midday."

They let her go. She had wondered if they'd consider stopping her, but though they didn't like it there were no further protests. An escort took her back down to check on Seb, and then showed her the way out of the palace. Rennyn wasted a few minutes losing the person set to follow her, and removing the subtle little traces which had been 'chanted into her clothes, then spent the remainder of the day ensuring there was nothing in the apartment which would reveal too much. If they were persistent, they would find the place eventually.

Then she took the old lady's advice and slept.

EIGHT

T his is becoming intolerable."

As soon as she heard the deliberately raised voice of Lydia Norandar, Kendall snapped her book shut and sat up, straightening her stupid student smock. Just in time. The door was jerked open and three girls clattered in, all braids and exaggerated drama.

"Two hours," fumed Lydia to her companions, thrusting her books back on their shelf. Tall and golden, she'd be pretty but for a nose permanently elevated. "Two hours they keep us sitting around, and then sent back without a word of apology. My father will hear of this."

"Does he rank your education above the defence of the realm?" asked Helena Renton, a droopy blonde following the three into the dormitory they shared. "Surely it must have occurred to you that every competent mage in Tyrland has better things to do right now than prepare you for your Summoning."

Since Helena topped Lydia on the social scale that was Lydia's be-all and end-all, the girl only tossed her head, then glared at the last student to enter the room.

"If they're so keen on defence, they're being very lax," she said, with deep meaning. "If they're really hunting for supporters of the Black Queen, why are they ignoring the obvious?"

The obvious was the last of the students who shared the room, a tall girl with fine but colourless hair and daggers for nails. She didn't react to the pointed comment, returning her books to their shelf and leaving the room without so much as glancing at the other occupants.

"Truly, she makes my blood run cold," said plump Elsa, Lydia's chief crony. "Why are we forced to keep company with a creature like that, particularly when the Black Queen threatens us?"

"It shows a disregard for our safety," said Anaret, the second crony. "If you ask me, they should all be locked away, at least until this crisis is over. I mean, you never can be sure."

"Truly an excellent idea," Helena drawled, propping herself on the mound of pillows which had found their way to her bed. "With Tyrland suddenly plagued by the worst nightmares out of the Eferum, we should throw half the Sentene in prison. Because they're spooky."

"Because the Kellian were created by Queen Solace," Lydia said sharply. "You can't escape that. It doesn't matter what they've done in the past, how they've served the Montjustes. They were *made* by Solace Montjuste-Surclere. She's their creator, their god. Now that we know she's alive, how can we trust them?"

Helena shrugged. "Well, if you think Sukata Illuma is going to attack you in your bed, feel free to go home. Somehow, I don't think you're her type."

"I may well do that." Lydia turned her displeasure abruptly toward Kendall. "First the peasant, and now cancelled lessons every day. What kind of—"

Kendall didn't bother to stay for the rest. She'd heard more than enough about unlettered peasants being allowed into the Arkathan. Things had turned out much as she'd expected. Lady Weston had handed her over to the Head of the Arkathan, the school which was one of the three branches of the Houses of Magic, and had not been back. Kendall didn't blame her: a stray potential mage was totally unimportant when people were being killed, and there was all this talk about conspiracies to bring back the Black Queen. Besides, Kendall had made her own choice to try magery, and didn't want the Grand Magister treating Kendall as her business.

The problem was that the Arkathan was the wrong place to start. It was an advanced school, taking snotty nobles and the very cream of other young mages just when they were getting ready to summon their first focus, and grooming them for the Hand, or the

Sentene, or to be scholars of the Art – or just too powerful for their own good. It didn't matter whether Kendall had potential or not; she hadn't passed any of the stages required to enter the Arkathan. She hadn't been learning sigils along with her letters, and could barely sense power, let alone understand how to *use* it. The Head had given her a couple of books and told her to memorise them, found her a uniform and an empty bed, and left her to kick about on her own.

She didn't fit with the people either, of course. Not all of them were as bad as Lydia, who talked with a built-in flounce, but plenty had made it clear that they didn't like having a village girl shoved in unasked. Not just because she wasn't rich or titled like many of them, but because she hadn't *earned* the right to be there. Studying at the Arkathan was a privilege, a prize to be won or bought, while Kendall was some girl whose only qualification was that her home had been destroyed by the Grand Summoning. And when Kendall had chosen to feign ignorance of anything beyond that, she'd failed to even be a good source of gossip.

Like the Kellian girl, Kendall found it simplest to avoid the other students as much as possible. She shared a room with these five, only saw the rest at the dining hall, and concentrated on memorising ugly, crosswise sigils. With the dormitory no longer quiet, she took her book and headed to the only place she'd found to get any real privacy.

The Houses of Magic were set on a jutting section of Aliace Hill, within the circle of the palace but separate from it. Six buildings, three large and three lesser, stuck out around a thick central tower where the Grand Magister and the library were located. Each main building belonged to a different House, and the smaller ones held shared kitchens, stables and infirmary.

The infirmary was between the Arkathan and Sentene House, and outside that was a not very interesting garden which looked north-east to where the hill fell away. A stone balustrade guarded the drop, and Kendall had found that if you climbed over this there was a useful rock shelf a few feet down. It was sunny in the morning, and out of sight of annoying people. She slid down to it with a sense of relief, only to meet the startled eyes of a boy maybe a year older than herself.

"Guess I'm not the first person to notice this spot after all," the boy said.

Kendall hesitated. Thin, with very black hair and eyes, and wearing a loose set of pyjamas and a blanket, he looked worn and ill, slumping back against the rock as if he couldn't sit up properly.

"Are you hurt? Do you want me to get someone to help you?"

"Fel, no. I've had enough of being peered at." He paused, glancing from her shapeless black and blue smock to her book. "Are you one of the students here?"

Something about the way he tilted his head brought recognition. "Do you – do you have an older sister?"

The boy's face brightened, then his wary expression came back in force. "You've met Rennyn?"

"I don't know what her name is, though I guess she must be the one everyone is saying is a Montjuste-Surclere, come back to fight the Black Queen. She came to Falk."

His eyes widened, then for some reason he went red. "Are you the shed girl?"

"My name's Kendall," Kendall said, flatly. 'Shed girl' indeed.

"Ah, um. I'm Sebastian. I guess you have met my sister, then." He shuffled his feet and glowered down at them, adding in a stifled voice: "I owe you an apology."

"You do?" Kendall couldn't begin to guess why.

He nodded, then met her eyes. "I told Ren she shouldn't have done it, you see. Saved you. We were supposed to keep everything we did a secret, we weren't supposed to be noticed at all. But because Ren sent you away, the Sentene found out about us. And I'm – sorry I said that."

Kendall thought about being angry, but he looked so crumpled and unhappy that she decided it was no use yelling at someone who belonged in a sickbed. "Sounds like you should be telling her that, not me."

"I know. She must be furious with me. After saying that to her, what do I do but end up here. They knew Ren existed, yes, but–" He paused, and bit his lip. "Now it seems like everyone knows about us, and that's my fault."

"How?" When he just chewed on his lip more, she added persuasively: "If it's things everyone knows, it's not going to hurt to tell me, is it?"

"Maybe not. I wish I'd had a chance to talk to her before she left, so I knew just what she'd said. What are people saying about us?"

"Well, I hadn't heard anything about *you*," Kendall said. "Your sister apparently did something impressive in the middle of the Night Stalker invasion and saved the city. I'm not real clear on what. And she's going to do what Prince Tiandel did, and stop the Grand Summoning just before it finishes. But she's vanished, and no-one knows where she is."

"She's supposed to come back today. Is all that really common gossip? I was hoping it at least wouldn't go beyond the Sentene and the Hand."

"They had a debate about it in Council. Mainly about the Montjuste-Surclere right to the throne."

That won an incredulous stare. "How stupid."

"So, what was it you did? I've not heard you mentioned at all."

"Small mercies. I was – I followed Ren to where the incursion would be. She's the one that has to take all the danger, you see, while I'm just supposed to keep myself safe and out of the way. I wanted to at least see what she had to face. So I went there and hid myself on a roof, made myself invisible. Then – well, you know that the incursion was huge beyond belief. The Eferum-Get went everywhere, and the Sentene were chasing them. A building near me caught on fire, and some people came out. There were no Sentene near, and they ran straight into some Irisian – they're like poisonous scaled monkeys. I couldn't just *watch*."

"But you got hurt?"

"I didn't get the fourth one quickly enough. So now I'm stuck here, and Ren's in *more* danger because it sounds like the entire Kingdom knows exactly what she's doing."

"Wouldn't she have helped against the monsters anyway? Even if you weren't there?"

"Maybe. But me getting clawed by an Irisian left her with little choice about how to deal with the aftermath." He fidgeted restlessly, still slumped against the rocks. "You joined the Arkathan? Can I see what you're studying?"

Kendall handed over her boring book, noting how much trouble he had keeping hold of it. He flipped through the pages clumsily, then shook his head. "You've no background, right? What have they given you except this dictionary?"

"There's another one, but it's just more of these squiggles."

"What exercises have they given you?"

"Exercises? I've got to memorise all that first. I get tested on how well I know the sigils, and then they start to tell me how to make them work."

"You're reading a Sigillic dictionary? End to end? No exercises at all?"

"Don't I need to know the sigils to cast?" Kendall asked warily. "Like knowing the alphabet before I can write?"

"Since sigils are words, not letters, you'd only need to know the words that you're going to use, not the entire book. This doesn't even explain how sigils are structured. And you don't use words for Thought magic — that's the entire point. It's just raw will and power. Try moving that pebble."

"What? But—"

"Did they really just give you that book and tell you to teach yourself how to be a mage? What a stupid school this must be. Look — you can sense casting, right?"

"I can smell it."

"Do you ever feel anything when that happens?"

"My nose itches."

"So, look at that pebble. And concentrate on the smell. That's a bit like, um, if you're baking bread. When you're cooking, you can smell it. But the bread, the dough, smelled like something before that, just not as strong. So try and imagine what it smelled like before."

Uncooked thunderstorm? Kendall shook her head helplessly. "That doesn't make sense to me."

"Efera's everywhere, all around us, leaking into this world from the Eferum. Mages just happen to be able to tell that it's there, know when it's being worked. And have a kind of muscle that allows them to do things with it. So all the time you're smelling raw Efera, and you're only noticing it properly when someone does something to it." Sebastian lifted a hand and a fist-sized rock rose from the hillside. "Do you feel the change?"

"Maybe," Kendall said, doubtfully. She hadn't even known you could cast without using sigils.

"Making the link between sensing power and actually doing anything with it is the biggest and maybe the hardest step. When you start casting Sigillic, you'll push the power into the path charted by the sigils. Thought magic is more basic: there's a rock and you want it to move. You know it's surrounded by Efera, so you push the Efera at the rock, wanting it to move."

"But – push it with what?"

He grinned, and flipped her book open again. "That's the hard bit. You know that there's Efera here. You know that you've got a muscle that can work it, a muscle that you can use by *wanting*. So move the pebble."

"You're not a very good teacher."

"And you didn't even try." He turned his head toward the rock still hovering in the air and this time Kendall knew a moment beforehand as the stone broke into dozens of little pieces. "Thought magic exercises. Both for precision for when you need to Thought cast, and for strength that you'll eventually be able to push into Sigillic casting. Sigillic casting is for complex, more permanent things, but don't neglect Thought." He turned a page, not even watching the stones spiralling above his head.

"*And* a show-off," Kendall muttered, but glowered obediently at the pebble, trying to picture herself surrounded by mysterious forces which she could reach out with an invisible arm and poke. Nothing happened, of course, and she began to suspect he'd been playing games with her.

"So why the shed?" he asked, after she'd been glaring at the pebble a while.

"What?"

"Why were you living in a shed?" He flushed at her expression, but continued: "We've lived in a few places, and the hardest thing was getting people to leave us alone. Always expecting us to help out with something, or trying to arrange things for us, and gossiping endlessly. I can't imagine getting away with living in a shed. The Holier-than-the-Dawnbringer types would have kicked up the hugest fuss."

"Trying to take you over," she said, understanding. "I lived there because it was mine. When Gran's house burned down, a lot of them wanted to take me in. Some of them wouldn't have been so bad, but it wouldn't be mine, not a place I belonged. And they would have thought it gave them the right to tell me what to do."

"Don't people do that anyway?"

"I suppose." Kendall sighed. "I bet no-one tells your sister what to do."

Sebastian laughed. "All the time. But she doesn't often listen."

"I'd like that kind of power. To be able to do what I want, not what other people want me to."

He looked at her, then slowly closed the book and handed it back to her. "She does that sometimes, I guess."

The rock shelf had moved into the shade, and no longer felt so comfortable. Kendall frowned, fingering the worn cover of the book. "Is there really a conspiracy to kill you?"

"A conspiracy?" The glance he gave her was wary. "I don't know. Queen Solace is definitely returning, and I'm sure she doesn't want us to stop her. And someone did kill our great-grandfather, so we have to assume that there's someone willing to help her, and avoid giving them the chance."

"Do you think you're safe here?"

"No. Yes and no. There's an awful lot of people who pass through these buildings. The Sentene guard the door to the infirmary, but – can they really be sure of everyone? I've been testing my food for poison."

"You don't believe what they say about the Kellian, then? That because the Kellian were created by the Black Queen, they consider her their god, and are secretly loyal to her?"

Sebastian ran a hand through his tangled hair, shifting uncomfortably. "We thought of it, of course," he said, after a moment. "It would be stupid not to at least consider the question of their loyalties, and it's one of the reasons we were planning to avoid the Sentene. But – a Kellian killed the Irisian that was attacking me. And they've had plenty of chances to kill me since. My father used to say that the Kellian are the last people who would want the Black Queen to return."

"Really? Why?"

"Why would the children of slaves want the slave-master to return?" asked a light voice, and Kendall looked up to see Sebastian's sister leaning on the balustrade gazing down at them. Worse still, she was flanked by two tall figures in the black uniform of Sentene.

"Ren!" Sebastian, face alight, floated abruptly upward. "Are you all right?"

"Better than you'll be if I find you've been levitating yourself out of any more windows."

"You wouldn't have stood a single day of it, Ren. Being gawked at like a bear in a menagerie."

"I'm sure. But still, you won't recover properly unless you work your body against the effects of the poison. You can use a cane, but not magic, in any further escape attempts."

Sebastian ducked his head, then looked sideways at his sister's escort. Not wholly oblivious after all. Hauling herself over the balcony less showily, Kendall hoped the climb would excuse her burning face. She was glad to see one of the Sentene was Lieutenant Danress, but the other was Captain Faille.

"Hello again," said Rennyn, smiling at Kendall. "I was wondering where you'd ended up." To Kendall's dismay she then turned to the silent figure on her left. "And do the Kellian regard Queen Solace as a god, Captain? That's not a theory I've heard before."

With half his face hidden by the uniform, and the midday sun transforming his eyes to gold disks, Kendall couldn't decipher any kind of reaction in the grim Captain. "The Kellian were created without voices," he said, just when Kendall had decided he wasn't going to respond. "Their purpose was to be tools in the hands of their Master, no more. A hammer does not worship the smith."

Rennyn Montjuste-Surclere stared up at him, then inclined her head, as if he'd done her a courtesy. "And it is the Phoenix who wields you now. Well enough." She turned back to her brother. "I brought you clothes and a fresh journal, Seb. Given the library here, I think you'll be well supplied with study material. Now, can you walk if I help you?"

Balancing with help of the balustrade, Sebastian made a doubtful movement and began to teeter, recovering with another surge of magic. His sister gave a gesture of permission, and he steadied and began floating again. The little group headed off, Sebastian glancing back and waving at Kendall when his sister did.

Kendall watched them go, then bent to pick up a pebble.

NINE

Rennyn took the time to reassure Seb, then narrowly avoided an audience with the Queen. Another reason to stay away from the palace as much as possible. She'd been neither pleased nor surprised to hear her name on every street of Asentyr, and could only appreciate the magnitude of her failure. Three hundred years of secrecy, smashed to ruins.

The Sentene were keen to reach the next site before sunset, and she found herself being very efficiently bundled into a coach, part of a small cavalcade. The dark, over-quilted interior made her sleepy, so she curled up on the seat and dreamed confusedly of being shaken until she was woken by a light hand on her shoulder. The red-headed Lieutenant, Danress, standing in the doorway of the coach.

"You haven't really recovered, have you?" the woman said. "Will you be able to do what you need here?"

"It's nothing difficult," Rennyn replied, running her fingers through her hair, the bandages catching at strands. She'd be able to rid herself of them soon, but it was true that sleep hadn't balanced the physical toll.

Peering past the Sentene mage, she saw they'd stopped in a well-established encampment. The group she'd been travelling with had joined up with an equal number who'd gone ahead to the rough location she'd named. "How solid is this plan to build a shield to contain the Eferum-Get?"

"With time to prepare a properly constructed circle it seems workable. Just because we usually build them to keep things out rather than in doesn't mean the principle alters. And we have plans to create something rather special here – it should hold even another Azrenel. The incursion is due at dawn, yes? How long before you're able to pinpoint the exact location?"

"I'll do that now."

They were a few hours east of Asentyr, on a road trailing over gorse-studded hills notable only for sheep and a cold wind. It wouldn't be long before the sun set. Rennyn climbed out of the coach and glanced over the encampment, ignoring the expectant interest directed back at her. Ten pair of Sentene, five members of the Hand, and an impressive number of Ferumguard. Captain Illuma had called this a war, and Rennyn found herself with troops, not quite at her command, but following her lead.

Absurd to resent it. But she recognised that feeling as a gloss over underlying worry. She didn't want to work with the Sentene, and certainly not the Kellian. Not because she feared they would run her through, but because they seemed so dutiful. Loyal servants of the kingdom, ready to spend their lives for its protection.

Unhappy with her thoughts, Rennyn took one of her bags from the coach and slid the ring attached to Solace's focus over her finger. Already the pull was there, so she followed it, trailed at a discreet distance by an escort of five. Up the hill, not all the way to the crest, but a long walk. When she stopped she stood on a patch of grass like all the grass about it.

"I can't predict the width," she said.

"It is enough to have a starting point," said the senior representative of the Hand, a man she vaguely recalled being named Barton or Martin. He stepped forward, gazing eagerly at the ground. "A priceless opportunity, not only for our defence but to study a breach in formation. Katznien, have this space cleared and flattened while it's still light."

The Ferumguard accompanying him signalled, and the camp below stirred. Battle lines would be drawn.

"They'll have prepared a meal, if you're hungry," said Lieutenant Danress, who appeared to have been assigned the particular duty of ushering Rennyn about.

Rennyn shook her head and walked a short way up the hill. "I'll go in now," she said, finding a jutting rock which was suitable for her purposes. "I'm trying to gauge how much she's grown in power." She gestured, shearing off the top of the rock so she had a flat surface to work with, then began marking out her circle with swift strokes.

"Can I ask you a question?" Lieutenant Danress asked, when Rennyn had finished and was checking for errors. The woman had opened the front of her cloak so that Rennyn could see her face, and her apologetic smile. "We've been instructed not to antagonise you with constant interrogation, to simply observe as much as possible, but I'm too curious not to ask. Ignore me if you don't want to answer."

"You'd need to ask either way," Rennyn said, amused by the idea of them being ordered not to irritate her.

"Why is your focus *black*? I've never seen or heard of anything like it. And, well, it's smaller than mine, but I'm nowhere near as...as obscenely powerful as you."

"How many times have you summoned?"

Danress lifted her focus on its chain. "Twice." There was a hint of pride in her voice, understandable because the stone was large for only two summonings. Rennyn drew her own focus free of her collar and considered it. Certainly smaller.

"Two hundred and eighty-five," she said.

There was a clatter from further down the slope. One of the Sentene had dropped an iron bar which was apparently part of the plan for a shield. "Kellian have such sharp hearing," Rennyn murmured wryly. The one called Faille had been sitting outside the infirmary window listening to Seb chat to the girl from Falk. Not that Seb was likely to say anything too revealing. And every one of the Kellian at the breach site had looked up when she'd answered Danress' question.

"It was an experiment in summoning," she explained. "I was following the debate on what the dark layer separating multiple focuses is. The layer always appears, no matter how much power you succeed in summoning. I decided to build it up by tiny degrees, rather like a pearl. It's certainly slower, but less dangerous. I would say the result is purer."

"Quality over quantity." Danress looked thoroughly disconcerted. "Have you truly been in the Eferum that many times?"

"Every morning for six months, at one time." Rennyn was still watching the reaction of the Kellian, who were now gazing up at her, openly listening. "My father made me stop summoning more than once a month because it does things to you, the Eferum. Like not being able to go out in the sun, or eat cooked things."

Satisfied that her sigils were correctly drawn, Rennyn moved to the centre of her circle and poured power into the sigils until they took her away from her audience. The chill quickly sapped any annoyance she felt at the transparency of Danress' ingenuous approach, and she turned her attention to her appearance, checking that her presence was properly cloaked.

This very basic precaution had become less of a rote exercise, though she could see no unusual activity nearby. The Eferum was vast and black and very quiet. Not wasting any time, she slipped free one sheet of paper from the small pile she'd brought with her, a casting which would measure the force of any movement of the Efera. Like most paper-wrought castings, the power she put into it burned the sheet to ash.

The shield the Sentene were constructing was very visible, blazing with such power it blotted out the moving motes around it. Rennyn shook her head, and closed her hand around Solace's focus. Hard to guess how the Eferum-Get would react to that, but if they broke away from the breach then she was at risk, for she would need to drop the cloak during the attunement. Usually not such a dangerous thing, but if such a mass of Eferum-Get were loose in the vicinity, the chance of an encounter was much higher.

Her divination was reacting to changes in the currents about her, so she gripped the focus tightly and, forewarned, only pressed her lips together when a stream of moving shadows rushed toward the breach. No possibility of coincidence: they had to be working with Solace. Wasting no time, she made the attunement at the first possible moment, then immediately stepped back into the world.

It was a cold, wet dawn. The sun was a hint on the horizon, a wan ghost compared to the light coruscating around the shield.

Inside was a tangle of claw and wing and dark flanks, all pressed together in a writhing mass. Any touch of the walls confining them produced a burning flash, and outside the fiery glow of the shield were the scorch marks of a larger circle. Slowly, it was compressing.

The stench was stomach-turning. Rennyn stared for a long moment, then began walking at an angle down the hill toward the camp below, keeping well away from that circle of extinction. The faintest tread behind her warned her that she wasn't alone. One of the Kellian, scarcely visible in the light, and soon joined by Lieutenant Danress. Persistent irritants, though they at least had the sense to keep silent. Few Eferum-Get had more than an animal intelligence, and the vast majority were predators that considered humans an excellent meal. But they were screaming, these monsters. Screaming as they burned.

CRSO

The northwest of Tyrland climbed into mountains and forests and what was once the Duchy of Surclere. It had a grand and lofty air, and a habit of producing waterfalls unexpectedly around corners. The roads were fantastically bad.

Even with enchantments the jolting made it very hard to read, and impossible to write, so Rennyn spent her time staring out the coach window. It had taken more than a day and a half to travel from the third incursion point to this far into the mountains, and she was weary of the journey. She had long loved this part of Tyrland, but today its isolation just felt inconvenient.

They drew to a halt beside the worn remnants of a wall, barely visible beneath a rampant mass of morning glory. The tracery of a road danced down through a sunlit valley, disappearing before it reached the tumble of stones forming the outline of a building. A pair of spiralling birds were the only sign of movement.

"Surclere Manor," said one of the Ferumguard, as Rennyn climbed out of the coach. Her escort had been reduced to six Ferumguard and the four Sentene whose primary task was keeping her alive: Meniar, Faral, Faille and Danress. "We'll not be getting the coaches down there. The horses should manage."

"The road's fallen away completely in a couple of places," Rennyn said, slipping the strap of her smaller bag over her shoulder. "It's a nearly two hour walk."

"You've been here before, then?" Danress asked.

"I summoned my first focus here." She gazed across the valley. "I knew I'd need to know the place."

Lieutenant Faral, a female Kellian of particularly willowy proportions, was examining the ground by the wall. "No sign of recent tracks. But this is only the obvious approach."

Captain Faille nodded, and with a brief hand gesture assigned two of the Ferumguard to remain behind. Rennyn had yet to see him even move without reason, let alone speak unnecessarily. But, like all the Sentene, he got things done quickly. She did not have to wait long while they prepared, and they soon started down the ancient road.

It was wonderfully quiet. Wind, and the occasional call of birds. The loudest thing was the crunch of their boots. This area had never been precisely populous, but it had withered after Surclere Manor had burned. The village further into the mountains had faded altogether, and the one they'd passed on the way had been less than prosperous. But the people owned a remote pride, and had watched with heads held high as the Sentene passed.

The walk helped clear her mind. There were times when Rennyn found the plan too much, when her certainty faltered and she doubted her resolution to end this. The screaming of the Eferum-Get had unsettled her. They were monsters, and they ate people. Their existence in Tyrland was an obvious wrong. But they still felt pain.

Her greatest issue was the effectiveness of the cage. If she had chosen to work with the Sentene from the start, the disaster in Asentyr might have been completely contained. Over a thousand people. She had always known that people would very likely die, but with every passing day she wanted a new solution, one which was safe, sure, and without cost.

All she could do was remember what she'd said to Seb. If she could prevent someone's death she would. It was a simple pledge, but she murmured it to herself as she led the Sentene along one side of the manor's remains toward the summoning circle.

"Wait."

Startled, Rennyn turned to Captain Faille. He was gazing at the circle through narrowed eyes, then reached slowly over his head and drew the sword he had strapped to his back. The other Sentene and Ferumguard followed his lead, though Rennyn doubted they could see whatever had made him suspicious. She certainly couldn't, and there was no sense of casting.

But – tilting her head to one side, she tried to puzzle it out. Not casting, not the sense of Efera being worked, but there was a kind of current, a thing she was more used to feeling in the Eferum. A distortion.

The Sentene split into pairs and spread to either side, with the Ferumguard forming a loose semi-circle behind them. Both Danress and Meniar had their slates out. Rennyn scanned the area. The summoning circle had been in a separate, smaller building near the main house, and sat a little lower on the hill's slope. With the walls gone, and dirt creeping past the edges of tumbled stone, the exposed floor looked like a white pool. Trees had grown around it, but she couldn't see anyone hiding in the dappled shade.

Then one of the shadows laughed. Rennyn glimpsed a shape, the line of a shoulder, of a man sitting with his back against one of the larger blocks of stone.

"A Montjuste-Surclere with a Kellian bodyguard. I do like irony."

The words dragged and echoed unnaturally. The figure shifted again, and through him Rennyn could see moss-covered stone, and a fragment of fern.

"It's – some kind of illusion, Captain," said Meniar.

"Truly, the blood has weakened. Following that traitor's course without deviation. So predictable, so unoriginal."

Dropping the makings of a Thought-shield she'd instinctively drawn, Rennyn walked forward and stared at the man in the shadows. Black hair, black eyes. A heart-shaped face, delicately made. She could feel the distortion more clearly as she came closer, but there was none of the stamp and scent of worked Efera. He turned his head to study her, the motion oddly too quick and too slow, the black eyes full of mockery and malice.

"A projection," she said, scarcely believing her own words. "It's a projection out of the Eferum."

"Not entirely dull-witted, then. Come closer, little cousin. I want to look at you."

She wanted to look at him too, but she only circled a short way to her right to get a better angle.

"You will not object, I hope, if I name you cousin? A few too many 'greats' to describe the proper relationship."

Rennyn narrowed her eyes. "You look like your brother," she said, and was rewarded with a sudden flash of fury. He moved incautiously, and the entire projection flickered out of existence for several moments, then returned.

Back in control, he reassumed his air of pleasant malice. "Different enough," he said. "Far less dead, at any rate. The shield was unsporting, little cousin. Did your friends not feel equal to the hunt?"

"Have you anything of interest to say, or are you merely here to talk at me?"

His mouth curved up, wider than it should. "I'm going to *enjoy* you." He leaned forward, almost as if he meant to approach her, adding: "Shall I tell you something useful? Change your tactics."

Before Rennyn had to think of a response he was gone, the sense of distortion fading to nothing. A bird called, and the drone of insects rose as if to underline their previous absence. Rennyn stared at an innocuous rocky stone, then sighed and found a different one to serve as a seat.

"Well, that was unexpected."

"I – you have a gift for understatement," Lieutenant Danress' voice wavered, then she shook her head and allowed the spell she'd been holding back to dissipate. "The brother you were talking about–?"

"Tiandel." Rennyn felt light-headed, and worked to adjust. "We have a portrait of him."

"How does this effect your plans?" asked Captain Faille, not one to waste time exclaiming.

"It's always been the differences between the first iteration of the Grand Summoning and the current which have posed the greatest risk. I can't say any of my family ever predicted that Solace would bear a child to – whatever it is she's allied herself with. This confirms, at least, that the size of these incursions is no coincidence. In terms of attuning the younger focus – if their purpose is to stop me, it means they know every step, and are no doubt able to calculate the locations as we did."

"If?" asked Lieutenant Danress sharply.

"Her need for the attunement wouldn't have changed. The question is whether she is willing to risk me being able to use it, or if she thinks she can take it from me. There's over a day between the final attunement and the conclusion of the Grand Summoning, and I expect that to be a challenge to survive. Tiandel's attack on Solace was successful primarily because she did not expect it. Still, she may not choose to risk a second attunement, and instead find another way to deal with the size of the new focus. To that point, I suppose I need to try and discover whether this second son has done anything clever here."

She spent some time divining, trying to imagine any way a person in the Eferum could interfere with this stage of the attunement. The problem was, she was still struggling to believe the projection was possible. Even casting an image out into this world, let alone one that could react, that could hold a conversation–! The distortion was an incredible obstacle to overcome, and that projection told her that this second son was an extraordinary mage.

In any case, she could not find sign of a trap, so she turned to preparation. The Sentene and Ferumguard alternated scanning the horizons for enemies with watching Rennyn as she marked a circle and set out the components. She wondered if they'd really been ordered not to bother her with questions, or if that had been Danress' invention. They certainly obediently shut up whenever she showed a lack of interest in talking, and she was sure it frustrated them immensely. She wished she'd decided to come here alone.

The vessel for the younger focus marked a major stage of the attunement. The pieces had been prepared by her great-grandmother – two halves of a hollow crystal sphere which could be bound together with bronze and copper bands. Rennyn pulled Solace's younger focus from its wire loops and placed it within the sphere, then carefully worked the bands into position. Placing it in the centre of the circle of sigils, she stepped outside to cast.

This was the most technically complex thing Rennyn had to do, and she set all her concentration to the task, eyes not wavering from the sigils as each illuminated. Casting of this level was not simply a matter of thrusting power through the shapes of sigils, but of taking an absolute view of their meaning, requiring an understanding of every nuance of intent. And since the overarching spell, the attunement, was more Symbolic than Sigillic, she faced the risk of the spell becoming rather more than she asked for.

On the far side of the veil, a mass of power was being worked into a thing which would become an extension of Solace Montjuste-Surclere. Rennyn had three times allowed the younger focuses to taste the edges of that power. Solace's power. Because they were a part of Her, they were also a part of It. They were in two different places, yes, but then that place was the origin of the younger focuses as well.

The air before Rennyn grew heavy, and the overhanging branches sagged, leaves and twigs falling and being whirled away before they could land within the circle. Everything seemed taller, with the Sentene and the trees and the mountains all looming above a sucking well, pulling at them, trying to drag them through the veil to a vast blackness.

The vessel made a tiny clicking sound and settled fractionally. Done. As the distortion faded, Rennyn straightened and took a few deep breaths, then flexed her fingers. She tended to clench her fists during this kind of casting, and the skin had not fully recovered from their burns.

Lieutenant Meniar, who was a brown, slim man with an attractive smile, appeared at her elbow and offered a flask of water. "It worked, then?"

"Try to pick it up," Rennyn said, taking the flask.

Meniar was quick to step forward, but his hand slipped off the sphere when it didn't lift as he expected. He shot her a quick, surprised glance, then wrapped both hands around the outer bands, shoulders bulging with an effort which brought no reward. He stepped back, face flushed. "Keste," he said, "You try."

Lieutenant Faral looked first to Captain Faille for permission, then approached the vessel at a slight tangent, as if it was a horse she thought might startle. Rennyn wondered briefly if the attunement would treat a Kellian differently, but Faral was no more successful than her partner.

"It's a link to both the Grand Summoning and the bloodline," she explained, picking up the bound spheres, now the size of two fists. It was a solid weight, but as yet no heavier than it appeared. "It will reject anyone who isn't a Montjuste-Surclere."

"Of which there are now four," Danress said.

Rennyn nodded, and looked restlessly at a particular moss-covered block. "He didn't come through the previous breaches, and we've blocked that passage now. And he can't complete the attunement within the Eferum. But—"

Change your tactics. Rennyn looked over her bodyguards and worried about what that meant.

TEN

The pebble skittered and bounced down the hill. Kendall watched it disappear, then sat back with an exhausted sigh. The throbbing in her head subsided a little, and she blinked, trying to decide what she was doing wrong. It had taken four days before anything at all had happened, and being able to make a pebble wobble and occasionally skip a bit was less than impressive. Especially when it took so much to manage any movement. Kendall could carry a thousand pebbles to the top of the palace with less effort than it was costing her to poke this one with magic.

Her stomach growled, and she decided she was more than ready for lunch. At least here every meal wasn't a matter of careful planning and scrimping. So far as Kendall could tell, she could spend her entire time refilling her plate in the dining hall and no-one would protest.

Climbing back up to the garden, she found Sebastian Montjuste-Surclere leaning against the balustrade clutching a thick wooden walking stick. His face was flushed with effort, but he seemed much less limp and ill than last time.

"Congratulations," he said as she clambered over the barrier.

Surprised and a little uncomfortable, Kendall glowered. "How did you know?"

"Oh, once you start casting, you get a good deal more sensitive to changes in the Efera. Enough to tell location, the power of the casting, sometimes even what's being cast. You weren't doing anything loud, but I was close enough to tell the direction."

Not loud about described it. Kendall had expected more of herself and turned away, shrugging her shoulders. Then she saw two men, Ferumguard, standing near the infirmary wall watching them.

"Do they follow you about?" she asked, interested.

Sebastian flicked an irritable glance at the pair. "There's always someone watching. They've the most fantastic library here, and I can't bear to read because I know someone's watching me do it. That's why I'm out here."

"They're still watching," Kendall pointed out. Her stomach growled again.

"Inevitably. But I want out of that infirmary, I want a room with a door I can shut, and they won't let me until I've improved more."

"Walking practice?"

"Something like." He gave her a diffident look, and added: "You'll be hungry after Thought-casting. How about you show me where to get something to eat? That should be enough that they can't say I need a nurse-maid."

"But they know you can use magic to go places, don't they?"

"I'm not allowed to, except in emergencies. Come on. Do we go back through the centre?"

"Quickest way," Kendall said, watching dubiously as he took a couple of steps, swinging his legs like he'd forgotten his knees. But he managed to get going at something faster than turtle pace, so Kendall led him left around the hallway which circled the Library Tower.

There were three dining halls bracketing the Halls of Magic's kitchens. The smallest and fanciest belonged to the Hand, and had lots of smaller tables and some pictures on the wall which Kendall had liked a lot, even though they only showed bowls and jugs and grapes. She'd snatched an enjoyable ramble in there, stroking velvet cushions and inspecting the carvings of the chair backs. Fine stuff.

The Sentene had their own area, but Kendall hadn't more than poked her nose in. It was sparse and tidy and looked like it wasn't often used. The third hall was well battered, crammed with long benches and always too full of people. The Arkathan was the busiest section of the Halls, with students ranging from Kendall's age all the way up to their twenties. People were always coming and going here, grabbing plates from the gleaming stacks and moving through the serving trays, taking their pick. The noise made

Kendall want to leave: too much chattering, clattering, benches scraping back, mugs clunking.

They arrived just as all this was reaching lunchtime peak, and Kendall took Sebastian's elbow and made sure he got across the hall upright. She filled their plates too, not trusting his ability to juggle his cane, then moved them to one side of the servery so she could look for a place to sit down.

"Is it always this crowded?" Sebastian asked, for there were precious few spare seats.

"The first couple of days I was here, when there were more classes, it didn't get so bad," she said. "People would rush in, and gulp things down and then rush out. Now they all sit around gossiping and blocking—"

She broke off as a loud scraping of benches brought a sudden hush to the room. At one of the corner tables everyone had stood up at once, and were walking to return their plates, all very stiff-backed and correct. Sukata Illuma, who had obviously just sat down, gave no sign that she'd even noticed their departure, or the murmur of discomfort mixed with enjoyment which ran through the room.

Kendall nearly lost her own balance when Sebastian moved forward. He'd gone white, with spots of colour highlighting his cheekbones. Really angry. And then he stalked across the hall. Even balancing on the cane he managed dignity and outrage with every step. Kendall trailed in his wake, spotting his Ferumguard minders watching with the interest shared by the entire room.

"May we join you?" Sebastian asked, and didn't wait for an answer before sitting down opposite Sukata. "I'm Sebastian. This is Kendall."

"Sukata," said Sukata.

Kendall suffered a slight shock on seeing Sukata's expression. In the little time she'd been at the Arkathan she'd learned Sukata was master of the art of being correct, so perfect that all the slights and snobberies of students and faculty had no power. Like all the Kellian, nothing seemed to touch her. But she wasn't that way about Sebastian. She met his determined eyes and actually changed colour. So extremely startled and uncertain she was not quite able to hide it.

There was some noise from a nearby table, and Sukata's expression flicked back to normal. But the talk wasn't down to her. A tall boy, three or four years older, had stood up and was staring at their small group. Beside him, a much younger girl with the same fine, fair features was asking him questions in an excited voice, demanding until he responded. The girl bounced gleefully at his response, and wriggled out of her seat.

She wasn't much more than ten years old, dressed in a floaty wisp of rose silk. A fairy-princess, Kendall thought, and realised how well that fitted when the girl ran straight up to Sebastian and announced: "Justin says I have the right to call you cousin."

"Do you?" Sebastian ran fingers absently through his hair and blinked at the girl, then looked past her to her elder brother, approaching with a little train of friends behind him. With some difficulty he stood up, and bowed carefully. "Exceedingly remote cousins, Your Highness."

"But the link's still there," said Prince Justin. "And that's all that's important to Sera. She's been longing to meet you." He laughed. "I can't say I haven't been more than curious myself. May we join you?"

Kendall suspected Sebastian wasn't altogether pleased by this development, but he agreed. The eight-person table was quickly over-filled.

"Why did your sister snub Grandmama?" Princess Sera asked, making mischief clear as day. Kendall's eyes widened, then she settled back to enjoy the entertainment. Sebastian hadn't become general gossip, but the royal family had obviously been informed, and weren't overly shy about confronting him. And Princess Sera had all the makings of a sugar-glossed brat.

"I hadn't heard she had," Sebastian said. He was still pale, but not at all nervous. "What makes you think it?"

"Grandmama summoned her to audience, and she said she was too busy and left!" Princess Sera made a great play of looking shocked.

"Well, my sister does have to be at certain places at certain times, even if that means missing out on meeting your Grandmother. The incursions won't wait for her to arrive."

"What is she actually doing?" Prince Justin asked. "I've heard so many different things."

"Building a weapon," Sebastian said, after a slight pause. "The same thing Tiandel used."

"Something to use against the monsters?" Princess Sera's eyes were round and innocent, but Kendall wouldn't trust her an inch.

"No, just against the Black Queen. The Sentene and the Hand are dealing with the Eferum-Get." Sebastian turned from the princess to the Kellian girl making herself unobtrusive in the corner. "I wanted to ask you if you're related to Captain Illuma. You look very like her."

"My mother."

"She saved my life. I need to thank her, but haven't found a chance."

"It is her duty," Sukata replied , putting down her knife. Kendall was sure she wasn't the only one who looked at the girl's hands. Like most of the Kellian seemed to, Sukata clipped the nails of one hand, but left the other pointed and alien.

"Maybe. Is duty any reason to honour her less?" He turned his head to meet Prince Justin's eyes, and his gaze was so uncompromising that Kendall heard a couple of indrawn breaths. The prince flushed.

"I should get back," Sebastian continued, struggling again to his feet. "Kendall, you don't mind leading me?"

"Sure," Kendall said, taking a last hasty mouthful, then pushing aside her plate. She had no intention of remaining at the table to deal with the aftermath of that stoush. Sukata, she noticed, wasted no time collecting the plates and retreating herself.

"So what did that achieve?" she asked as soon as they were out of the room.

"It made me feel better."

"Your sister snubs the Queen and you turn your nose up at her heirs. Not really sensible."

"Maybe." He scrubbed a hand over his face, and she noticed darkening shadows under his eyes. "I suppose I lost my temper. He ranked everyone there, watched them act like that, and made no protest. As good as countenancing it. He has a responsibility toward the people who serve his family. Besides, that wretched little girl was working toward asking if Ren really, truly wants her Grandmama's throne, and I didn't want to dignify that idiocy with an answer."

"Do you think that's where she was going?" Kendall wouldn't have been surprised. "Not that you acting like the whole room was beneath you isn't going to put fuel on that fire."

"The entire question's bizarre. The last thing I thought we'd have to contend with. Though–" He smiled. "The Surcleres were famed for two things: magic and arrogance. If it's the family reputation driving this, I guess I should stop trying to live up to it."

He was leaning on her more by the time they reached the infirmary, and dropped heavily to the bed, dislodging a couple of books. Kendall picked up the nearest. It was written, not printed, and even when she made the effort to decipher the scratchings, it made little sense. Something about the way the Eferum was a globe around the world, but inside and through and behind or similar nonsense.

"Control's the thing you need to work for now," Sebastian said, kicking off his shoes. "You work on control your entire life, but the least you should aim for is to be able to move an object with the same exactitude as you would with your hands. It's amazingly hard to manage, so start with just lifting and holding the pebble in place. Hold it unmoving as long as you can. Hugely dull, of course, but it will make a change from your Sigillic dictionary."

"What do I need to be able to do to be a Circle-Turner?"

"The basic ones about villages, you mean? Not much. Get a proper understanding of the sigils involved – there's about thirty in those 'don't cross' circles. Beyond that, just have enough control to maintain a flow of power to activate sigils. Most of those Circle-casters are as much mages as a boy with a broom is a knight."

"Speaking of Surclere arrogance." Kendall shook her head when he grinned. "But how strong do you have to be? Nothing like your sister, I guess, but – are mages ever not powerful enough to turn circles?"

"I don't suppose most travelling Turners have even summoned a focus, which is a good deal harder. The virtue of those circles is built up with constant reinforcement, not a single big casting. There's no huge power requirement." He gave her a swift glance. "The pebble felt like a mountain, right? That's not a gauge of your strength – you're using a limb you've never even felt before. It's like comparing a baby's strength to an adult's."

"Then how can I tell how strong I'll be when I've practiced more? It matters, doesn't it?"

"To a degree. The better mages have more strength in their focuses than intrinsically. The Force magic exercises will allow you to develop some of your natural potential. That will take quite a long time, and should also give you some idea of how much fine control you're able to achieve. Strength, control and sense are the three basics. Willpower is their foundation. And by then you'll probably know enough about magic to know if you're really a mage or not. Presuming they ever give you something other than a dictionary to read."

"Whether I'm a mage or not? Is this more Surclere snootiness?"

"Perhaps. Are you really a mage if you just follow the patterns set out by other people? The difference between a painter and someone who copies other people's paintings. Most of these people calling themselves mages, even in a place like this, just follow well-travelled paths. They'll never cast a Sigillic someone hasn't written for them, they don't even bother to try Thought magic. Symbolic they run scared from. Most of the major castings will be beyond them because those castings aren't just a matter of following a recipe, of writing a bunch of sigils and thrusting power into them. You need to be able to think, to see how it all fits together, and glimpse more."

There was an impassioned little throb in his voice. Kendall looked from him to the piles of musty books, dry and dull. "You really love this stuff, don't you?"

"It's what I am. I couldn't stop if I tried. Even Ren, who swears that if she lives through this she's never going to cast again, and will spend the rest of her life lying on a couch reading novels and eating cream cakes. She wouldn't be able to go more than a couple of weeks before some idea occurs to her and she has to experiment with it."

"It's what you are." Kendall considered him doubtfully, then shrugged. "Well, even those broomstick knights get paid more than enough. If you're right about the strength, that's a reason either way to see what kind of mage I can be."

"I've probably made you some enemies," he said, the thought obviously just occurring to him.

"Maybe. But it was fun to watch."

"Seriously, though. My fault for getting angry."

Kendall thought about it, then shrugged. "I know where to bite to make people let go, and they've rules here that make it risky for the students to hurt each other. They already ignore me, thank Fel. I guess they could try and get me kicked out."

Sebastian leaned back on his pillows looking tired and concerned. Not just making noises, but genuinely worried that he'd caused her trouble.

"There's no cost to me, see? I didn't particularly want to come here, and it would probably suit me better to go find someone a bit lower level who would teach me instead of giving me memory exercises. Whether I'm a 'real' mage or not, it's a bankable talent, and I'm smart enough to get myself 'prenticed pretty easy. And if I don't like it – well, I can read and write and run errands."

"And you were envying Ren." He sighed, his eyelids sagging. "You've something neither of us have."

"What's that?"

"The ability to walk away."

ELEVEN

Darasum House, the home of Earl Forinth, rested white and shimmering at the crest of a gentle hill. Before it, in what Rennyn was told was the Verisian style, was a great sweep of grassland exactly bisected by a series of terraced, stone-edged pools stretching halfway down to Carnell Lake. Spear-slim cypress in pale stone urns marched down the centre of the pool, with a rigidly kept herbal border keeping exact pace on either side. Between house and pools bloomed a rose garden of scrupulous symmetry.

The Earl had been informed well in advance that an incursion had been predicted to take place on his estate. He was a bluff, slightly pompous man in his forties, all rosy cheeks and moustaches. Rennyn had found his mixture of affront and stifled pleasure in the proceedings rather endearing. Then Solace's focus had led them a third of the way down that magnificent, carefully-tended stretch of grass and the day had ground to a halt.

Feeling sorry for both the Earl and the two Hand mages trying to calm him, Rennyn wandered back up the lawn and explored the roses. She was joined by the Earl's wife, Lady Risdale, a heavyset, red-faced woman who told her the names of different flowers and watched imperturbably as her husband gesticulated and shouted in the distance while the mass of Ferumguard and Sentene waited to one side.

"How very out of place they look," Lady Risdale remarked. "Like some fantastical flock brought on the wind. Shall I go calm him? You must be anxious to prepare."

"The breach isn't due till late afternoon." Rennyn glanced up at the high sun. "This parkland is worth a few minutes' protest."

"Grass will grow back. And it will give him something to point to and boast of." Lady Risdale smiled indulgently. "He has been very excited, and will remember the alternative soon enough. He will dine out on what he sees tonight for years."

Rennyn glanced sideways at the noblewoman, at the lines of care and humour on her face. "Don't," she said. "Watch them build it if you wish, but not the rest. Go into the village for the evening. And send your servants away."

"You think there is a risk some will escape this shield?"

"I think you would not be able to describe what happens tonight and stomach a meal."

Lady Risdale's smile faded, and she stood motionless as her husband made a dramatic gesture and began striding toward the house. "I have already sent the children to my mother. I will – wish you luck, Lady Montjuste-Surclere."

Murmuring her thanks, Rennyn walked back down to the cluster of uniformed figures as they switched into action. By the time she reached them, Earl Forinth's sweeping lawn had a large circle cut out of it, beetles and earthworms squirming away from their sudden exposure. A spot toward the outer edge of the expanse of scythed grass seemed near enough, and Rennyn cleared and marked a far more modest circle, then spent some time casting defensive enchantments on herself. The Sentene had been discussing ways to overcome the practical difficulties of protecting someone in the Eferum, but if that was even close to easy, summoning focuses would not be so perilous. Captain Illuma was playing bodyguard today, and all she could do while her charge was in the Eferum was wait for her return. Rennyn thought she detected faint approval for her precautions, but doubted any of the Kellian enjoyed having their hands tied.

Returning from Surclere, her small group had found almost the entire complement of Tyrland's Sentene and more than half of the Hand waiting at Fenlis, the village abutting Darasum Park. 'Change your tactics.' They weren't certain this referred to the shield, but Lady Weston had wasted no time after reviewing the report Captain Faille had sent ahead about the projection. She would not risk a repeat of Asentyr.

Rennyn, stretching after a tedious round of casting, nodded brief farewell to Captain Illuma and fed the Sigillic until it shifted her into the cold embrace of the Eferum. Solace's focus, now attached to a chain and heavy bracelet, immediately dragged at her hold and nearly slipped free of her fingers. It had taken a major step toward being one with the Grand Summoning, and she shuddered at the weight of power it allowed her to sense.

She'd prepared for an ambush by Eferum-Get, but the dark sea showed no unusual signs of life, and her divinations revealed only minor creatures some distance away. Perhaps, now that the Sentene were sealing these major breaches, there would be no more attempts at spectacular incursions.

Still cautious, Rennyn next triggered the divination which would measure the force approaching her. Soon. She cupped the vessel in both hands and waited, having no plans to linger a moment longer than necessary. The wave was coming.

And a tiny star came with it. Rennyn frowned, but it was not headed for her. A single Eferum-Get, one of the scaled and winged Darensi, was guiding a compact mote of tightly-wound Efera toward the forming breach. Some kind of casting? It looked like the hint to change tactics had been a warning that the Eferum-Get were about to alter theirs.

Knowing there was little chance of being able to return before that thing had gone through the breach, Rennyn concentrated on making the attunement, choosing the best moment rather than rushing. The younger focus pulled at her till she felt she was a fisherman who had hooked a whale. She would have to set her circle further from the breach next time, or risk being dragged in.

"Hello cousin."

As shock sent a cold spike down her spine, arms closed around her waist. And, far worse, two injunctions settled on her as he spoke, binding her from casting and moving. Immediately she tried to break them, to overwhelm them with her sheer strength, but they were an odd structure, layered as if she were wound in a thousand cords which flexed instead of snapping. She couldn't stop Solace's second son as he tightened his arms, pressing against her back.

"We have so much to talk of, cousin, but first I think a moment's silence only appropriate. You must say goodbye to your little friends."

Rennyn couldn't make the adjustment to look through the veil, couldn't see what that mote was doing. She couldn't even close her eyes. But the hot circle of power which was the shield abruptly flared and vanished, leaving her surrounded by darkness.

She pushed harder against the invisible bonds, feeling them stretch and fray. It would break, strand by strand if necessary, but the question was how much time she'd have to do it. Rennyn had never met an injunction so well built, its strength not drawn from any massive amount of power, but the intricacy of structure. What kind of mage was he? She'd not been able to detect his presence, but he had unerringly found her. She hadn't had time to trigger even one of her defences. But he hadn't killed her yet.

"How your heart is beating, cousin." The arms around her waist tightened further, and he rested his cheek against the side of her throat. She could feel his heart beating too. Fast. Excited.

"My name is Helecho," he continued, in a conversational tone. "I thought you should know. I'm going to have you, you see. You're mine from the moment I walk into your world. You should know the name of the one who owns you."

With unhurried deliberation he undid the top four buttons of her shirt and pulled it loose at the throat, then began to kiss the side of her neck. The touch of his lips sent a blank incredulity through Rennyn, but the jolt woke a spark of hope. He wasn't going to kill her, not right away at any rate. And no matter how well-built these injunctions, she had the advantage of strength. The longer he delayed, the more certain became her escape.

An injunction was an unequal battle of strengths. Structured magic was always stronger than the pure will of Thought casting which was the only recourse of a person under an injunction. Rennyn had been able to break Lady Weston's injunction quickly because she was that much stronger than the Grand Magister, and the woman had not been prepared and so used a very straightforward Sigillic spell inscribed on a bracelet. This Helecho's injunctions hadn't used even half as much power as the Grand Magister's, but their layers stretched instead of obligingly snapping.

Anger helped. All she was able to do was stand there while he nuzzled and licked her throat, his arms wrapping so tightly back around her waist her stomach felt bruised. It was revolting, infuriating. And then he freed one arm so he could slide a hand inside her shirt, beneath her thin camisole to fondle her breast. Outrage roared through her and she stoked it, concentrated it, fed it. Thought magic was as much will as raw strength, and the injunction was becoming badly frayed.

"I can't promise to treat you well," he murmured, nipping lightly at her skin. His teeth were sharp. "Rather the opposite. But you mustn't give in. Too dull, if you crumble straight away."

He was so pleased. Enjoyment of her situation radiated off him, and his excitement was reaching a fever-pitch as he bit her again and again, each time coming closer to breaking the skin. He squeezed her breast in painful accompaniment, twisting soft flesh cruelly, and made a little noise in his throat, one of triumph and satisfaction, and it was too much. It was enough.

Shedding fragments of the casting, Rennyn thrust him furiously away, and triggered one of the spells she'd prepared. The Efera all around her ignited, white fire blasting out into the darkness. Without pause she followed it with three expanding circles which would cut through anything, but they sliced into nothing. Unlike her, he could easily move through the Eferum.

"So powerful." The gloating words drifted out of the darkness, out of her reach. "I *am* going to enjoy you, little cousin."

Shuddering, Rennyn refastened her shirt as she tried to isolate from which direction the voice had come. "Not if I see you first, worm." She guessed a direction and spent her anger in a meaningless bolt of pure force, but there was no sign that she'd hit anything. This was his home ground and there was no value in lingering, so she made the shift back to the far side of the veil. And fell.

Strong arms caught her. Rennyn gasped, and clutched at an unseen shoulder, then stared about her. She'd forgotten the mote of worked Efera.

It was night, with a low sliver of moon. The carefully smoothed earth where she'd marked her circle was gone. Most everything was gone, replaced by a massive crater, a dozen feet deep in the centre. It covered a quarter of the lawn, shearing the stone-lined pool in two. The explosion hadn't reached the house or even the rose garden, but dirt and stone had been flung in every direction, sparing little.

The arms holding her tightened, and Rennyn looked up. Captain Illuma, faintly luminescent in the moonlight. There were others: Danress, Faille, and Illuma's partner Vesan. Waiting patiently for her return.

"How many dead?" Rennyn asked, struggling to control herself.

"Three," Captain Illuma replied, and started walking out of the crater. "But few escaped without injury."

Looking around, Rennyn was surprised there hadn't been more deaths. "The shield didn't contain the blast?"

"The shield was the blast," Lieutenant Danress explained. "Some kind of spell which converted the shield's energy. You were a long time returning."

"Yes." It was a dry little word, and Rennyn closed her eyes to push away the sudden roil in her stomach. "Solace's second son calls himself Helecho, and he is enjoying himself far too much. I don't think the intention was to kill me, though. He didn't even try to take my focus, and he could have very easily. A taunting kind of creature, this uncle of mine. Playing games."

They had reached flatter ground, so Rennyn slid free of Captain Illuma's hold, concentrating as tightly as she could on business, on what must be done. "I learned a couple of things. He's at a disadvantage in terms of power. He can't have summoned a focus of his own, perhaps is unable to without coming to this world first. So though his castings might be technically skilled, there's a limit to the scope of them."

"Broad enough." Danress' voice was bitter.

"He's nigh-undetectable in the Eferum," Rennyn continued. "So I will change my approach there. I think I should be able to avoid another ambush. What do the Hand say about using the shield again?"

"They debate the point," Illuma said, leading the way toward the drive. "And will put the question to the Grand Magister."

Rennyn nodded, then retreated into silence for the walk to the coaches and the ride to the nearby village. She was tired, cold, hungry, and had been...wounded. And three more people were dead. Just for the night, she wanted a way to stop thinking. She wanted her father.

"Why are you frightened?"

Startled, Rennyn looked up. She hadn't even noticed the coach draw to a halt, or the door open. Captain Faille was a pearl-tipped shadow blocking the way out. "What?" she asked, not equal to any better answer.

In the pause before he responded Rennyn could hear the sounds of people moving about, of horses. They'd reached the inn the Hand had commandeered.

"You are perhaps not so arrogant as you pretend," Captain Faille said finally, in his soft, attenuated voice. "But you are secure in your abilities. You did not so much as flinch when we met at Finton. During the incursion in Asentyr your plans were completely overset, and that casting was one which had every likelihood of killing you. It barely made you hesitate. In Surclere, this second son's existence was simply a new factor to include in your calculations. But now you are frightened. Why?"

Rennyn stared, resenting the uniform which hid so much of his face, and the lighting which always conspired to make Kellian impossible to read. Surely she could not be so transparent as he made it sound. How much more had he seen? He was risky, more dangerous than she'd realised. But, all the same, the question deserved an answer.

"I was raised to do everything I could to stop Solace," she said. "Or to die trying. I'm used to that idea. But I never pictured anything but a quick death. The idea of being...brutalised by this son of Solace, that is new to me." Her skin crawled at unwanted memory, and she pressed her lips together to control them.

A slight shift of position was all of his response, and then he stepped aside. Rennyn escaped upstairs, to the room she'd left her bags in hours ago. A tray of food had been set out waiting but, hungry as she was she couldn't face it, and stood by the fire clenching her fists. Frightened. It was true. It was what that gloating snake had been trying to achieve.

A tap at the door broke into her angry thoughts, and Rennyn turned a less than pleasant expression on the two maidservants who opened it.

"You ordered a bath, M'Lady?" the first girl asked uncertainly, balancing one end of a large tin tub.

Rennyn hadn't, but realised it was precisely what she needed and nodded stiffly, then went to the food tray and forced herself to eat while the maids carried in bucket after bucket of steaming water.

Captain Faille saw entirely too much.

TWELVE

T he stables of the Houses of Magic were crowded, for most of the Sentene had returned to Asentyr ahead of Rennyn's small party. Re-grouping to lick their wounds and make new plans. The undoing of the shield had been a bad blow.

"Can you tell Lady Weston I'd like to talk to her when she's free?" Rennyn asked, lugging her bags out of the coach.

"Of course," Lieutenant Danress replied, not managing to hide a flash of curiosity. Rennyn saw her give Captain Faille a quick glance, but the man only turned to remove his overlong sword from the second coach.

"I'll be with my brother." Rennyn wandered off, cheating a little with the weight of the bags. She hadn't slept and was still very tired, but felt herself again. So long as she didn't think too much.

Asking about, she was directed to a small room in the Sentene's building. "I see you're making good use of the library," she said.

"Ren!" Seb jumped to his feet and hugged her tight.

She was glad of it, holding him close for a long moment before she let him pull away.

"You look terrible."

"Thanks. Have you heard much of what's been happening?"

"Hardly. They see me as babysitting, nothing more. The way they moved me this morning, I had a feeling they needed the infirmary."

"Yes." Rennyn cleared a few books from the bed, then took him through the events of the past few days. The excitement died from his eyes, but then he frowned and shook his head.

"It shouldn't make any difference, really. Well, not to our plans, though if we think of any way to help the Sentene with the incursions, we could make a few suggestions. But – this Helecho – do you think he's as loyal a son as Tiandel?"

Seb was always quick to the vital points. "The Summoning will be taking most of her concentration, so that...creature gives her a free agent. Whether he was supposed to come through a breach himself and work from this side, or whether this invasion attempt was even part of her plans, that I can't guess. The Eferum may have changed her to the point where having a horde of Eferum-Get loose in Asentyr is acceptable to her."

"If he's making a play of his own, he'll not want her to complete the Summoning. Which would be reason enough to not kill you when he had the chance. It may mean things won't play out as we expect." He looked at her anxiously.

"Possible, I suppose." Rennyn sighed. "Though there's no proof he's not acting on her instructions. Either way, he's a nasty creature."

"Ren..."

"Mm?"

"The way this ends–"

"I know. I'll try my best." She clasped his hand, forestalling anything else he might say in this place where anyone could be listening. "How are your treatments going?"

"The worst is gone, but it'll be a couple of weeks yet before I'm clear of it. I'm clumsy, can't write properly, and if I stand up too long I go all shaky. In a way – in a way I'm glad it happened, that I came here."

"Yes." Rennyn looked down at her hands. "It's better to face some things, isn't it? No matter the complications."

"Speaking of which – I may have been a little tactless." With a certain amount of relish he told her of an encounter with the royal heirs.

"You do get these righteous fits."

"You'd have done the same thing."

A knock at the door ended the conversation, and it opened to reveal Lieutenant Danress.

"Lady Weston is ready to speak with you now."

Rennyn blinked. The Sentene mage had her uniform fully fastened, hiding the lower part of her face but totally failing to disguise simmering fury. Rennyn reviewed her conversation, wondering what she could have revealed, but then she realized that Danress was barely looking at her. This was nothing to do with the Claires.

Exchanging a blank look with Seb, she allowed herself to be led away. It wasn't just Danress. Rennyn caught a glimpse of several people having what seemed to be a heated argument in the Sentene's central hall. The whole atmosphere was charged with sudden upset. Decidedly worrying.

Lady Weston was alone in a cavernous and slightly musty study. She looked old, closer to her true age instead of the forty-ish woman magic allowed her to remain. She didn't seem surprised when Lieutenant Danress, instead of politely delivering Rennyn and departing, abruptly launched into speech.

"M'Lady, please, is there nothing you can do?"

The Grand Magister made a quelling gesture, fond but stern. "There are some battles it's better to concede, Jolien. This is one."

"But it's uncalled for," Lieutenant Danress said, tugging her collar open as if it stifled her. "They've done nothing to deserve it. And it's so ungrateful. Not to mention unjust."

"Justice and politics rarely walk together," Lady Weston said.

"Has something happened?" Rennyn asked, though she had a suspicion.

Lieutenant Danress turned to her, with a hint of doubt which told its own story. "The Queen has ordered that the Kellian be placed under injunction and put to the Question," she said, her voice quavering with anger.

"Someone's actually taking the idea of them worshipping Solace seriously?"

"Perhaps not worship. But the demand is growing that they submit some proof that there remains no lingering allegiance." Lady Weston shook her head. "The Kellian have their enemies, and this is naturally an ideal moment to strike. It comes as no surprise."

"An ideal moment?" Lieutenant Danress took a frustrated step, as if she were longing to hit someone not there. "Haven't they noticed what's been going on? There couldn't be a worse moment! Don't they understand anything at all about what the Kellian do for us?"

"Possibly not," Lady Weston said dryly. "But this is a command from our Queen, Jolien. The time for argument is past."

Rennyn was finding it very hard not to think about Captain Illuma catching her and carrying her out of the blast site. Nor of a badly-needed bath. She had been spending more than a little effort, these past couple of weeks, trying not to think constantly of the Kellian. It would have been so much easier if she'd been able to avoid working with them until the last moment. But Seb was right.

"Where do I fit into the interrogation schedule?" she asked, and smiled at their arrested expressions. "After all, I am Solace's direct descendent, and head of the Montjuste-Surclere family. If anyone's going to be accused of lingering allegiances, it should surely be me."

"You would allow that?" Lady Weston's surprise was palpable.

"I don't guarantee to answer everything, but somehow I suspect the questions they'll ask are ones I have fairly definitive views about." She considered Lieutenant Danress. "You're a descendent of one of those Eferum Travellers, aren't you? Maybe you should be interrogated too, just in case you're some kind of advance spy. Really, is there anyone in the Sentene who can truly be considered above suspicion? Questioning only the Kellian is a trifle lax, Lady Weston."

"That is an excellent point." Lady Weston glanced at Lieutenant Danress, who nodded eagerly.

"If it's the only way to balance this," the younger mage said. "Gladly."

"Very well." Lady Weston pulled a sheet of paper from the reports spread on her desk, and began writing. "Take this to Councillor Allerton, Lieutenant," she ordered. "And then pass my command to the Senior Captains."

"Yes, M'Lady!" Lieutenant Danress said crisply, and strode out of the room. She looked very happy for someone who'd just been added to an interrogation list.

"A show of solidarity is little enough, but it will make all the difference to morale," Lady Weston said. "There are few Sentene magi who don't owe their lives to their partners. Particularly after Darasum House. Only the Kellian could have saved that situation."

"Oh?" Rennyn sat down in one of the high-backed chairs before the desk. "I wondered how they'd managed so few casualties."

"Instinct." Lady Weston shook her head, then rang a bell, summoning a secretary to send for spiced tea. "The Kellian have a command, Full Clear – they train it, but I've not heard of it being used before. It means 'take your mage and run'. Their speed and Faille's instinct – which is the best among the Kellian and as close to precognition as anything is likely to come – is all that prevented almost the entire Sentene from dying to that exploit of the shield. They managed to get most of the Hand present out too, and the Ferumguard were fortunately further back. But there were still deaths, and many injuries."

"Not a good moment for spiteful interrogations."

"No." Lady Weston gave Rennyn a searching glance. "I admit that I'm surprised. I had an impression you were less than eager to associate with the Kellian."

"True enough," Rennyn said, thinking over what it was safe to admit. "But that's nothing to do with their loyalties."

"Then why?"

"Guilt, I suppose you could say." She shrugged at Lady Weston's startled expression. "Queen Solace did two major things during her rule. The Grand Summoning is the thing she's known for, but it's the second which is perhaps the larger achievement."

"She created a race."

"I don't think it was deliberate. The original Kellian were designed to be long-lived, but nothing I've read suggests that she intended them to breed. That's Symbolic magic: you get more than you ask for. But even if it was only a question of the original ten golems – my family has devoted itself to dealing with the Grand Summoning; we took responsibility for it. But the Kellian – after Solace was gone, Tiandel ordered the Kellian to leave Tyrland and never return. They were...barely people. Not mindless dolls, but they existed for a specific purpose. It was everything they were. They didn't have personal goals, personal desires. They couldn't even speak. And Tiandel told them to go away and not come back."

"Does avoiding the Kellian who exist today balance that?"

"Not at all. But – do you know, that horrible second son of hers saw it straight away? 'A Montjuste-Surclere with a Kellian bodyguard'. I don't want them protecting me. I hate the idea of – using them. Besides, I just as strongly feel that I shouldn't be talking about 'taking responsibility' for them. They're people, not children, not tools. Between feeling I should do something for them, and knowing I could get them killed – it's cowardly, I know, but I just wanted to have as little to do with them as possible. Mainly to spare my own feelings."

They were interrupted by the arrival of tea and cakes, and Rennyn was glad to have been stopped. She shouldn't have tried to explain. "Complicated, you see," she said, busying herself taking several slices of something particularly sticky and rich. "Do they have so many enemies?"

"Enough to matter. It's not merely their appearance, or even the fact that they are superlative killers. That watchful repose rouses suspicion, and this is not the first time they've been accused of conspiracies, of keeping themselves separate, of being loyal not to Queen and country, but to themselves or in this case Solace Montjuste-Surclere. It's amazing the impression a lack of casual chatter can make. If they behaved more like humans, fidgeted and complained, schemed and drank, bickered and laughed, they would be accepted far more readily, no matter what they looked like."

"Yet their magi partners are so upset at the idea of them being interrogated."

"Yes. I spent a brief period in the Sentene, many years ago. My partner was Korion Asaka. I swear he didn't say two unprompted words to me during our first five assignments. Even when I asked him questions, his answers were so brief I felt I was being rejected. But – he made it is his business, first and foremost, to keep me alive. And I very quickly started finding Korion a most reassuring presence, his silence simply a part of his nature. After many assignments I was bold enough to ask him why he did not speak more, and he told me, 'I forget that I can'. It wasn't that he was blankly passive inside, either; he simply rarely brought any of himself to the surface. That is what the Kellian are. They behave the way they do not out of any belief in their superiority, or dislike of humans, but because smiling or laughing or even talking are not automatic responses for them. It doesn't mean they don't feel, or that they aren't proud, or loyal. There's not one among them who isn't fiercely protective of Tyrland. Once they recognise that, most of the Sentene mages grow very protective of the Kellian in return."

"What's the Queen's attitude? She is allowing this."

"The Queen – Her Majesty's reserve is born out of their origin, I believe. The Kellian are a remnant of the Montjuste-Surclere rule. And whatever else can be said of her, there's few that will not acknowledge that Solace Montjuste-Surclere had a right to her throne. When the children of the original Kellian came to Tyrland, over one hundred years ago now, they asked to be allowed to serve the kingdom. They consider it their homeland. That was during a particularly bad outbreak of Eferum-Get, and the King of that time saw the Kellian as useful to his plans for a special force of hunters. And they *are* very useful to the kingdom, invaluable. But the Montjustes have always considered the Kellian a group with no loyalty to *them*."

"The uniform was specifically designed to distract from those wearing it, wasn't it?" Rennyn had thought as much. "Though from what I've seen of them, I'd say the Kellian do keep themselves separate."

"To a degree," Lady Weston conceded. "They are not human: they live longer than all but the most skilled mages, their senses are sharper, they mature differently, respond differently. Even after three hundred years, there are only some sixty individuals. They will develop friendships and relationships with humans, and very occasionally they marry outside their kind. I believe they make an effort to avoid in-breeding. But to the casual observer, they must seem a closed community."

"Sixty deadly people loyal to each other," Rennyn said.

"Some are convinced that there is a Kellian ruler dictating the decisions of the group, and the re-emergence of the Black Queen only adds fuel to this fire. But there is no conspiracy to be found, and no leaders. A kind of unspoken accord, perhaps."

"No leaders? Truly?" Rennyn had not had that impression.

"Outside the structure of the Sentene, no. They'll take ranks and give orders as part of their duty, but on a personal level Kellian strongly resist imposing their will on each other. The Illumas, for instance: it is immensely rare for Kellian to show the ability to be mages. Sarana is only the second, and all the Kellian were, I think, tremendously pleased when Sukata Illuma showed the same ability as her mother. But none would suggest that Sarana try and have another child for the sake of increasing the number of Kellian mages, or try to force the issue if Sukata chose not to study the art. It's very rare that they'll even give their opinion unasked, because an opinion is itself a kind of expectation, a suggested direction. You look sceptical, Lady Montjuste-Surclere."

"I can't tell if you're idolizing them or not. You obviously care about them greatly."

"Indeed. They are a complicated group, misunderstood by most. Perhaps I misunderstand them too. But I do trust them. And I *do* consider them a responsibility, even though they are, as you say, people. To me they are simply people worth protecting."

Rennyn was starting to see she should have paid more attention to Tyrland's politics. It would probably not make a great deal of difference until the Grand Summoning was complete, but might complicate what vague hopes she had for the rest of her life.

"Do you have a map of the area around Sark?" she asked, deciding she really needed to stop talking about the Kellian. She'd asked to see the Grand Magister for an entirely different reason, and proceeded to further spoil Lady Weston's day by using the measurements she'd been making to calculate the eventual diameter of the area of distortion emanating from Falk. While the expansion would probably not cross Sark's circle, it would come very close. More people than Rennyn cared to imagine would need to be moved.

Lady Weston had barely time to call another secretary when two men dressed in the resplendent red and gold of the Royal Guard appeared with a summons for Rennyn. Unsurprised that they'd leapt at the chance to question her immediately, Rennyn followed obediently along behind.

The guardsmen took her deep into the Old Palace, to a room focused around a box-like podium constructed of marble heavily worked with sigils. This was the Hall of Question, where any injunction to tell the truth would be massively reinforced by this permanent working. It made even half-truths immensely difficult, though not impossible. Even the strongest-willed could not outright lie here. That was the risk in making this gesture. They might hit upon the right questions, and a refusal to answer could reveal almost as much as the truth.

Seated at the long table before this podium were the seven who were conducting the questioning, though a reasonable audience had been allowed in as well. Mostly Councillors, Rennyn assumed. There were also two powerful shields, one around the podium and one enclosing the section of seats to the right of the Hall. This area was half-filled with Kellian waiting their turn. Many of their mage partners had joined them, including Lieutenant Danress, face set beneath her bright hair. Captain Faille was currently being questioned.

Rennyn was immediately struck by the fact that none of the Kellian were wearing their uniform coat. She'd seen them remove it so it wouldn't hamper them in battle, but never otherwise outside the Houses of Magic. A gesture, a very deliberate gesture: they had removed the Montjuste Phoenix. The Kellian might have accepted this questioning, but they were far from impressed by it.

Her entrance had caused a little stir, which was immediately overshadowed when below to the left a small but grand door was flung open and a very upright and decorative man strode in, crying: "All rise for Her Majesty, Queen Astranelle." Since Rennyn was already standing, she stayed where she was and curtseyed on cue when, after a stream of minor courtiers, the Queen entered the room.

Astranelle Montjuste was in her sixties, and had the timeless appearance that anyone with access to powerful magery could achieve, though Rennyn understood she was no more than a competent caster herself. She was small-boned, her ash-blonde hair drawn up into tidy confinement except for soft curls framing her face. She was not astonishingly beautiful, but looked...sweet. A lovely, blue-eyed delicate creature in floating blue and turquoise silks. Queen of Tyrland, and by all accounts an intelligent and practical woman.

Queen Astranelle surveyed the room until she found Rennyn, and then stood gazing at her. Given the foolery about challenges to the throne, Rennyn supposed it was unfortunate that she was standing at the top of the stairs, forcing the Queen to look up at her. Magic was not the only arena where symbols had power. With that in mind, Rennyn curtseyed again, as deeply as she was able without falling over. The Queen inclined her head in return, then sat down, and people began to move.

After some murmured consultation with a member of the Queen's entourage, one of the people conducting the questioning said, "Thank you, Captain. That will be all for now," and the official in charge of the shields made some adjustment which opened a passage to the waiting area. It seemed that although the Queen had ordered their interrogation, she had no real interest in what the Kellian had to say.

Without any hint of surprise, Captain Faille bowed and left the dock. Remembering his little catalogue of her reactions, Rennyn suspected the man was probably rarely surprised by anything – when he did bother to speak his comments were always perceptive and on occasion exceedingly dry. She watched him covertly as she started down the stair, but Danress' whispered explanations provoked no change of expression. He simply sat down to watch.

"Rennyn Montjuste-Surclere, you are called to Question."

The official opened the shield for Rennyn to pass through, and she stepped up to the podium. It was a thick marble box, reaching as high as her chest, with a gap cut in one side for people to pass through. Interesting how just standing in it made her feel like a criminal.

Rennyn looked out at her audience and remembered she was tired. Politics did not amuse her. Touching the cold marble gingerly, she gauged the power running through it. A strong shield. She wondered what that monster Helecho had used to convert the Sentene's to an explosion.

With the injunction settling around her, Rennyn reminded herself that she'd chosen to do this. Exploding shields would not be necessary.

THIRTEEN

P lease state your full name," the person sitting in the centre of the examiner's table said. She was a woman with short-cropped brown hair, a voice of warm smoke, and a most suspicious gaze. Councillor Allerton, perhaps.

"Rennyn Helena Montjuste-Surclere," Rennyn replied, then added, "Though Rennyn Helena Claire on the Dawnbringer's Register. And various aliases."

Interesting. She'd answered rather more than she'd been intending. It was a clever spell, encouraging thorough explanation, a potentially fatal chattiness. Narrowing her eyes, Rennyn concentrated on the task of choosing exactly what truth she would tell, and no more.

"Can you prove that?" asked a dark-bearded man sitting at the far right of the table. "Evidently you believe that you are a descendent of Solace Montjuste-Surclere, but that may merely be something you have been told."

Startled, Rennyn had to laugh. "It would be an elaborate ruse, if so. Let me see. I don't imagine the usual paternity castings would cover such a distant connection, but feel free to devise one. I have a few centuries of documentation, various objects which belonged to the family. I–" She paused, then shrugged. "There's a collection of letters from King Eliathas. One has the official seal on it. That would establish Tiandel's survival, at least."

"King Eliathas was aware of the ruse?"

"Pretending to die is perhaps not so hard. Pretending to die after moving your most precious belongings out of your house and shuffling your fortune about in interesting ways, that requires a little collusion."

"Reasonable," the man continued. "What other members of the Montjuste-Surclere line survive?"

"My brother, Sebastian. Solace. This new son of hers, Helecho." The name sat bitter on her tongue.

"After three hundred years, only two descendents of Tiandel remain?"

Rennyn shrugged. "Three hundred years of experiments with the Eferum. It's not the safest preoccupation."

"Experiments based around the Grand Summoning? It is true, is it not, that this would involve continuing research into the function of the spell? That you would have the means to recreate the Grand Summoning?"

"Quite true." She did not look down, did not dwell on the day her father had not returned, of the void that had left. And she never allowed herself to think of her mother's death.

"Have you ever planned to cast the Grand Summoning yourself?"

"No."

"Have you supported, assisted or colluded in any other individual casting the Grand Summoning?"

"No."

"Have you, or do you intend to assist or aid Queen Solace in completing the Grand Summoning?"

"No."

Lady Weston's voice suddenly interjected, "Do you know of any way to stop the Grand Summoning before it completes?"

Rennyn blinked, turning. The Grand Magister had arrived unnoticed to sit beside the Queen. The map of Sark was open before them. Even at this distance Rennyn could see the sharp line she'd drawn along the outskirts of the city.

"Yes." Rennyn ignored the murmur which ran around the room. "The obvious way: go into the Eferum where she is and attack her. She will have the means to fight back, and it now seems possible that she's guarded by Eferum-Get, but a sufficient force, well-prepared, should overwhelm even that. After all, people die all the time in the midst of summoning focus stones. The problem is what happens with the power she is manipulating. Even if she'd been killed as soon as the Falk expression had appeared, the minimum consequence would be a backlash which could have shattered Aliace Hill and sent pieces of it raining down on the city. To be clear, other than using the attuned focus to push her back during the last moments, I do not know of a way to stop the Grand Summoning without destroying large pieces of Tyrland in the process."

"What do you intend to do after her defeat?" the Queen asked, her voice a very resonant one for such a small woman. Her gaze was steady and unwavering, reserved but not hostile.

"If Solace is pushed back into the Eferum, she will not have been defeated," Rennyn explained. "So I would inevitably have to prepare for her return. But − either way, if I pushed her back or were to succeed in killing her, I..." She shrugged, for she had never found this question easy to answer. "For a while at least, I would do the things I haven't been able to spare the time to do now. Trivial things. Beyond that I can't say I've made any firm plans. Travel. I've not been able to risk leaving Tyrland."

The Queen had listened with an air of polite attention. "You have heard of the recent debates regarding your claim to the throne?"

"Yes. I was surprised by it. I have no claim to the throne. Tiandel abdicated."

"The argument is that if Solace still lives, Tiandel had no throne from which to abdicate."

Rennyn was trying to work out what was going on. It didn't seem to her that the Queen was concerned in the slightest about the legitimacy of any claim to her throne.

"Well, given that Solace still lives, it's her claim to the throne which seems to me the point of contention," Rennyn said. "Either way, Tiandel removed himself from the line of succession. Which would make that creature Helecho Crown Prince. Perhaps you should take this discussion up with him?"

The Queen said something softly to Lady Weston, then sat back. Rennyn found the entire exchange confusing, and could only presume that some political point had been made.

"Were you aware of this Helecho's existence before your encounter in Surclere?" Lady Weston asked.

"No."

"Do you believe it is he who was responsible for the death of your Great-Grandfather?"

Rennyn paused, then said dubiously. "I suppose that's possible. But it doesn't seem to me very likely. I don't believe he has a focus stone. If he was able to open a gate to our world, he would not lack that. But, focus or not, he is a dangerous thing, perhaps more dangerous than Solace. Eferum-Get might have various abilities, but they are not usually mages."

Lady Weston nodded, then gestured to return the floor to the Councillors conducting the questioning. This time the woman second from the left took charge: a prim blonde brimming with righteousness.

"What is your opinion of the Kellian, Lady Montjuste-Surclere?"

Deliberately, Rennyn looked at the collection of Sentene waiting behind the shield. She'd been careful not to glance toward them until now, and couldn't help but wonder what the Kellian thought of her. What did the children of slaves think of the children of the slave-master?

"Which one?" she asked.

The answer, or perhaps Rennyn's flat tone, caught the woman off-guard. But after a startled moment she said: "All of them."

"I haven't met all of them," Rennyn said, reasonably. "Are you asking me to give an assessment of their morals? Or their ability to wave pointy bits of metal about?"

The man to the woman's left murmured something softly, an instruction. "I am asking whether in your opinion the Kellian pose a potential threat to Tyrland," the woman said briskly.

"Ah." Rennyn glanced at the Kellian again, waiting so impassively. "Of course they do."

That produced a nice reaction, a ripple of shock which ran through the room. Rennyn watched the two Councillors thoughtfully, seeing the way the one of woman's hands tightened on the sheet of paper she held, how her eyes brightened. The man was less unrestrained, but he, too, definitely wanted to hear bad things said of the Kellian.

"It's the speed, primarily," she continued, blithely. "Skill with weapons, strength, and the interesting effects with light are one thing, but the ability to react quicker than anyone else, that truly takes them to a different level. But then—"

She reached out her hand, touching her fingers to the shield. Tiny shimmers of light gathered, then intensified as she poured raw power into it. The air heated, taking on a distinct odour of stressed metal, and she watched the shield retreat in a perfect circle from around her hand. She held it just long enough for the shield to really strain, then allowed it to snap back, whole once again. She could swear the entire room let out its breath at the same time, the explosion at Darasum House no doubt at the forefront of everyone's minds.

"It's a relative thing, isn't it?" she said, looking over the table of now very attentive Councillors. "Once you start talking about potential threats. Any weapon you use to defend yourself can be turned upon you. But I have no interest in anything but defeating Solace, and I've seen no sign that the Kellian want to do more than protect and serve this kingdom. Since it seems you do want moral judgments, you'd best ask someone who knows them better. The most I can say is that they seem more inclined to swallow insults than I am."

The smile she offered the woman was thoroughly unpleasant, and it was probably a good thing that the moment was cut by a dull rumble. Rennyn could feel a vibration even through the thick stone beneath her feet.

"An attack?" said one of the men in the audience, and there was a small flurry of activity around the doors. Most of the Kellian were on their feet before the vibration had died away, but were waiting before reacting further. Rennyn's senses were currently overwhelmed by the shield, but she closed her eyes to try and feel for worked magic beyond the usual background enchantments of the palace. Nothing major sprang to her attention.

Captain Illuma, who had remained seated, casting, stood abruptly. "My Lady, there are Eferum-Get loose in the palace. At least five." She didn't pause for a response, leading the Sentene out through the iron-bound door at the rear of the shielded area.

"Is this one of the Grand Summoning's incursions?" the Queen asked, unshaken but frowning. "I understood their time and location to be already known."

"It must be a natural breach," Lady Weston said. "They will increase in frequency as the Summoning progresses. But it is an unusually large number of Eferum-Get for a natural–" She looked sharply at Rennyn. "Could the man Helecho have the ability to open breaches?"

"If he had, I expect Tyrland would already be overrun," Rennyn said. "But recall, I said it was possible Solace has Eferum-Get guards. Any breach or gate within the palace could well be opening among an army's ranks."

"How convenient for the Kellian," said the man on the left of the examiner's table, flushing. "Before their activities can be properly investigated, they are handed a dramatic opportunity to prove themselves. Are we supposed to believe this is a coincidence?"

"Do you propose I should recall them, and allow the palace guard to deal with this?" Lady Weston asked, and turned away. "You had best move to a safer location, Your Majesty."

The Queen stood unhurriedly. "Continue your questions at a later time, Baron Ridehalt. I fail to see how this will change the answers you will receive." She nodded at Rennyn. "Thank you for your candour, Lady Montjuste-Surclere."

Wondering if that was meant to be ironic, Rennyn turned expectantly to the official controlling the shield, and stepped down as soon as he dropped it. She crossed to Lady Weston, who had paused to cast a divination.

"Don't deal with it as an ordinary breach," she advised tersely. "If there is real organisation among the Eferum-Get, then this lot very likely have targets. To which point, I'm going to stand over my brother."

She looked for the nearest shadow and twisted it around herself, taking herself back to Seb's room. It wasn't a safe method of travel when moving out of line of sight, but she was worried, and more so when she arrived to find Seb gone. Given the bonds cast between them, it was easy enough to divine his direction, and she strode swiftly through the Sentene's barracks, crossing to the Arkathan.

Ignoring a bothersome woman who wanted to know her business, Rennyn quickly found her way to the second floor, and a small room with a matched pair of Sentene and royal guardsmen standing outside it. She hadn't encountered this particular pair of Sentene before, but since they appeared to be bodyguarding, not responding to the breach, she paused a moment to let them know what was going on.

"Do you have any information about the type?" asked the Sentene mage, a barrel-chested man so wide his uniform turned him into a Phoenix-embossed wall.

"None. I'm going to put a shield up around this room. Stay in or out as suits you."

Rennyn opened the door to find a classroom where her brother appeared to be playing teacher to a half-dozen youths around his age. He broke off when he saw her. "What's happening?"

"Small outbreak of Eferum-Get," Rennyn said, studying the diagram her brother had been busy creating. "Why are you inflicting your theories about Eferum distortion on defenceless minds?"

"Eh, well, Kendall wanted an explanation of why the Eferum runs at a different pace. Sukata found us an empty room. Everyone else just poked their noses in."

Rennyn considered the diagram again, then smiled at the girl from Falk. "Seb's the last person I'd ask to explain the Eferum. He thinks he understands it."

"Does he?" the girl asked, with extreme doubt. Seb's explanation had obviously reached the convoluted stage.

"More than most. I'm going to shield this room, so if anyone wants to go elsewhere, do it soon." Leaving the door open, she moved to the nearest corner and began to chalk a line of sigils down the wall.

"You think one might stray all the way out to the Houses?" asked one blond youth, presumably Crown Prince Justin since the decorative guardsmen had hurried to stand on either side of him.

"Depends on what they're hunting." Rennyn made a correction to one of the sigils and moved to a different corner.

"Is your sister in the building, Highness?" Seb asked abruptly.

"She shouldn't be," Prince Justin said. "I told her to go back to the palace." He turned to one of his bodyguards. "Ridgeway, go check the dining hall. Bring her back here if you see her."

The guardsman went off at a run, and nervous conversation broke out, which Rennyn ignored, concentrating on chalking the long series of sigils in each corner and at the halfway points of the walls. If the shield was necessary at all, there was likely little time left to finish it.

The Sentene, being charged with the protection of more than just Rennyn's brother, herded the occupants of neighbouring rooms in to fill most of the seats. This produced an annoying babble, rising when the guardsman returned with a small blonde girl and her own set of attendants. Rennyn climbed on one of the desks and scribbled on the ceiling.

"But it's daytime!" the girl protested, though she was plainly enjoying the drama. "The walkway between the Houses and the main bit of the palace is all open and sunny. Night Roamers couldn't come here."

"Only the weakest and the strongest Night Roamers are killed by sunlight, Highness," said the wall-like Sentene, coming into the room. "All dislike it and many are hurt by it, but there's more than a few which can venture out into it."

As Rennyn climbed off the desk, she glimpsed another Sentene pair out in the hallway. Reinforcements. She knelt and rapidly began chalking the last set of sigils in the centre of the floor. They wouldn't have sent reinforcements if the incursion had been defeated already.

"Five Escaton-types have been located in the palace," the Sentene mage continued, dropping his voice a little, though the room had immediately fallen to a fascinated hush. "It won't be long before they're dealt with, but Captain Illuma's divinations show curious results, and there's been reports and signs of something large moving which we can't isolate. Almost as if it's shielded."

Food for thought. One thing Eferum-Get didn't usually do was cast shields on themselves.

"Could it be him?" Seb asked, leaping to the same conclusion.

Rennyn finished the last of the sigils first, and stood up. "I doubt it. His personal shielding was perfect. But I wouldn't put it past him to cast shields on Eferum-Get."

"And send them after me?"

"He may not even know you exist, Seb. But as wicked uncles go, I think this one would take great delight in getting something to eat you in front of me."

"Should we move, Your Highness?" one of the guardsmen asked Prince Justin. "There is a well fortified room in the Houses' central tower."

The prince glanced at the Sentene in the doorway, then shook his head. "We would need to take some of this room's defenders with us. And—" He offered Rennyn a little bow. "I've heard enough about Lady Montjuste-Surclere's strength to suspect this might be the safest place on Aliace Hill."

Rennyn just started casting. Safety would only come when the shield was complete.

FOURTEEN

Kendall was entirely envious of Sebastian's sister's ability to ignore people. She acted like she couldn't even see the twenty Arkathan students sitting at and on the desks around her, let alone hear their whispered comments. Turning away from Prince Justin, she gave the sigils on the floor a sharp look and began pumping power into them.

It really was becoming clearer. Not just people casting, but already existing enchantments. Kendall could even tell when she'd crossed an active circle. None of it made much sense yet, but it was a far more positive sign than the long days of failing to do more than make pebbles jump unpredictably.

The sigils began to glow as Rennyn Montjuste-Surclere spoke softly beneath her breath, bluish light working from the top to bottom of each row at the same time. Kendall couldn't see the shield which was being created, but felt like she was being boxed in. There was a moment when the final sigil flared and, even though the door was still open, Kendall knew she wouldn't be able to walk through it. It was like the room itself was telling her so.

"Sealed for air as well?" asked the gigantic Sentene mage, his rumbling voice more curious than concerned. Unlike the royal guardsmen, the Sentene just looked alert and interested.

"You think this will take so long we'd have to worry?" asked Rennyn, then shrugged and followed her brother as he moved back to where Kendall and Sukata were sitting by the windows closest to the chalk-board.

Kendall seized the opportunity. "Can I ask something?"

"Why not? It's my day for answering questions."

"Your brother was trying to explain how everything goes slower in the Eferum. That an hour there is like two days or more in the real world. But if that's so, then wouldn't the Black Queen have only been in the Eferum for a year or two?"

"Not far from that. The distortion is variable, and we don't know anything of what it's like when you move away from this world. But I doubt more than two or three years would have passed for her."

"Then, if it's – if what everyone's been saying about her having a second son, one born in the Hells, is true – why isn't he still a baby?"

"Mmph. Have you heard any of the theories on the origins of the Eferum-Get?"

"Not really." They were monsters. They lived in the Hells. They ate people. What more was there to say?

"A common idea is that the Eferum-Get are the nightmares of this world, conjured into existence by our fears. I can't be sure exactly how my Wicked Uncle came to be, but I'd be surprised if Solace went through any form of pregnancy. Maybe he sprang fully-formed from her forehead."

Kendall checked the expressions of those around her, not certain if she was misunderstanding an attempt at humour. "You mean she just thought him up?"

"It's entirely possible, though it's equally possible she went through some form of ritual or...activity with a thing which could be called his father. Certainly the dominant school of thought is that Eferum-Get 'come into being', rather than do anything so mundane as breeding – that they only become capable of doing so when they reach this world and begin to adapt to its nature. In either case, it wouldn't make this Helecho any less her son."

"The Eferum operates on an entirely different set of rules from this world," Sebastian put in, because he always would try and explain anything and everything, no matter how much Kendall discouraged him. "There's no physical surfaces, no air. You float in Efera, raw magic moving all around and through you, without any need to eat or breathe. It's very easy to lose your sense of self. A weak-willed person venturing into the Eferum is more likely to forget to come back than be attacked. A strong-willed person, someone able to hold back the tide of magic, blazes with a sense of

Self which can leak through the best shielding. It's a place of the mind, of emotion, and most importantly of will."

"Have you summoned a focus already?" asked Princess Sera, playing the wide-eyed and innocent card again. "You don't look nineteen."

"Unregistered mages are so bad about keeping all sorts of rules," Rennyn Montjuste-Surclere said before her brother had to answer, studying the young princess as if she were deciding whether to step on her. She obviously hadn't missed the mischief behind the question.

"Summoning my focus was the most daunting thing I've ever done," Prince Justin said, taking Princess Sera's hand and settling with her at the desk just across the aisle. "How you can bear to venture there frequently I can't guess, Lady Montjuste-Surclere."

Kendall would bet Sebastian and his sister found it harder to bear all this fascinated attention. Scary and dangerous as the Hells sounded, it was the source of all the magic in the world, and to this pair probably bunches more fun than being in a room with gossip-hungry strangers. If it wasn't for them acting so much like they were in charge, it would look like they'd been backed into this corner and trapped there.

Feeling a little cornered herself, Kendall turned to look out the window, down at the Reading Garden, the grassy patch between the Arkathan and the dining hall which had little tables and seats scattered about it for the students to use. When this was over, the tittle-seekers wouldn't accept any more excuses of having only met Sebastian looking for the dining hall. Once she was out of this box she'd either have to do some fast talking, or make herself scarce.

Outside it was warm and sunny. Except for the glowing sigils, she couldn't see the shield at all, though it did make the grass seem all wavery – in a weird, moving patch. Concerned, Kendall nudged Sukata and pointed at the tree that looked like it was under water.

"Guise shield haze!"

Sukata was abruptly on her feet and holding a long knife she'd pulled from somewhere. The huge Sentene mage cursed and moved to look outside while his partner slid one of those overlong Kellian swords from the sheathe on her back. Everyone else moved forward or away depending on how brave or stupid they were, but Kendall was still by far the closest when the room's four tall windows smashed apart.

There was – it was – only a few inches away from her face was a wet white tube. It was thicker than her leg, pulsing and twisting as it jabbed at her again and again. Over all the noise, all the breaking glass, scraping furniture and screaming, the noise it made as it pounded at the shield trying to get at her was the loudest thing Kendall could hear.

Then Sukata was there, a hand on Kendall's arm as she drew her away, got between her and That. Moving back only gave Kendall a chance to see it properly, to understand the pale background blocking out the sky, surrounding that horrid, fleshy...mouth? As tall as the room, it looked like an upturned crab, but between hard-shelled and spindly legs there were thick tentacles, the blue-tinted suckers ranging from coin to saucer-size.

More pieces of wall and window broke away as the tentacles searched for a better grip on the side of the building. Little stalks with eyes poked from ridges at the front of the shell, then withdrew as it climbed upward. A leg, tipped like a spear, jabbed downward. Sukata's long knife looked pitiful before it – even the Sentene's four-foot sword was nothing to this thing as it began to rip the roof off trying to get in with them. One of the royal guards fired his pistol, filling the air with stinging smoke, but the shot stopped dead and dropped to the ground.

"For pity's sake man, no need to tax the shield any further," growled the Sentene mage, pulling down the arm of another guardsman. "And be quiet, the rest of you!" he shouted. "Calm down. It's not getting in here with us and squealing like stuck pigs isn't helping."

His voice was loud, and certain enough to get the attention of the scrabble of people trying to claw their way through the shielded door. The shrieking dropped to a panicky babble, and the lone teacher who had been herded in with them made shushing noises, but Kendall wasn't alone in looking worriedly at Rennyn Montjuste-Surclere, who was still sitting at the next desk down, her chin propped on one hand and her eyes half-closed. Almost as if she was bored, but Kendall was near enough to see the set of her jaw, and knew that keeping the shield up couldn't be nearly so easy as she made it seem.

As the Thing outside sent bits of wall and ceiling flying, Rennyn Montjuste-Surclere turned her head and said: "Prince Justin, will you perform an experiment for me?"

The prince hadn't moved, was holding his sobbing sister tightly. His voice was unsteady as he said: "What is it?"

"Go stand at the other end of the room."

The prince stared blankly, then went even whiter than he'd already managed. But, still holding Princess Sera, he struggled to his feet and walked swiftly along the centre aisle between the desks to the far wall, close to the clutch of people pressed against the doorway. Immediately the monster stopped pounding at the shield by Kendall and, with a writhe of tree-trunk tentacles and a skittering of long legs, went after Tyrland's heir.

"I don't recognise the type," Rennyn Montjuste-Surclere said over the renewed shrieking, not pursuing the subject of the monster's target.

"Not one that's been classified," said the Sentene mage. He and his partner gathered the two Montjustes back from the far end of the room, their attention never straying from the Thing which was now making a show of destroying the roof.

"What happens if it pulls the whole building down around us?" Kendall whispered to Sebastian, but he didn't reply, busy writing in chalk on one of the tables.

"The shield is anchored to the point where the sigils were," Sukata answered instead. "It doesn't matter if the surface they were written on is gone."

It would matter when the shield went away, Kendall thought, and grimaced as the Thing crawled down the wall behind them. When it pulled apart the stone, the chalkboard and a fine shaving of wall fell on the inside of the shield as well. Shifting most of its bulk into the room next to them, the monster began pounding on the shield with its tentacles and legs. It was an eerily unreal attack despite the noise and the light which bloomed around each blow. Kendall could barely feel the impacts. The shield seemed immovable. The 'inside' of all the walls fell off, as well as the part of the door projecting into the room, but it was because the building had shuddered and shifted around the box which was keeping them safe.

How long would the shield last? Everyone said Rennyn Montjuste-Surclere was an incredibly powerful mage, but this Thing was so *strong*. It was demolishing the Arkathan as easily as kicking over a bucket of milk. A single blow would squash a man like a roach.

With a screaming sizzle bolts of white arched up from outside and slammed into the nearest tentacle. The monster flinched and bucked, destroying most of the floor in both rooms. It fell into the room below as another series of bolts punched into it.

"Thank the Dawnbringer," breathed one of the royal guardsmen, as the monster reoriented in the wreckage to face a row of black-clad figures standing on the far side of the Reading Garden, the Montjuste Phoenix shining.

"It's not damaged," pointed out another, dismayed. This was true. The bolts had obviously hurt, but the thick tentacle wasn't a bit crisped.

"Some Eferum-Get are resistant to magic," the Sentene mage explained, and Kendall noticed that he stood just a little straighter. He'd been worried too, though he hadn't been showing it.

Rennyn Montjuste-Surclere bent her head back and looked directly up. Kendall followed her gaze and saw golden men and women. Kellian, blazing in the sunlight, standing on the exposed shield. One glanced down at them, and she recognised Captain Faille as he gave the signal to attack.

For people who always seemed so still, Kellian could move beyond fast. Almost, it was as if they had gone from roof to grass with no part in between. But, like a lantern swung at night, they left a little trail of light to show the path taken. They'd jumped down *onto* the monster, and made a bunch of cuts on its tentacles before leaping out of its reach.

The Thing let out a gurgling roar and writhed after them, but though it was faster than you'd expect for something so large, its blows only succeeded in creating deep dints in the ground and earned it a few more slashes. Its blood was treacle-brown. In another moment it was surrounded, and was being cut at from every side. Kellian wasps, stinging, always moving.

Just when Kendall was about to let her breath out in relief, the Thing changed tactics, charging toward the dining halls. It brought down one of the trees in the process and, picking it up, hurled it at its pursuers. Kellian scattered to all sides, and the tree slammed into the Arkathan as the monster scuttled straight at the Sentene mages.

A streak of golden light resolved into Captain Faille, running right between the tentacles and jumping up onto the blue-tinted shell. He thrust his sword beneath the ridge protecting the Thing's eyes, then leapt away as a tentacle swiped at him like a fly on a horse. The monster turned for another charge.

A rock fell from the sky. More than fell – it hurtled down like someone had shot it from a cannon. The crack it made as it struck the monster's shell was sharp enough to hurt Kendall's ears, and the Thing staggered. The next stone went straight through one of its legs and made a black hole in the ground.

"They're throwing bits of the Arkathan at it!" exclaimed one of the students, and a cheer went up as a third stone was followed by a positive rain of broken bits of wall. While the Kellian had been keeping it busy, the Sentene mages had cast a spell which lifted pieces of the destroyed rooms high into the air and smashingly returned them. Even the monster's thick shell couldn't stand up to this, and it was rapidly reduced to a pulpy mass which the Kellian went and poked swords into until it stopped twitching.

"One day you too will be able to throw rocks," Rennyn Montjuste-Surclere said to Kendall, and stood up. Everyone in the room suddenly rose a foot in the air, and before they'd had a chance to do more than gasp, the shield went away and the desks fell through the holes in the floor while all the people floated to the ground outside.

Kendall wondered if this was the spell Sebastian had been casting. It felt rather more like his sister had just picked them all up. She turned and stared back at the Arkathan, at the hole in the side of the building. This from only one Night Roamer.

"They said there were hundreds of monsters during the Black Night," she said, amazed. "How in the Hells did you kill them all?"

"I didn't kill any of them," Rennyn Montjuste-Surclere said matter-of-factly, watching a handful of Sentene approach. "Besides, this was something rather special."

"A new type," said one of the approaching Sentene, an older version of Sukata. This must be Captain Illuma.

The group stopped before Prince Justin and bowed very formally, which was an eerie thing when most of them had yellow disks for eyes and sunshine hair. "Your Highness," Captain Illuma continued, "it would be best if you returned to the main palace."

"Do you believe there are more on the loose, Captain?" the prince asked, sounding calmer than he looked.

"None that we can divine, but if Eferum-Get are now able to guise themselves, a physical sweep will be necessary."

Princess Sera, all eyes and no mischief now, wriggled loose from her brother's arms. "You must come with us!"

"You will be escorted, of course, Highness," Captain Illuma replied, without missing a beat. "And the circles and defensive spells around the throne room are the strongest in Tyrland. A creature such as this could not overcome them."

The princess didn't put up any more argument, once she saw that four of the Sentene would go with her. Kendall was disappointed to be herded off with the rest of the students. She had particularly wanted to hear the discussion the Sentene would surely move on to once their audience was gone: just how had the Night Roamer been able to find, in the mish-mash of the palace, the boy who happened to be heir of all Tyrland?

FIFTEEN

Rennyn lay watching Seb making notes as he read. He never remembered he was holding a quill, and had managed to draw a delicate squiggle from the corner of his mouth down past his chin. Each year he grew more like their father: as soon as he was caught up in something he found it hard to focus on anything else. The shadows under his eyes had already told her that he was burying himself far too deeply in the Houses of Magic's library, but it was hard to lecture him when she'd had to borrow his bed for a few hours to balance a night without sleep and some unexpected shield-casting.

"So why the lessons?"

Seb started, then smiled over at her, shrugging. "Kendall. I wanted to see how much she took in. And I'm trying to make her see what she's missing."

"How do you mean?"

"She went from nothing to the beginnings of using Thought in a few days. Her memory's almost as good as yours – she really is memorising those dictionaries they gave her, without any context. She has enough willpower for two, and the questions she asks are sharp, well-observed. But she never sees magic as anything but a means to an end. Can she really have that much potential, and absolutely no *feel* for it?"

"The world's full of rote mages, Seb."

"It's just such a waste." He dropped his quill into a stained cup and crossed to the door, smudging a line on a pattern of chalk symbols already drawn there, then putting power into it. A muffling spell.

"So what's been happening?" Rennyn asked when he finished casting.

"Eh, they don't exactly come and report to me. Nothing else has tried to eat anyone."

"Do you know how many–?"

"Eight, and a few injuries."

Rennyn sighed. "I keep asking how many people died, but it's just numbers. I feel like I should find out their names, try and–"

"What? Apologise?" Seb thrust out his chin. "We're not the ones responsible for this, Ren. We're trying to fix it, yes, but we're not–" He broke off, grimacing.

"Not as bad? Not the ones killing people?" Rennyn sighed and sat up, combing fingers through her hair to sort out the tangles. "Ignore me. I'm still tired, and I don't like how this is playing out. There's too many things we didn't plan for."

"How do you think the prince was being tracked?"

"Hm. Why bother seems more relevant to me, but I suppose it could simply be a message, a demonstration. To do it – the link between Solace and the Montjuste bloodline is a lot weaker than the one she has to us, and the Queen has more than enough relatives to confuse any casting. Either our Wicked Uncle has found a way to track a person without any real knowledge or connection to the target, or someone's stolen the prince's hairbrush. The Hand are pursuing the theory of a conspiracy targeting us, of course, but that investigation hasn't been getting anywhere. Divinations aren't much use for events that happened so long ago." She glanced at the door, wondering which Kellian was on duty, and whether Seb's spell was successfully keeping their conversation private.

Seb followed her gaze. "They're really keen for you to stay here. Lieutenant Danress asked me if I could convince you, to stress what might happen if one of those things attacked when you were too far away for the Sentene to reach you."

Rennyn snorted. "Fel knows, I would rather have thrown rocks at the thing than sit behind a shield. Today's little drama makes me want to move you out of here, not the other way around."

"I figured. They just want to – do you know what Kendall said to me this morning?"

"I'm sure you're going to tell me." Rennyn considered her brother curiously. The girl from Falk seemed to be figuring very large in his life.

"She shares a room with Sukata Illuma. She said Sukata behaves differently around me than she does with anyone else."

"That's hardly surprising, Seb."

"You don't think–?"

"I think it's hardly surprising," Rennyn repeated firmly. "I haven't been able to work out whether they actively dislike the fact that we've turned up, but the Kellian would have to feel very ambivalent about us, at best. Even ignoring the fact that Solace created them, the purpose, the whole reason for existence of the originals was to protect the Montjuste-Surcleres. And Tiandel abandoned them. Wouldn't you resent us, in their position?"

"They don't." Seb was quite certain. "You've seen that, haven't you?"

It took time to decide her answer. "It's rare that they're ever anything but totally correct around me. I know my refusal to stay here frustrates them. They don't think I'm being sensible, but it's just as much that they want to...observe me, and – I don't know."

"How would you feel if the reason for your existence showed up and wouldn't let you protect her?"

Rennyn pulled a face, then sighed and hunted about for her boots. "I would be astonished if the Kellian considered you and I the reason for their existence. More a hangover from their past which complicates their present. Which reminds me, if you come through this alone, leave Tyrland – at least for a while."

"Don't talk like that."

"Hush. The politics surrounding us are apt to get sticky once we're no longer a critical factor in Tyrland's survival. So far as I can make out from the farce today, the Queen doesn't believe the Kellian conspire to anything, or that I have any legitimate claim to the throne. Yet she allows this public interrogation, a slap in the face to a group of people integral to this country's defence. Just to placate some Councillors who've been making a fuss? I wouldn't have believed her rule so tenuous."

"How did you end up being called to Question? I couldn't believe it when I heard."

"I volunteered for it. I was annoyed."

He laughed. "Enjoy yourself?"

"Not really. Some meaningless posturing." She finished tugging at the laces of her boots and stood up, glancing at Solace's focus but leaving it on Seb's desk. "Do you want to stay here? Or go back to the apartment?"

"Don't you think that maybe, after all, it might be an idea for you to stay?"

"I'd just have to leave again. But I guess that means you're staying, so you can do some research for me." She explained the kind of spell she was aiming for, and shrugged at his expression. "This uncle of ours is worse than revolting, and I don't want to find myself under another of his injunctions with no way out. I do want you to put some proper wards up on this room. I'll be back in two days."

"Take care."

It was early evening, and the Sentene's barracks were quiet. Rennyn glanced around and with some difficulty spotted Captain Faille sitting on the bottom step of a nearby stairwell, a small book balanced on his knee. Something to speed the time while waiting outside the rooms of sleeping mages. It must be fantastically boring for a Senior Captain to play bodyguard, and she wondered if he ever regretted the instincts which made him the safest person to use.

Faille disposed of the book somewhere between Seb's room and the entrance of the barracks, and Rennyn found herself disappointed to have not caught a glimpse of the title. She didn't look back again until she was out of the palace gates, to check that he was trailing her as she had been previously followed. Without the Sentene cloak it always took a moment for her eyes to resolve him, even with the bright street lighting of the Palace District. She continued down Aliace Hill and was nearing Crossways when she looked for him a third time.

"May I ask you a question, Captain?"

His answer was the lengthen his stride until he walked at her side instead of ten steps behind.

"What happened to the original Kellian after Tiandel ordered them out of Tyrland?"

He didn't appear perturbed by the question. "For several years they lived directly over the border, among the wilder mountains of Vandaluse. Eventually the Vandalusians noticed their existence and hunted them, as invaders or mistaking them as Eferum-Get. Rather than fight, they crossed the Sands of Denara."

The noise and bustle of Crossways overwhelmed his thin voice and he stopped speaking as they walked into an evening reaching its highest pitch, with crowds lining up outside the playhouses, and taverns and food stalls doing a roaring trade. Rennyn ignored the strident demands of a stomach neglected since tea with the Grand Magister, and only gazed at the excited press. A remembrance ceremony had been held only that morning, and already the Black Night, as people were calling the incursion in Asentyr, might never have happened.

"On the borders of Verisia they encountered a runaway bondswoman," Captain Faille continued, as they started along the main road of the Temple District toward the Docks. "Aurai Falcy. This woman became their Voice, and taught them to write. In her company they roamed for many years, and finally settled in the fringes of the Forest of Semarrak."

Even Rennyn, whose geography outside of Tyrland was vague on account of being irrelevant, had heard of the Forest of Semarrak. It was inhabited by creatures which may once have been Eferum-Get, but were now far more complicated. The Kellian would probably pass as unremarkable there.

The Temple of the Devourer loomed ahead, and Rennyn paused to look up into the shadows of its portico, then moved slowly on toward the Docks. It had been a very sparse account, the barest of facts. The attenuated voice had been detached but his attention, she was sure, had been divided between watching for attacks and keenly observing her reaction. She might not be able to guess how the Kellian felt about the reappearance of the Montjuste-Surclere family, but whenever she was with them there was this sense of observation that went beyond the business of bodyguards. In their place she'd be both resentful and wildly curious, and expected the Kellian were not so very different as to not feel those things.

"Why did they have children?"

The question bordered on rudeness, along with sounding very strange. Yet Rennyn knew in great detail how the original Kellian were devised, and how they had functioned before their exile. It was difficult to imagine them deciding to take lovers and raise families.

"The first was a child of rape," Faille told her. "Those who dwell in Semarrak, the inhabitants older than the Kellian, are considered creatures of great good fortune, to be captured and used as talismans. A man of ambition mistook his prey."

It made him angry to speak of it. Not at her, but at a long-dead beast who had seen a Kellian, perhaps in strong sunlight or moonlight when they were at their most exotic, and somehow managed to force himself on her. Rennyn wasn't entirely certain how she knew the Captain was angry – in the dimmer light of the Docks she had no hope of gauging his expression, and his voice hadn't changed. Perhaps because he suddenly seemed ten times as dangerous.

"The child was a daughter. They named her Faille, which is a Verisian word meaning 'incalculable'."

She'd certainly blundered straight onto sensitive ground. There were no good responses, so Rennyn swallowed the awkwardness and guessed: "Experiencing that child prompted them to seek more?"

"I believe she gave them some purpose beyond existing."

That matched Rennyn's understanding of the golems Solace had created. Raising and protecting their children would fill the void Tiandel had left. Wondering what the runaway bondswoman had been like, she turned off the main road into the back streets of the Dock District, where great hulking warehouses were interspersed with tight, cramped housing. It wasn't a pleasant smelling area.

"We are being followed."

"I don't expect to leave the palace and not be followed," Rennyn said, amused given that he'd trailed her out as well. "And, frankly, unless it's a small army, I would only feel sorry for them if they were stupid enough to attack."

He'd warned her because the area she was heading into was increasingly secluded. The noise of the magelight-studded main road died away, and as she found her destination there were only her own footsteps and not a single light except that of the stars.

"The street completely devoured by the Azrenel."

She took the unprompted comment as a sign of increasing curiosity. Walking down here had been an impulse sparked by her empty stomach, and the challenge of tracking a guised creature to which she had no powerful connection. Magic was both greatly limited by distance and tremendously dangerous when asked to perform a vague or imprecise action. To find a familiar thing nearby was easy. To find an unknown at a distance was very near to impossible. The map-based divination which allowed her family to pinpoint the first expression of the Grand Summoning was one of the most complex pieces of magic she knew, and only worked because her family had both exacting knowledge of the spell, and a real and tangible link to the caster.

Rennyn reached back and pulled free the long black ribbon she used to hold her hair away from her face. Knotting it into a large loop, she threaded her fingers through and then clasped her hands together. She needed a link.

"*Unaet*," she said. "*Temaru. Arlaeth.*" Dark. Cold. Hungry.

Turning, she walked back down the street, repeating the names of three sigils over and over. *Unaet. Temaru. Arlaeth.* Dark. Cold. Hungry. Here, to this place the Azrenel had come. Here it had feasted, drawing out life after life, but for an Azrenel it would never be enough. Hungry.

Her stomach was a pit, echoing, and her breath puffed out in clouds. As she reached the head of the street and turned toward the river, she brought the night with her, streaming behind like a cloak, dripping from her hands. Dark. Cold. Hungry.

Ahead was the broad, flat expanse of the Murian River, stinking liquid black, but before that was the band of inscribed paving stones which marked Asentyr's circle. All circles were literally that, as perfectly round as they could be made. It was Symbolic magic, a thing many didn't realise, though they understood well enough that circles couldn't cross each other. Circles within circles were acceptable, such as the circle around the crown of Aliace Hill, but to cross a circle with another was to weaken both. The city of Asentyr had dozens of circles clustered about the edges of the main, like the two immediately ahead: one large enough to encompass a tavern and several houses to the right, and another filled by a lone warehouse. Little islands of protection, with darkness between.

When Rennyn crossed Asentyr's circle, it shuddered. Reinforced countless times, the circle's entire purpose was to keep Eferum-Get out, to protect the city from creatures which would feed on the living. When she crossed the circle, she was remembering a time when cooked food made her ill, and she was hungry all the time but nothing seemed to satisfy. That craving filled her as she stopped in the empty, unprotected point between the three nearest circles and looked back into the light of the city.

Just before her were several people. Captain Faille, a sword in one hand, and three others she couldn't spare thought to recognise. Between them was the thick border of the circle, and trailing streamers of night trapped in the shield. Mist curled around her, lifting from the ground, and she gazed upward as something drifted down from the sky, an insubstantial thing drawn to her, attracted by the memory of an Azrenel's feasting just as it would be to a sleeping and undefended human.

"Life Stealer!" exclaimed one of the people, and drew power. But that wasn't needed.

Unclasping her hands as she lifted them, Rennyn held up a cat's cradle made of black ribbon, criss-crossing lines trailing darkness. The Life Stealer, no more than a wisping grey shape, was tangled, trapped, and Rennyn held it out toward the shield as it writhed impotently.

"*Unaet,*" she said again, pushing the creature into a shield specifically designed to keep it out. Light bloomed where it touched, a delicate purple haze. "*Temaru. Arlaeth.*"

Power poured through her and into Asentyr's shield. The light spread, dancing in gem hues, racing along the boundary of the circle, lifting into the sky. The shield shimmered into visibility, shifting slowly from dome to a pillar of colour rising straight from the ground all through the area it protected. Swathes of green and red, orange and purple, thickened the air. Around the palace and various other minor circles the colour flared into brighter points of white, but these did not impede the flow of her casting.

"*Senyatel,*" Rennyn said, when all the city blazed with a peacock aurora. "*Senyatel.*" Revealed. Revealed.

The Life Stealer burned into nothing and Rennyn staggered and fell forward through a shield which no longer resisted her. Faille managed to get an arm between her and the ground and set her easily back on her feet as the light display faded abruptly away, leaving only two colourful motes on Aliace Hill. Raindrop beacons spearing the sky.

"What did you do?" asked one of her audience, and she recognised Lieutenant Meniar, the Sentene mage who was part of the detail to accompany her to Surclere.

"Spectacular, but–?" asked the woman. A member of the Hand. Rennyn wondered how many others had followed her from the palace.

"That was some kind of divination, wasn't it?" said the last, a well-dressed young boy Rennyn didn't recognise, his red hair dimmed by eyes brimming with amazement.

"Like calls to like," Rennyn explained. "The only thing I could think of to counter guised Eferum-Get roaming inside a circle."

Captain Faille's attention had been on the two remaining motes of colour, but he looked back as Rennyn went and sat heavily on a nearby crate. "Meniar, get a message to Captain Illuma," he ordered. "Have squads investigate the target of those lights. And give Lady Montjuste-Surclere your coat."

"Yessir." Meniar wasn't in uniform either, but his coat was still large and warm and a welcome relief. He gave her shoulders a little squeeze as he put it around her, then retreated and began the difficult task of sending a message by magic.

"Do you suppose that tavern serves anything edible?" Rennyn asked, tucking her hands in her armpits in the hope of unfreezing them. Her already healthy appetite had become an urgent need to replace lost energy.

"I'll go look," said the boy, and after a moment's hesitation the Hand mage followed him, for it was not the kind of place noble youths could walk into safely.

"Will your brother be able to complete the attunement if you cannot?" Captain Faille asked.

"Yes. Though I would prefer that he didn't have to." Rennyn considered the man, who wasn't quite criticising her, but who obviously thought she'd taken an unnecessary risk casting such a massive spell. And might well feel that permission should be gained before altering the city's main protection. "If my Wicked Uncle comes into this city, I want to know it. If anything comes near my brother, I want more warning than we had today."

"How long will the divination last?"

"Anywhere between a few weeks and a few centuries." She shrugged, and gazed at the lights of the city. "Long enough."

Her stomach hurt. Too convinced by her spell that she, like the Eferum-Get, was a bottomless void, an emptiness that even a thousand lives could not fill. "What prompted the Kellian's departure from the Forest of Semarrak?" she asked, hoping to distract herself.

"Tyrland is our home."

"That's the answer to a different question," Rennyn pointed out, looking up at him. "Had the last of the originals died?"

During the silence which followed she could hear Lieutenant Meniar sounding out each sigil he activated, and a gust of laughter from the tavern. It was the first time she'd asked something that it seemed Faille might not answer and she studied his profile as best she could when he blended so well into the night. Despite obliging with answers, this man was as far from the obedient ciphers of the originals as it was possible to be. Grim courtesy could not mask a sheerly incisive mind, and a tendency not to express his opinions did not leave her in any doubt that he had them. He weighed every word she spoke, and judged whether she deserved any response.

"Nine of the Ten remain."

Remain? He meant they were still alive? Rennyn stared at him. The original golems would have been long-lived, true, but she would not have expected their life-span to be more than one hundred and fifty or perhaps two hundred years.

"One was killed in battle," Captain Faille continued. "The rest...grew weary. To wake, to move, to do more than subsist, became beyond their strength. But they do not die."

Words failed her, and she shook her head in futile denial. Still alive? Unable to die? But she saw what was behind this. She understood the rules which bound the Kellian golems' existence, and could see a reason. Unless they were killed through violence they would not die.

They hadn't been given permission.

SIXTEEN

Stupid, stuck-up, full of himself, know-it-all, pampered...
Kendall ran out of new things to call Sebastian
Montjuste-Surclere and started the list over, stomping a foot
in time to each word. What business was it of his to look down on
her? *She* hadn't been learning magic since she could crawl.

Well, enough was enough. Sebastian could admire himself as
much as he liked. The idiots at the Arkathan could gossip and
nudge and whisper and smirk at each other. Kendall didn't need to
hang around for that. She had money enough to find a place to
stay, and smarts enough to find a job. She'd practice holding
pebbles in the meantime, and if it ever looked like she might be able
to do more she'd find a teacher. There were plenty of mages
outside the Houses of Magic. Better mages.

At least, now that she'd decided to leave, she would be able to
see the city. Who would have thought she'd have spent all this time
in Asentyr and not even looked around? It was a stupid rule that
students of the Arkathan couldn't leave the Houses of Magic
without permission, and Kendall felt as if she was kicking off chains
as she marched down Aliace Hill.

Someone walking the other way stopped and turned around,
following after her. Busybody. Kendall shot them a withering
glare, which didn't have much effect on Rennyn Montjuste-Surclere.
The woman only seemed entertained by Kendall's expression.

"Been arguing with Seb?" she asked, unexpectedly perceptive.

"No!" Kendall increased her pace, but found her elbow taken
in a firm grip.

"Let's go eat something. There's a nice-looking teashop down
here."

"Don't you have a kingdom to save?"

"Tea first, then kingdom."

Kendall debated pulling free. "Look, Lady Mon-"

"Oh, call me Rennyn. I don't have a title and we'll dump the stupid surname as soon as this is over. Rennyn Claire, no more complicated than that."

"Then why introduce yourself as Montjuste-Surclere?"

"Because it's simpler right now. Expediency excuses many sins."

Her voice was so bitter that Kendall had to stare, and she was curious enough to follow meekly into a tea-shop full of snotty types who were even less impressed with Kendall than the lot up at the palace. Without the all-concealing blue and black uniform smock, her worn dress marked her as exactly what she was.

"Spiced tea for two and a selection of cakes, please," Rennyn Claire ordered, tucking her bags under the table and gesturing for Kendall to do the same. "So you bored of the Arkathan?"

"They weren't teaching me anything."

"Are they teaching anyone anything much at the moment? I understood the Arkathan teachers were covering the Hand's duties, while the Hand mages are off helping the Sentene, who are hopelessly overstretched. They can barely keep up with the natural breaches, let alone the larger ones."

"I know all that," Kendall said, crossly. "I'm not asking them to stop or anything. I'm just putting my own time to better use."

"Having argued with Seb."

"I haven't argued with *anyone*."

"Bah. What did he say to you that's annoyed you then?"

"You're as bad as he is – you always think you're right."

"That's because I usually am." Rennyn Claire smiled provocatively, then sat back as the snooty ladies filled their table with tea things and cakes. "So what is he wrong about?"

"This has nothing to do with your brother."

"If you say so. Have a cake."

It was early for lunch, so Kendall picked at a piece of seedcake, and watched Rennyn Claire put away enough for four. The woman ate with a straightforward enjoyment of all things sweet and sticky, her attention on the people walking past outside. Every time Kendall saw her the circles under her eyes were darker, but except for that brief remark about expediency she acted as calm as she had that day in Finton. Almost as insufferable as her brother.

"Do you think if you just sit there eating I'll suddenly decide to tell you?"

"I think that the more times I ask the same question, the less likely you are to answer. You're the one who has to decide whether it costs you anything to tell me."

In other words, she was curious but she didn't really care. And Kendall had to admit there was nothing stopping her from answering the question.

"...he called me a would-be rote mage."

"What, to your face? Seb's manners are slipping. Why does it matter what kind of mage Seb thinks you'll make?"

Kendall groped for words. "It's what he thinks matters. He acts like the world is full of two kinds of people: 'real' mages and everyone unimportant."

Rennyn laughed. "Not so bad as that. But – Seb is like a musician in a world of the tone-deaf. He loves magic and adores talking about it, and if people can't tell one note from the other they won't understand what he's saying. Does it matter to you what kind of mage you become?"

"A well-paid one." Kendall wasn't going to pretend otherwise. "Anything that will earn more money than I would selling vegetables and running errands."

"How much more? A deviser, one with the depth of understanding to do more than just repeat back spells they've learned, is ten times more valuable than any rote mage."

"Maybe. But I'm not going to suddenly be this magic-is-my-life person. I'll try and get good at it, but I'm not going to act like it's the only thing in the world worth doing."

"Fair enough, though treating magic as a profession doesn't prevent you from becoming a deviser – or being a 'real' mage if you want to call it that. The thing I don't understand is how leaving all the free food and accommodation helps."

"It lets me get some peace and quiet. The Arkathan is full of idiots who want me to tell them everything about you two, and won't leave me alone when I won't."

"So tell them. I doubt there's anything that most of them don't know already."

"I'm not there for their benefit."

"Hah." Rennyn drained her teacup and dropped some money on the table. "If nothing else, being able to stand your ground will come in useful when you're casting. How about this – for the next five or so days I get to be dragged about Tyrland pinpointing incursion points again. Come with me and I'll give you some tedious lectures on magical theory. When you get back you can decide if it's worth hanging around the Arkathan any more."

Kendall glowered at the woman while she worked their bags free from beneath the table, but waited until they were outside to say anything.

"I'm not some charity case."

"Would you like me to charge you for lessons or something? It's not going to cost me anything to talk at you, and will pass some time for me since I don't find it at all easy to read or write while travelling. Though I do warn you that I'm planning to sleep most of the way to Knifecliff."

"That's where the next breach will be?"

"Just south of it."

The idea of returning to the front row of the drama of Tyrland's defence was a good deal less attractive after seeing one of the Night Roamers far too close up. Kendall would never forget that crab-thing's fleshy mouth. But still, to be able to witness one of the battles which would shape the whole kingdom's future: it was definitely tempting. And she had to admit that the Montj– the Claires at least acted like they knew more about magic than everyone else put together.

"They'll start to fret if I don't show up soon," Rennyn said, starting back down the street. "Come if you're coming."

Kendall went.

CR&O

The stable yard of the Houses of Magic was full of horses and coaches. After Rennyn found them the right coach to put their bags in, she disappeared into the Sentene's barracks. Kendall went to collect her dictionaries, which she'd left on her bed with her smock and a snippy little note resigning from the Arkathan.

Sukata Illuma was reading it. She gave Kendall a long look when she came in the door, then handed the note over. "What changed your mind?"

Kendall hesitated. She liked Sukata, so far as it was possible to like someone who kept herself separate and hardly ever spoke. It wasn't so much explaining that was the problem – it was convenient that someone was around for her to give a message to – it was just that it was Sukata. Not only was her mother probably going to be in danger on this trip, but the offer of personal tutoring from Rennyn Claire was something Kendall suspected most would-be mages would value a good deal more than she did. And that wasn't even counting how strange the Kellian were about the remnants of the Montjuste-Surclere family.

"Guess I saw the sense of not cutting off my nose to spite my face," Kendall said slowly. She chewed her lip. "Sukata – why do you stay over here if your mother lives in the next building?"

"That is a rule of the Arkathan. Few are granted an exception, though of course many have now been given leave to return to their families for the duration of the Grand Summoning. And while the building is repaired."

"Are you going to go into the Sentene when you've finished with the Arkathan?"

"Perhaps. Sentene mages need to learn how to apply their knowledge in trying situations. It's a good proving ground."

"Proving what?"

With rare physical expression Sukata lifted one shoulder. "Whether I am capable of more."

More. Just as Kendall had guessed, Sukata wanted to be a real mage. "Walk back with me," she said, picking up her uniform. "I don't think I've much time left."

Kellian could be deceptively obliging. Even though Kendall had barely spoken to her before today, Sukata had answered her questions and followed along now quite as if she would do whatever she was told. But that, Kendall would bet, was because she was more than curious about what was going on. Kendall went back to the stable yard, reaching it just before Rennyn, who was carrying a funny-looking crystal and metal thing attached to a chain.

"Wait here a moment," Kendall told Sukata, and followed her would-be teacher around the other side of the coach. "You can lecture two people as easily as one, can't you?" she hissed.

Rennyn glanced in the direction where Sukata waited, hidden by the coach. For a moment there was the faintest hint of – dismay? – on her face, but then she shrugged. "True enough." She moved so that she could see Sukata, whose wide eyes and frozen stance made clear that Kendall had spoken too loudly. "Though, unlike Kendall, I expect there's people you'll want to ask permission of before going on tours of Tyrland."

"I – yes." Sukata recovered rapidly, making a smart little bow. "Thank you, my Lady. I will be quick." She vanished through the increasing tangle of Sentene and Ferumguard getting ready to depart.

"Nice gesture," Rennyn said, when the Kellian girl was out of sight. "I didn't expect it of you."

"I knew it would really matter to her," Kendall said, ducking her head. "I couldn't just tell her where I was going, knowing that."

"Troubling to have a conscience, isn't it?"

That was the sort of comment which made Kendall remember that this woman was a descendant of Black Queen Solace. Rennyn climbed into their coach and sat fiddling with the crystal thing, fixing a thick bracelet around her wrist, but Kendall stayed outside watching the Sentene and Ferumguard organise themselves. Sukata must have run at full Kellian speed, returning clutching a small bag just as Lady Weston showed up flanked by Captain Faille and Captain Illuma.

"Well, child. You do have a talent for attracting would-be teachers." Lady Weston's wry tone acknowledged that she herself had failed to teach Kendall anything. "It is good of–" She broke off, looking into the coach, then shook her head, smiling. Rennyn Claire was curled up on one of the seats, deeply asleep. "I will save my speeches, then," Lady Weston continued in a lowered tone. "Take care, you two. Follow the orders you are given. I need not warn you of the dangers, since you have already witnessed what you may face. Most of all, listen. Make the most of this opportunity."

Be good and listen hard. Kendall muttered something appropriate and climbed into the coach, deciding that Rennyn Claire was just as good at taking people over as Ma Lippon. Deciding how things should go, and getting her way by pretending not to care whether you did what she wanted. Or, no – more that she knew you'd do it, because her way was the right way. Surclere arrogance.

Not that Kendall hadn't just done the same thing to Sukata, who was sitting very upright gazing out of the window not because she was interested in the stable yard, but because she'd really rather stare at Rennyn Claire. Her face was perfectly composed and her eyes were totally lit up. Happy beyond words. Maybe this was why they did it, those people who tried to take you over, who thought they knew what was best.

More likely they just wanted to make themselves feel good.

SEVENTEEN

L ike a mother duck and her ducklings."

This made Sukata's eyes widen, and Lieutenant Meniar laughed outright, then tried to pretend he hadn't. It was true though. They'd stopped somewhere south of Knifecliff, on a white road cut through rolling greenery. Rennyn Claire had started walking about, dangling the big round crystal which apparently held the Black Queen's focus, and a little deputation of Sentene and Hand mages trailed behind her, while everyone else watched. So serious they made Kendall's teeth ache.

The road, overlooked by a farmhouse and plenty of sheep, ran alongside an abrupt fall from pasture to a sliver of sand edging the endless blackness she was told was the Deridian Sea. It stretched further than Kendall could see, and she was unable to resist standing close to the edge of the proper, solid world, drawn and repelled by the mass of water.

Right now, she was betting the Sentene wished they were anywhere else, as Rennyn Claire walked straight up to the cliff's edge and, after the briefest pause, right over it.

"Barin," said Lieutenant Meniar. "Go up to that farmhouse and ask them about tides. Everything about tides."

"Yessir," said one of the Ferumguard, sounding just about as pleased as Meniar. Kendall watched her supposed teacher walk from the narrow beach to ten feet out over the water, then stop. She glanced back at the beach and with a gesture brought a man-sized boulder flying toward her. It sank into the dark water beneath her feet.

As Rennyn floated herself back to the top of the cliff one of the Captains ordered most of the crowd to setting up camp, leaving only a small group to stand about being dismayed.

"You did say something about Sentene mages and trying situations," Kendall muttered to Sukata, and then scooted herself in at the back to listen to the senior Hand mages yak on about whether their clever shields would work under water.

Captain Illuma turned to Rennyn when she set herself down beside Kendall. "Can you delay entering the Eferum until this is settled, Lady Montjuste-Surclere? We may need your advice."

"I'll be delaying entering the Eferum until the last moment anyway," was the response. "Since it seems I can't reliably conceal myself, it's the simplest way to limit my exposure." She glanced restively down at the waves. "The cliff top should be within range, so I'll set my circle up here, too."

"This is a situation we've not encountered before, My Lady," said one of the Hand mages, a twittery, dark-skinned woman who was a good deal sharper than she made out. "We are aware that natural breaches open over water, of course, but given the difficulty of studying them, we have little information."

"Mm. The water's about ten feet deep where I put that rock, and the bottom drops sharply." Rennyn's attention had drifted back to the waves with a touch of the same fascination Kendall felt. "I'd abandon any idea of that shield," she continued after a moment. "If you hadn't already. There's too much confluence between deep water and the Eferum, which is why I need to keep my circle at a distance. This breach will be very large, its strength enhanced by the environment, and will form at the surface, wherever the surface happens to be. Still, few Eferum-Get do very well in water, so if there is another horde, some of them may drown."

"We should look at nets," Captain Illuma said. "Reinforced and cast over the area to drag them under. Use the water to our advantage instead of taking it as an obstacle."

This suggestion produced lots of nodding, and a detachment was sent back to Knifecliff to wangle some nets. Kendall followed Rennyn as, rubbing the back of her neck, she wandered off to the coaches to ferret around in her bags. Kendall had seen her eyes open more than once during the journey, and wondered if there was anyone who could order the woman to go back to bed.

For a group who usually travelled in pairs, the Sentene acted like a well-drilled army. Or perhaps it was mainly the Ferumguard, whose normal role was keeping villagers out of the way and searching out any remaining traces after a Sentene pair had taken care of whatever thing had been ravaging the countryside. In any case, they had a small town's worth of tents erected in little clusters, food cooking, the horses rubbed down, and the local farmer soothed, all before Rennyn had finished dissecting her luggage. A handful of mages were busy constructing two temporary circles to keep out stray Night Roamers – those that were stupid enough to come anywhere near a Sentene camp.

At least the meal, a salty mix of buttered grains and vegetables, made Rennyn look a bit more alive, to the point where, sitting in front of one of the tent clusters as the afternoon started thinking about twilight, she turned her attention on Kendall and Sukata.

"So, tell me what you know about magic."

"Aren't you supposed to tell *us*?" Kendall retorted.

"It helps to know where to start. You know the differences between the three so-called spheres of magic?"

"Force, Sigillic and Symbolic," Kendall said, reluctant because there were at least half a dozen people unashamedly eavesdropping. "Sebastian found me a book which explained a bit. Far as I can tell, Clumsy, Complicated and Scary magic."

"You're not far off," Rennyn said, laughing. "Though that's more the usual outcome than the sphere itself. Casting is just a mage trying to tell Efera to do something, but you have a choice of approach. How have you been going with the exercise Seb set you?"

Hunching her shoulders, Kendall glowered at the small wooden bowl she'd recently set down. It jerked to one side. "It goes everywhere but up," she muttered.

"And you, Sukata?" Rennyn asked. "The first step of Thought magic – to lift and hold steady a light object."

"The Teremic approach–" Sukata began.

"Goes on interminably about the relative uselessness of what they like to call Force Magic, and counsels those who would use it be well-grounded in Sigillic before attempting anything. You're a couple of years off summoning your first focus, I presume?"

"Yes."

"Can you lift up that bowl?"

"I–" With more than a hint of reluctance Sukata turned her eyes on the bowl, but it didn't do anything and she shook her head.

"What about you Lieutenant Meniar?"

Meniar stopped pretending to be busy watching for attackers. "Ah...I'd better not."

"The Teremic approach is like putting off learning to walk or talk until you're twenty or so – an excellent way of discouraging you from starting. Because you've no magical strength yet, Kendall, there's a limit to how much damage you can wreak while you're trying to find out how to order your thoughts. Lieutenant Meniar has apparently reached the point where he thinks he might kill someone if he tries."

Kendall was astonished. All this time watching pebbles hop about, she'd thought she mustn't be particularly talented at magecraft. "But – they can cast – why is it possible for them to cast at all if they can't do that?"

"'Thought magic'. Telling Efera what you want simply by thinking it. It's an exercise of will and mental discipline. Sigillic magic puts a buffer between the Efera and your thoughts, and uses an entirely different 'muscle' – as if you were using your arms instead of your legs, for instance." Rennyn searched about in her pockets and produced a small wooden box containing sticks of chalk. Calling the bowl to her with a gesture, she wrote a bunch of sigils on the curving wood, then pushed power into them until the bowl rose a short way into the air and stayed there. "Although mages usually think or even speak the name of the sigils as they power them, they're not making any attempt to do anything with Efera except run it through the shape of the sigil. Whatever they've written shapes the result of the casting. Complicated is a good description, since, because the casting is at one remove from the caster, factors such as duration need to be taken into account. You'll see few good Sigillics which don't have some limit or cut-off mechanism – a word or a phrase. But that's the structure of the casting. The act is the same whatever the spell: push power to the sigils and let the sigils form the outcome."

"It's easier to make the sigils do things than it is to hold up a rock? Sigillic magic is the *easy* kind?"

"During the activation. It's the safest method, and allows even those with no particular mental discipline to cast. More importantly, it allows the creation of spells which are really beyond the ability to compass in a 'single' thought, and can be used for castings which persist after the user has stopped thinking about it, or even putting power into it. Thought magic takes a good deal more effort to produce the same outcome, and usually only basic outcomes can be achieved. Picking up a rock."

"Are the sigils magic themselves?"

In answer, Rennyn released the bowl, cleaned it off and then wrote on it again, this time in neatly printed Tyrian script. Again she pushed power into it and again it obediently lifted a couple of feet off the ground and sat there.

"Efanian, the language of magic, reaches well back into the beginnings of structured magic. The Wizard Corela, one of the early great practitioners, invented it, although it has naturally been constantly refined. The sigils were designed to allow each symbol to be a single word, and the language attempts to remove all ambiguity, so there are no homonyms – no words that can mean more than one thing. Think, for instance of telling Efera 'to make something light', 'to light a fire', 'to conjure light'."

"How would you make it float with Symbolic magic?"

"Mm. Not the most appropriate candidate for Symbolic casting. Make a soap bubble, perhaps, and then use either Thought or Sigillic magic to suggest that the bowl is like a soap bubble. Symbolic magic takes advantage of characteristics of objects and concepts to transfer those characteristics to the subject of your casting. The problem is a symbol is often worse than a homonym – the colour red can symbolise anger, passion, blood, romance, death, or indeed anything the caster thinks it means. Some argue that even things that the caster doesn't know it means matter in Symbolic. With a soap bubble, the bowl would probably float, but since I consider a soap bubble a symbol of the ephemeral, it might also pop out of existence when I next touched it. To cast Symbolic magic, there must first be a sense of...rightness, of surety over what symbols you have chosen and the result they will bring. In a way you have to dominate the outcome, by being certain in yourself what your symbols mean. Otherwise you could end up with almost anything. Scary magic, as you say."

"What kind of magic do you mostly use?"

"Mostly? The best casting is usually a combination. What do you think circles are? A symbol of perfection, of a cycle, of a line not to be crossed which has no end."

Kendall was fascinated, enjoying this explanation far more than she'd expected, not least because: "You're saying that almost everyone learns magic the wrong way round."

"Not precisely. The Teremic Approach would be appropriate – a necessity – for people who don't have a great deal of strength of mind. Advanced Thought casting is absolutely more dangerous than anything except perhaps Symbolic, and I would not recommend any move past the simple exercise Seb gave you unless precise control is gained. But if you don't start with it, you're unlikely to ever use it. The stronger you become the more damage you'll be able to do."

"So what *can't* you do with magic?"

"In theory, nothing. In practice, you are of course limited by your ability to convey your intention, and your strength. Understanding exactly what you're trying to do is fundamental. I, for instance, probably wouldn't have done very well getting that poison out of Seb. To be a good healing mage, you need to understand how people work, and my studies have focused on the Eferum and divinations, not blood and bile and flesh.

"Size and distance also limit you. The further you try and send a message by magic, the less likely it is to arrive. Think of the difference between looking into the next room, and looking into a room on the far side of the country. Scrying is one of those things all the legends show the great mages doing, but no-one knows how they structured the spell. It seems a simple thing doesn't it? One of Tiandel's sons spent a great deal of time trying to work out a way to scry over distance, and when he finally succeeded the casting took all his energy and killed him."

"But he succeeded?" Lieutenant Meniar took a step forward eagerly. "A functioning distance scry? Truly?"

His excited advance brought a shutter down over Rennyn's face, but then she shrugged and plucked the still-floating bowl out of the air. "Yes and no. It's technically functional, but even I'm not powerful enough to cast it." She handed the bowl to Kendall. "Distance is a huge limitation, but choosing to learn only Sigillic is merely a self-imposed constraint. It's up to you two whether you attempt Thought casting exercises or not. It's not necessary to becoming a Sigillic mage."

"What about being a 'real' mage?"

Rennyn Claire paused, turning her head toward the darkening horizon and the line where the grass stopped and the sky began. "The question would be whether you can truly understand magic if you ignore all but one of the ways of performing it. And that's all Seb means by real mages – people who understand magic, and have the full set of tools to manipulate it."

There was a little silence, a weirdly upset pause, and then a shadow between the two tents behind Rennyn resolved into Captain Faille.

"What time do you wish to be woken, my Lady?" he asked.

"Midnight, I suppose. Three hours ahead should be safe enough."

Kendall was impressed that Captain Faille had managed to give Rennyn an order, just by not giving it to her. As soon as she had gone into her tent, everyone who had been lingering about shifted away, some only a short distance to stand guard and the rest to the busier end of the camp, where the noise immediately dropped to furious whispers. Kendall, retreating obediently with Sukata, considered the rearrangement appreciatively.

"It's like she's got a hundred nannies. The scariest woman in the kingdom, and they all tiptoe around her like she's made of glass. She doesn't strike me as fragile."

Sukata didn't respond, heading for the cliff's edge. She was obviously upset, though Kendall had only begun to be able to spot the signs. It was in the way she held herself, and the fact that she wasn't being so proper and correct. Kendall held off prodding, and peered cautiously down. The water had moved, the beach growing to half again its width, and the Sentene had found a way to pick their way down the cliff to the water, where they were conjuring balls of light.

"Going into the Eferum here is already risky," Sukata finally said. "Going into the Eferum when obviously in need of a full day's sleep is courting disaster."

"She probably has nightmares," said Kendall, who had suffered enough herself in the past few days. "Why is it so risky going into the Eferum here?"

"The ocean is said to be like the Eferum – cold and dark and full of currents. When travelling between two such similar places there's a danger of missing your direction."

"She didn't seem that worried about it. Was what she said about Thought magic right? How come people do this Teremie stuff, if it means you get all messed up? Is it really that hard to do?"

The Kellian girl sat down on the cliff's edge, which was more than Kendall was willing to do. "Force magic – too often children died trying to master it. The accepted wisdom is that it is simply not worth it. What can it accomplish that a well-constructed Sigillic cannot? It wears on the caster far more, and the danger of interruption or lapses of concentration is considerable. The basis of the Teremic approach is that a dead mage can't cast any kind of magic, and the speed of something as crude as Force magic doesn't balance the risk."

"Then why did everyone act like she was welcoming Fel to dinner? Hearts in boots and trying to put a brave face on it."

"There – there has been a great deal of debate over how much of what Lady Montjuste-Surclere does is Force magic. During the Asentyr incursion she was seen to use highly advanced Sigillic circles culminating in a Symbolic summoning, but much of her casting must be either pre-prepared or not Sigillic. I'm not sure she even carries a slate. She is powerful enough to maintain a number of pre-cast spells, it is true, but that casting after the palace incursion–"

"What casting?"

"You remember, an hour or so after sunset, there was a wash of colour? And then some lights in the sky?"

"I didn't see the lights."

"It was a casting which altered Asentyr's main circle so that it would pinpoint any Eferum-Get within its bounds. And it revealed two, both of them guised as the larger had been. Spies. Eferum-Get spies." Sukata's voice dropped with the enormity of this idea, then lifted again. "From what I have been told, Lady Montjuste-Surclere went to the place the Eferum-Get attack had been most destructive and set up an 'idea' of what Eferum-Get are like, and then used that idea to call to her a Life Stealer to cause a reaction with the shield. During all this she simply chanted three words which might count as Sigillic magic except she didn't write them on anything, and the names of sigils alone do not constrain Efera. Which means that the spell was almost entirely Symbolic and...Thought."

"So, more than just lifting things."

"How do you describe red to a blind man?" Sukata asked as she fidgeted with the hem of her smock, another sign that she was really upset. "Sound to the deaf? That is the lesson we've just learned: that Force – Thought magic can be used to say what words cannot. It has only been considered crude because we have not used it with any level of skill. She just told us that none of us are real mages."

"Do you think Rennyn's cruel?" Kendall asked, after a moment. "Nasty, just for the sake of being nasty?"

Sukata stared at her blankly, then shook her head.

"If she thought it was impossible for you to learn Thought magic – properly – she wouldn't have told you to try and pick up the bowl. Besides, it sounds to me that the thing that kills would-be Thought mages is being distractible or just not able to think in whatever way it is you're supposed to think. You don't exactly strike me as the scatty type."

"I have spent years developing my strength," Sukata said, her thin voice dropping so Kendall had to strain to hear it. "I would not be encouraged to take such a risk."

"Pft – far as I can tell from what was going on back there, we were allowed along because everyone else wants to listen in on these so-called lessons. If they have that much respect for her opinions on magic, are they going to argue about what she tells you to do? And there's plenty of empty fields in Tyrland to practice in."

"I–"

"Afraid you'll die?"

"No."

"Afraid you'll fail, then."

Sukata curled her fingers shut. "And you?"

"Dunno. Might give it a few more days."

"You are very pragmatic."

"Even if I can only use it to move things about, it seems worth trying to me," Kendall said, shrugging. "Could earn some money rescuing kittens from trees."

"Worth trying," Sukata repeated, then looked down to the darkening water, where her mother stood directing groups of mages to stand about writing on slates. Even though Sukata wasn't smiling, Kendall could tell that she'd made her feel better.

This needed to stop. She was letting others mind her business, and worse still she'd started minding theirs. Where would that get her?

Annoyed with herself, Kendall found a pebble and made it hop.

EIGHTEEN

Rennyn stepped into the Eferum in a blaze of power. Until she discovered a better way to hide, her approach would be to play on her strength, and it gave her a good deal of satisfaction to send deadly bolts shooting in every direction hoping one would meet her Wicked Uncle. She kept up a steady assault on the emptiness around her, chopping and changing between a number of pre-prepared offensive spells until Solace's focus warned her it was time to get down to business.

Relying on one last pulse of force to hold back immediate attack, Rennyn allowed her attention to be taken up by the attunement. Even as far back from the breach point as she was, the strength of the attraction between the focus and the Summoning dragged at her, but it was easier to resist when she was prepared for it. Done.

A small cluster of Eferum-get were approaching the breach, and she paused to blast them with raw power, incinerating them in a most thorough and final manner. Nothing like stopping an attack before it even started. But there was no wisdom in lingering in the Eferum congratulating herself, so Rennyn stepped back into the world.

Dawn. She'd managed to get in and out in only a few hours. The gentle hills to the east were picked out in pastel shades, with a hint of mist between clumps of sheep. Below, in the shadow of the cliff, the Sentene waited beneath their summoned lights for an incursion which would not come. A gull called, muted and distant.

"It went well?" Lieutenant Danress, standing at the very edge of Rennyn's circle.

"Uneventful. There were a few smaller Eferum-Get heading for the breach, but I had an easy chance to kill them. Duramoi, I think. They weren't carrying a shield-breaker this time, that I could see."

The faintest ring of metal made her turn. Captain Faille had drawn that overlong sword and was gazing out to the western horizon, his entire body taut with energy. In the delicately-tinted light he was a roseate gossamer man, and she saw in him an unexpected beauty. Dawn was the hour of the Kellian's creation, and would be the time of their greatest strength.

"Captain?" Lieutenant Danress asked.

The grim lines on either side of his mouth deepened. "Something is coming." He turned a fraction toward Rennyn. "Bring them up from there. This is another trap."

Wryly reflecting on Lady Weston's opinions about Kellian leaders, Rennyn obediently hoisted sixty people up a cliff. Since people and especially mages had an intrinsic resistance against Thought magic worked directly on them, this was not such an easy thing as throwing individual rocks about, and she was glad of Lieutenant Danress' steadying hand on her shoulder. She'd already used a lot of energy with her offensive spells in the Eferum, and had to take them in clumps.

"Arrowhead formation," Captain Faille ordered, underlining the command with a brief hand gesture. The Sentene rearranged themselves immediately, drawing the Hand mages with them so that only a small line remained on the cliff's edge and the rest spread back in a triangle. "Return to the camp, my Lady," he added to Rennyn.

Rather than divide his attention, Rennyn retreated: not to the camp, but back and to the left. Faral and Meniar shifted out to flank her. And they all waited. There was no sign of whatever attack was coming. The breach had closed, and Rennyn had killed the Eferum-Get before they'd even reached it. Still, she was learning to recognise that the Sentene trusted Kellian instincts for good reason.

Her world was growing more complicated. She wanted to protect them. A sense of responsibility for the Kellian had overtaken her, along with a growing attachment. It was exactly as she had anticipated and very much not wanted. She hadn't missed that they were all calling her "my Lady" now, and not just because it was a deal less clumsy to say than "Montjuste-Surclere". A return gesture for her grandstanding in the Hall of Question.

"There!"

Out beyond the shadow of the cliff, where the sea had lightened to stripes of oyster and pearl, a black shape had broken the shining lines. At first Rennyn thought it was a ship, but then it vanished, only to resurface a few moments later, much closer. Something very large, swimming.

It was moving at an incredible pace. If they hadn't been all staring out to sea from a cliff-top vantage there would have been almost no warning. As it was, Captain Illuma gave several curt orders and everyone moved further away from the drop to the beach. A few of the Sentene mages began writing on slates, but most of them had already cast their offensive spells, and were simply holding them on trigger till their target came within range.

The swimmer struck the rock below, ramming it like a goat in rut. The impact was enough to shake more than a few mages from their feet, and a large section of the cliff fell away. The thing made a booming, moaning noise and then rose so they could properly appreciate what they were facing.

A column of muscle, greenish-grey with a pattern of scales overlaid by a sheen of slime. It was well over fifteen feet in width, and would tower over every building and most trees Rennyn had ever seen. The head, rising well above the top of the cliff, was a massive wedge of streamlined bone, crested with a frill of yellow and green, and most otherwise mouth.

Sea serpent. For all the tales of them wrecking ships, Rennyn had never begun to picture the scale of such a thing. It dropped its jaw to make its drawn and mournful cry, and display fangs as tall as she. The stench was sickening: year-old fish gone well beyond fetid. Its eyes were long and dark and Rennyn saw in them a gleam of sorrowing intelligence before thirty battle-ready mages released their arsenals.

Flesh fountained in every direction and the massive head whipped back, then fell out of sight, crashing to the water below.

Even the sea seemed to hold its breath, then Captain Faille gave a sharp hand-back signal and the Sentene hastily drew further away from the cliff's edge as the creature's long body began to thrash and spasm. Its death throes were brief but intensely violent, sending large sections of the cliff tumbling. Then – hush. The waves soughed, the gulls remembered their voices, and the Sentene approached the edge to look down at water churned to a bloody froth and coil upon coil of muscle relaxing in death.

The Sentene broke into squads: to recover their equipment from the beach, search out whatever was the source of the compulsion which had drawn the serpent here, and not incidentally shift a corpse. Unhappy to own the name Montjuste-Surclere, Rennyn walked back to camp. And here were Kendall and Sukata, eyes wide and weary. Her students. A study in contrasts and probably another thing she was going to regret.

"Did that come out of the Hells?" asked Kendall, for once more awed than pugnacious.

"No. Well, perhaps originally. As a rule a breach wouldn't be big enough or open long enough to fit something like that through, but it's likely it was Eferum-Get once. They adapt to this world after they reach it, just as we change if we stay too long in the Eferum. But nothing came out of the breach this time, so far as I could tell."

"Then how come–?"

"It was under a compulsion." One of the Hand mages, the stocky, short one whose name was either Intsen or Insen. He stalked up, scrubbing a hand across his face angrily. "Tell me, Lady Montjuste-Surclere, how is it that no matter what we prepare we are circumvented? Why are we always on the back foot?"

This was hardly answerable, and Rennyn only looked at him as others of the Hand and the Sentene Senior Captains came to join them: a council of war.

"Our opponent sees the advantage of constantly changing tactics," Captain Illuma commented neutrally. "We should not be surprised by that."

"Changing tactics is one thing," Magister Intsen said, setting his feet. "But this – how is what we saw today even possible for someone in the Eferum?"

"I don't know." Rennyn glanced at the lightening horizon. "The hurdles he has to overcome – we have days between each incursion, while he has only hours. And that attack was specific to the breach point being on the water's edge, which even we didn't know until yesterday afternoon. I suppose that unlike me he may be able to pinpoint the breaches ahead of time, but even with that, to bring that serpent here from outside the bounds of Tyrland–" She lifted her hands. "Perhaps he's come through a natural breach and is now operating in this world."

Not a comforting thought, and she wasn't the only one who glanced at the green hills around them, wondering if they were being watched. If her Wicked Uncle was no longer in the Eferum, the danger of everything coming undone had increased immensely. He could take Solace's focus and complete the attunement. Worse, he could decide to hunt Seb.

"Even if that is the case, he is likely to wait until the attunement is complete, and take the focus from you then," Captain Illuma said. "His current intent appears to be to reduce our numbers."

He was certainly taking a few pointed shots at the Sentene. Rennyn wondered how much of her Wicked Uncle's actions were within Solace's plans, and whether she could be fortunate enough never to meet him again.

Captain Faille signalled for the pull-down of the camp to begin, evidently not seeing much value in sitting around asking 'why?'. "We will no longer focus our preparations purely on attacks out of the Eferum," he said matter-of-factly, and headed back to the cliff's edge.

Feeling cramped, Rennyn went for a walk up the nearest hill, trying to pretend Faral and Meniar weren't trailing discreetly behind. She returned none the wiser as to whether her Wicked Uncle had an agenda of his own, but refreshed enough to face the coach journey. One of the Ferumguard handed her a steaming bowl of oats laced with honey and fruit, and she sat on the coach's step to eat.

"Is he a better mage than you?"

Kendall, eyes groggy from a night spent watching and waiting, had reverted to her usual charming self.

"Almost certainly. Just not as strong." Rennyn weighed the castings she'd experienced. "Though that, too, might have changed since our last encounter. If he's in this world, he can summon a focus, and I doubt he faces the dangers we do. The Grand Summoning may even impact focus-summoning, though hopefully not casting in this world."

She could see the girl methodically working through that one. "So, even if you stop the Grand Summoning, we might end up with some incredibly powerful part-monster running about trying to take over the kingdom? One that keeps Night Roamers for pets?"

"One that eats people himself, unless I miss my guess."

"What does he look like?"

"Human. Unremarkable. Like Solace, but with the Surclere colouring." With a curl of amusement, she considered the girl's cropped head. "*Not* like Seb."

The girl pulled a face, her now-familiar glower darkening her eyes. "So where are we going next?"

"South-east, into the forests. We'll be going past Sark."

"And Falk?"

"As near as is safe."

NINETEEN

There was a valley where home used to be, flat and wide like some great round footprint. All the world which had been Kendall's for fifteen years was gone, had been stepped on.

Around the road they'd used, trees lay flat or splintered, radiating out from the heaviness' outer ring, where a crust of debris was oozing slowly up. At the centre a woman in white would still be lying. Kendall probably wouldn't have been able to see her, even if it hadn't been raining. Too far away. But the rain, a steady downpour, made it easy to judge just how big an area the heavy air now covered. It was huge, a grey dome where ordinary drops suddenly became a grey blur of needle-hard darts. They weren't allowed to go close enough to hold a hand into it, but Kendall could see the impact, the way those darts churned and stitched the ground. The whole of the world thrummed and was pulled by the weight of that air.

And everywhere were angry people. The cordon of militia, dripping and scowling as they blocked a road but not the fields beside it. The miserable clumps of townsfolk returning to view the wreck of their lives before the next expansion. The Hand and Sentene mages, faces hidden by hoods they'd attached to their uniforms, silently surveying a magical problem so immense they couldn't even go near it, let alone fix it. And the Kellian.

Angry Kellian were scarier even than the crab-thing. They were all grey and unseeable in the rain, but so intensely there they were like storm clouds lowering. They didn't frown or mutter or anything like that, but energy, a coiled readiness for action, rolled off them until Kendall could hardly stand to be near them. Even Sukata felt like someone who might turn and rip your head off at any moment, if she decided you were to be held to account.

Only Rennyn Claire seemed unmoved. She'd eyed the dome critically, cast a couple of spells, then pulled a big book out of one of her bags and sat in the coach making notes. The Black Queen's focus hung from her wrist, awkward and obviously heavy, but she'd made no move to take it off since leaving Asentyr.

Ignoring the wet, Kendall drew back from the coach so she could watch the way everyone moved about Rennyn. The Hand mages hovered, itching to see what she was writing. The Sentene mages and Kellian, angry as they were, still kept a protective eye on her position. Militia and townsfolk angled for a glimpse in the coach door, wondering who warranted such heavy protection. Captain Faille standing near the rear wheel, surveyed everyone else because it was his turn to be bodyguard. He only moved his eyes, and felt liable to crush anyone who came near.

Not that any assassin had a chance. They were travelling with a third of the Sentene: some had stayed behind another day to deal with the natural breaches which followed the ones they knew were coming, and another group had gone ahead to prepare the ground at the next site. Like the White Lady, no outsider could get near Rennyn.

Kendall headed back to Rennyn's coach just as Captain Illuma, becoming a little less like an imminent storm, crossed as well. "Do you wish to observe the next expansion, my Lady? We have time enough to delay."

"No need." Rennyn peered out the coach door, studying one of the big cracks in the ground which radiated out from the heaviness. "Have there been earthquakes?"

"It is a stable region. But the last expansion was felt well into Sark. That helped speed the evacuation."

"My best guess is that the final expansion will fall short of the southern edge of the city. But there will be considerable damage purely from the concussion." Rennyn turned back to Captain Illuma, started with, "Have—" then stopped, and looked fleetingly annoyed. "I've added minimum and maximum range for the final distortion to the map, but the range of the concussion and debris is outside my expertise."

"Where are they putting everyone?" Kendall asked.

Captain Sarana looked down from her unnecessary height and said: "Esson, Nelk, a dozen other locations. Mages of the Sentene and the Hand have been working with the non-specialist forces in ensuring that there are strong circles, and some kind of shelter. Temporary measures, since a large portion of the evacuations are merely precautionary and only the very southern fringe of the city is expected to be left uninhabitable. Much of Sark will be able to return to their homes and repair."

And a lot wouldn't, would be looking for places to live. Bundling her wet smock and trying not to drip on everything, Kendall thought about where Mayor Dorstan and the Lippons and everyone from Falk had ended up as Captain Illuma nodded and set them moving toward the military camp coordinating the evacuation.

Kendall cast a sideways look at Rennyn's face. She never seemed at all concerned about evacuations, never looked at the groups of angry folk they passed, even though there was supposed to be some great evil conspiracy of people out to get her. Was that likely? There'd been attempts aimed at the Sentene, and the royal family, but the only attack on the Claires had been Sebastian getting in the way of some Night Roamers. From what Kendall had heard, even her Night Roamer uncle had seemed more interested in talking to Rennyn than killing her. The gossip about her answers in the Hall of Question made it clear she wasn't interested in helping the Black Queen, or becoming Queen herself, but that didn't mean she didn't have her own agenda.

Kendall was uncomfortable with her thoughts, but mulled them over all the way south from the camp to Sanlecey, which was a big town not far from the Lecey Forest, where they nicely filled one of the larger inns, and another down the road. While everyone settled in, looking after the horses and setting up guard stations, Kendall watched the crowd which formed outside on the street. She'd be out there herself if she was a local. Sentene were an exciting enough sight, let alone a whole troop of them. Did they know that Rennyn Claire was with them? Was that why some of them looked angry?

Heading downstairs, she found Rennyn in the smaller dining room, sitting down to table for an early meal with a mix of the Hand and Sentene, including Sukata and her mother and Lieutenant

Danress. Kendall spent her time covertly studying her would-be teacher and thinking over Surclere arrogance. Though she sat at the same table with them, Rennyn was very much separate. She listened more than talked, lost in her own thoughts or in the meal. A real mage, a Montjuste-Surclere, with secrets.

"Why did Prince Tiandel betray his mother?"

Rennyn, who had been deeply involved in a gloopy trifle, looked up at Kendall's question. Her expression didn't change, which only reinforced Kendall's growing feeling that she was always guarding herself against them.

"What's the popular theory?"

Always answering questions with questions, buying herself time to come up with a story. "That the side-effects of the Grand Summoning – the stuff that's happening around Falk now – upset him. That he couldn't accept the price she was willing to pay in other people's lives."

"Mm – well, to be the fair, Solace didn't know the precise details of what would happen either. They both knew there would very likely be a general increase in breaches, that there would definitely be great stresses placed on the walls between worlds in a predictable pattern, and that there would be an initial outward expression of the spell. They both knew that people would probably die, directly or indirectly, as a result of the Summoning. The rationalisation was that in a war – for the threat of a Kolan invasion was very real – there are casualties. That for the greater good, sacrifices had to be made."

"And do you believe that?"

Rennyn Claire didn't answer right away. Everyone else at the table had stopped talking, and the only sound was the clink of her spoon as she put it down.

"Yes and no." Her eyes were completely black, face expressionless. "If I had to kill you, to stop Solace, would you think it wrong?"

"Of course I would!" Kendall said immediately, then faltered. She was here, alive, because this woman had chosen the exact opposite.

Rennyn smiled, and stood up. "Well, if it's any consolation, I don't plan to kill anyone if I can at all avoid it. But perhaps that was Solace's feeling as well. As to why Tiandel betrayed her, it was something she said to him just before she commenced the Summoning. The Council had been playing her off against the Montjuste Pretender in an attempt to increase their own power, and she was very much a Queen who believed that she should rule absolutely. She told Tiandel that after the Summoning, no-one would ever oppose her again. That gave him a lot to think about."

Moving to the door, she glanced at Captain Illuma. "An early start tomorrow?"

"Shortly after dawn." The Captain's face was particularly blank. Sukata, beside her, had that slightly hunched posture that said she was upset.

When Rennyn nodded and left, Kendall refused to get up and leave too. Though her face burned, she ate all of her trifle, ignoring the muttered conversation between two of the Hand, and the less obvious communication between the Sentene. She hadn't done anything wrong. Everyone tiptoed around Rennyn not asking the questions they should. Just because they were both enemies of the Black Queen didn't mean they were on the same side.

Finished, she pushed her chair back and went out, unsurprised but annoyed when Lieutenant Danress followed her.

"Let's go for a walk, hey?"

Kendall didn't want to talk, but she knew the Sentene mage wouldn't leave her alone until she'd said her piece, so she followed along silently, out a back door of the inn where there wasn't such an audience, and down one of the sloping cobbled streets. Danress wasn't wearing her coat, and in the long shadows of late afternoon they didn't draw any attention.

Sanlecey was a pretty town, with lots of up and down streets and tall, thin houses with dressing around the window – they looked like the dollhouse Nan Tikal had been so fond of boasting about. All of the houses had little patches of garden out front – not for vegetables, but full of flowers. Roses mainly, and sprawling bushes covered with purple and white daisies. At the bottom of the hill was a wide curving street edged with fancy stores on one side and a park on the other. There was a pond in the middle, and they sat on a bench to watch two swans drift about looking bored.

"How much of Sark will be destroyed, do you reckon?"

Lieutenant Danress grimaced. "Between hundreds and thousands of homes. Up to half of the city, though we are praying we will lose only the fringe. There's pressure to divert as many Hand and Sentene mages as possible into shielding certain buildings that lie on the edge of the predicted destruction. The Dawnbringer's Temple, for instance, is a work of art, truly glorious, and it's sure to be badly damaged, even if it's not crushed outright. They're removing the windows, hoping to preserve them elsewhere, but the carvings -"

"There's lots of mages who aren't in the Queen's service, aren't there? Can't they do that?"

"Some will be. But it's a question of numbers, and the danger. Shielding large areas against crushing force is a massive undertaking. You saw what it took Lady Rennyn to protect a single room. For us to protect entire buildings will take time to set up, and unless the mages are willing to trust the shields enough to stay within them during the expansion – a thing Lady Weston has forbidden for both the Sentene and the Hand – we will need to factor in duration. The shields will be set as near to the last moment as we dare, and then left."

"Saving buildings instead of people." Kendall had lived close to Sark all her life, but never been there, never seen the great glass windows of the Temple which were supposed to be so special.

"We can understand the reasons – the Temple, particularly, is one of Tyrland's jewels. But there are things we'd prefer to be doing."

She meant protecting Rennyn. Kendall scowled at a swan, which moved on unconcerned.

"Don't mistake what's happening here," Lieutenant Danress said. "We know there's things she hasn't told us, that there's some further complexity she's keeping back. Half-truths mostly, but the occasional bald-faced lie. She can act, but the omissions become obvious eventually."

"Could she take control of the power the Black Queen's summoned, instead of – whatever she's supposed to do?"

The look Lieutenant Danress gave her was so startled, Kendall explained the suspicion which had been growing in her.

"She doesn't want the throne, she's no friend of the Black Queen. She said she isn't going to cast the Grand Summoning herself. But couldn't she take all that power and make it hers?"

"I – I'd say that's impossible, but given Lady Rennyn's abilities, perhaps I shouldn't underestimate her. But that would be monstrously dangerous to the city and there's a vast difference between could and would."

"What other reason does she have to lie? She's – it's so obvious that she must be going to do something wrong. She just admitted that she'd be willing to kill innocent people to win. Lie about what she intends to do, and if she has to, kill people. Without even telling them why, without even giving them a choice."

Lieutenant Danress shook her head. "Lady Rennyn may be hiding something, but do you think we – let alone the Kellian – would not see through that kind of motive? There's no finer judge of character than a Kellian, and whatever else this is, they're sure Lady Rennyn isn't power-hungry."

Kendall glowered. "Don't you think the Kellian might be a little biased? She's–"

"A Montjuste-Surclere? Believe me, that hardly recommended her to the Kellian."

"They don't act like that."

"Hmph. Their current behaviour is dictated by the events of the Black Night. Keste – Keste Faral and I get along well and she tried to describe to me their first reaction, after we returned from Finton and were speculating over Lady Rennyn's identity. They found the idea of Montjuste-Surclere survivors annoying."

"Annoying?" That didn't match how they acted.

"People mistake the Kellian manner for a lack of will, but it's totally the opposite. They are – in a way they're very, ah, proud's not the word and nor is arrogant. They have incredibly high standards. They don't like to be connected with people who are...base. The Black Queen is their idea of base, and they don't consider Prince Tiandel was much better. They have a very low opinion of selfishness, of hurting others for your own benefit."

"They're all holier-than-the-Dawnbringer?"

Lieutenant Danress laughed, and shrugged. "Not really – they certainly don't go around trying to reform people. They just find certain people distasteful. Most of the rest they are unfailingly polite to, and some they consider worth knowing. When I was first assigned to be my Captain's partner, I was in dread of not living up to him."

Kendall would have just been in dread. "He's a scary man."

"Daunting," Lieutenant Danress agreed, in much the same tone she'd use for 'wonderful'. "Do you know – he knows more about magical theory than me – he just has no ability to cast? To be a novice Sentene and assigned to be his partner was a nightmare, but he gave me plenty of chances to prove myself and treated any mistakes as the minor things they were – so long as I did not make them twice."

Kendall thought Lieutenant Danress had a bad case of hero worship, but kept that to herself. Sukata was a bit the same way about Captain Faille, which Kendall just found perplexing.

"There's a reason Illuma and Faille are so respected," Lieutenant Danress went on, smiling at Kendall's expression. "They are extraordinary, both brilliant and fair. Not to mention very protective of their people. The idea of Montjuste-Surcleres resurfacing, linked with someone like Solace – as Lady Rennyn seemed she might be when we encountered her in Finton – well, they found it annoying, as I said. Like a sheep-thief relative showing up at a wedding.

"And then the Black Night, where Sebastian throws himself in front of a clutch of Irisian and Lady Rennyn – if we had taken even a minute or two longer in killing the last of the Eferum-Get, she may have died. And she chose that, to not let an Azrenel loose even at the cost of her life, because it was a worse thing than the Black Queen. The Kellian stopped finding their link to her a negative thing after that, and are almost possessive where she's concerned. While they very much want to know just what it is she's keeping back, they trust her overall goals."

"Even without knowing what they are."

"It's more the means which are in question. We are certain she truly intends to stop Solace."

"You could just ask."

"You think we haven't, directly and indirectly? The problem is the way she's been raised. All this was meant to be a secret, she was supposed to avoid us even knowing she existed. Not sensible, of course, but nothing we do seems to convince her that we can protect her adequately. She won't even discuss how to deal with the final incursion, which is in the Fens, until she's done the next partial attunement in the Hall of Summoning. We're almost certain she intends to cut loose from us after the Fens incursion, and make her own way to the Hall of Summoning. Frustrating, as you can imagine."

"Why does this attunement have to happen at all? Can't you just attack the Black Queen when she shows up in the Hall of Summoning, and kill her?"

"If only. She'll be shielded, and had at least a rudimentary command of Force magic. With her strength she'd swat us like bugs before we scratched her defences. With the kind of power she'll have at her disposal, even destroying the entire Hall before her arrival wouldn't cause her much bother. Not that we aren't going to prepare for a direct battle, should we fail to stop the Summoning, but–"

"What do the rest of the Sentene think of Rennyn?"

"Oh, we're all too busy lusting after her magical knowledge to have any opinion. Meniar made a good point the other day, though."

"What?"

"That the Council debates had some basis. That if Tiandel hadn't abdicated, Rennyn Montjuste-Surclere would be Tyrland's Queen." Lieutenant Danress looked at the darkening sky. "Shall we head back?"

Shrugging, Kendall followed the Sentene mage up the hill, her calves aching by the time they reached the inn, glad when Lieutenant Danress left her to make her own way upstairs. Rennyn's door was closed. Kendall frowned at it and tapped – too lightly to wake a sleeper – and bit her lip when the handle turned and opened.

The room was full of floating things. Rennyn lay in the bed, arms folded over the coverlet, and the Black Queen's focus sitting in her lap. Everything that wasn't nailed down was swooping around the ceiling, but it all settled back as Kendall came in.

"What's that in aid of?"

The woman reached out and picked her own focus off the coverlet, slipping it back over her head. "You never really stop with Thought magic exercises. Just like people who swing swords about, practice is important."

Kendall looked at her steadily. "Keeps you occupied, too. Like giving people lectures on magic."

This only prompted a faint, wry smile. "You wanted something?"

"My Gran used to tell me that the ends don't justify the means. What's the difference between you and the Black Queen if you're both willing to kill people to get your way?"

"Probably none, to any people I happen to kill," Rennyn said. She didn't seem surprised by the question, or particularly upset. "If there's any difference, it's that I'll feel bad about it after, and from what I've read of Solace's journals, I'm not certain she would."

"*Is* that a difference?"

"Well, I tell myself that it is. Are you trying to argue me out of continuing, Kendall?"

"N-no."

"Do you really think I'm as bad as Solace?"

"...no."

"Then why are you so upset?"

"She didn't start out bad, did she? The Black Queen?"

Rennyn's eyes widened, then she sat up, revealing a plain-cut linen nightdress. "Come here."

"Why?"

"Because."

Infuriating as ever, but Kendall didn't quite like to just walk out, so she moved slowly forward. And got hugged for her pains, a soft, quick squeeze. The Black Queen's focus swung against the back of her legs, cold and heavy.

"You surprise me again, Kendall," Rennyn said, letting go. "I will do my best not to become the thing I am fighting. You have my word on it."

Scarlet-faced, Kendall backed away. "Ask permission first," she said. "If you're going to change other people's lives. At least give them the choice."

This Rennyn didn't answer, only sat looking at her, so Kendall left, just managing not to slam the door behind her. A faint stir at the end of the landing showed her Captain Faille on guard, looking particularly ominous and not best impressed with her. Kendall escaped into the next room, where Sukata was pretending to be asleep already.

Queen of Tyrland all right, taking people over, acting like they were her business. Making decisions about other people's lives. A scary woman.

She'd smelled like vanilla.

TWENTY

Lecey Forest gave Rennyn a great deal of pleasure. It was very different from the forests of the north, which were grand and pine-scented and overwhelming. Lecey was full of smaller trees, none of which Rennyn had the knowledge to identify. Primarily twisty, black-barked ones, their canopies low overhead and the foliage dense. On a less well-favoured day it would probably be damp and gloomy, for there was moss and lichen decorating the undersides of all the branches, but the skies had been fortunately clear since they'd left Sark, and so the forest was a dapple-green playground for butterflies and sunbeams.

There were no convenient coach-roads running past the incursion point, but Rennyn had enjoyed being on horseback for an unhurried journey along trails winding between bushes and trees. There were plenty of berry brambles, too, offering a juicy selection of sweet and tart, and only a few scratches. Every so often the trees eased back, and they blinked at dazzling-bright clearings spattered with flowers.

The Sentene vanguard had widened and established camp in one of these, with fewer tents than usual and no provision for the handful of horses, which were taken back out again by the Ferumguard, since there was little room for them in the single circle of protection established. The trunks of freshly-felled trees had been pulled about a big central cooking area, and while they settled into camp one of the Ferumguard filled two frying pans with sausages, mushrooms and bacon, then broke eggs into the mix so they cooked together into savoury disks.

"Will you be able to locate the incursion today?" Captain Illuma asked, as Rennyn worked her way through lunch.

"Tomorrow morning at the earliest," Rennyn said, in a way glad to postpone the task another day. "Though I might take some readings later, to see what kind of reaction is detectable this far out."

After lunch, she checked how Kendall and Sukata were going with their exercises, and was surprised to see how far Sukata had progressed. Not that she could move something, but that she'd managed to rein in her own strength, and was nudging a small leaf about with a semblance of choosing the direction.

"The leaf's a good idea," she said, approvingly. "Less chance of embedding it in someone."

Torn between trying to escape for a private walk and feeling unusually settled, Rennyn watched the pair self-consciously struggling with the task, thinking over Kendall's accusation of the previous day. The offence not just of killing people, but of making decisions without their permission. Did all that come out of some past choice made on the girl's behalf, or just the sheer mule-stubbornness of her personality?

She heard Captain Faille take a step behind her, but didn't look back. She'd grown so used to his presence she'd started to notice his absences instead, and that made her hate the idea of Kellian bodyguards more than ever. Had it been inevitable that she end up surrounded by them, using them as Solace had? She was sure that Faille, like Kendall, would bitterly resent decisions made on his behalf. She wished that didn't matter to her.

Thinking about the man, Rennyn nearly jumped out of her skin when he reached down and touched one sun-tipped finger to the thick bracelet around her right wrist, pushing it further along her arm. He straightened as she looked up at him.

"Meniar," he said, "Find some way to shield Lady Montjuste-Surclere's wrists."

Lieutenant Meniar, who had been pretending to review his slates while he day-dreamed, gave them both a startled glance, then came across to study what Faille's sharp eyes had caught. Resigned, Rennyn removed the bracelet, cradling the focus carefully in her lap, and allowed Meniar to inspect the circle of bruises and rubbed skin. He shook his head, then fetched salve and bandages.

"How heavy is that thing? To you, I mean?" he asked.

Rennyn picked it up doubtfully, controlling the faint, ever-present wobble which was its reaction to the Grand Summoning. "About four pounds?"

"Is it necessary to wear it all the time? Is that part of the attunement?"

"It's to stop me dropping it," Rennyn replied, and placed the focus carefully on the ground. As soon as she let go it sank several inches, and then the earth around it trembled, compressing out in a series of rings which came perilously close to undermining the fire-pit. "You can imagine what would happen if it fell off my lap while I was in the coach," Rennyn added, as the entire camp stopped to stare.

Tenbury, one of the younger Hand mages, recovered more quickly than the rest and crossed to the depression, gauging it with probing fingers. "It mimics the distortion?" he said, more to himself than Rennyn, then looked sharply at her, adding: "You will allow us to divine this effect?"

His tone was more demand than request, but Rennyn shrugged, not inclined to spoil her day arguing. She didn't like Tenbury, who never succeeded in hiding his resentment when she refused to share information, but she knew there was little he'd be able to do with the focus.

She watched their initial attempts to pick it up while Meniar salved her wrist and cast an encouragement to healing. "The bracelet doesn't leave room for a great deal of padding," he said, winding on a thin layer of bandage. "Can you at least alternate hands?"

"Yes – the other's just more awkward, especially if I'm writing. I only really need to carry it when we're travelling. Or on marshy ground. Or in wooden buildings. It grows heavier with each expansion of the main distortion, but I doubt it will become impossible to cart about. That would defeat the purpose."

As soon as both her wrists were neatly protected with soft bandage, Rennyn changed her shoes and went for a walk, since the area in front of her tent was now crowded with excited mages. There were plenty of criss-crossing animal trails through the undergrowth, and she followed them at random. Berries, flowers, sun-spotted clearings, the occasional bird or small animal which would leap away. Guards. It was certainly the most well-protected bit of forest in all Tyrland.

She walked until the sun started slanting, stopping by a small stream, perhaps the same one which ran by the camp, though she had taken enough turns to have no idea where the camp was. There was a rock there which made a nice seat, and she studied the mix of sun and shadow on the water, then looked at Faille, who was as dappled as the forest. He moved near-silently, but she'd known he followed.

"The question of whether my distant uncle is loyal to Solace is giving me a lot of trouble," she said.

Shifting position from voiceless guard to consultative strategist without blinking an eye, Faille said: "The difficulty lies in the Azrenel."

Like Seb, he was quick to see critical points. "Hate us or not, sane or not, for Solace to loose an Azrenel is outside all expectations. Even if she *were* intent on destroying Tyrland instead of ruling it, to not do so personally is out of character. It was only through a fortunate set of circumstances that we were able to stop it so quickly. I just can't see her enjoying a return to an empty kingdom."

"It may be the bargain she has made."

That was true. Being trapped within the cycle of the Grand Summoning could have brought her to total desperation. "Again out of character," Rennyn said slowly.

"Three choices. Queen Solace allowed it. Prince Helecho arranged it outside her knowledge. Or the Azrenel was an opportunist, following the activity of the lesser Eferum-Get."

Prince Helecho. The title distracted, raising so many issues, but Rennyn put it from her thoughts. "The organisation of the incursions falls under the same question: with or without her knowledge?"

"If Prince Helecho is disloyal, there must be some bar which prevents him from simply attacking Queen Solace. Else, we would not be facing this."

"Tiandel did give her a lesson in trust. Helecho may be operating under a deep-set injunction, the kind of thing where he would have to at least obey the letter of her commands, if not the intent."

"Much as you answer questions."

She looked over at him, but matters were coming too close to the end for her to smile at the comment. "True enough."

"Is it so difficult to trust us?"

Faille's voice was even thinner than usual, and she met something exposed in his gaze. She should have known not to start a conversation, and realised she'd been drawn to do so precisely because she did trust him. Not just to keep the conversation to himself, but to understand the problem and help her see it more clearly. To support her.

"This isn't about trust," she said, not able to hold sunlit eyes. Not when the explanation she dreaded was only a few days away, and would change everything. Not when she was discovering that it would cost her to hurt him.

Then, because there didn't seem to be anything else to say, she started back to the camp, letting Solace's focus lead her. He followed silently in her wake, voiceless guard once again. Tool in the service of a Montjuste-Surclere.

CR&O

"And what is that one? To the right of the arrow?"

"Fel's Veil. Down below it is Rothyria the Wolf."

"A wolf? How?"

"Eh, just the head, I guess. Kind of squashed. The ears are pricked up and pointing east, see."

Kendall was introducing Sukata to the stars. City-raised, the Kellian girl had spent too much time in stone buildings, and not enough looking up. Besides, with almost everyone off standing around some random patch of forest waiting for Rennyn and any other monsters to come out of the Hells, there wasn't a whole heap to do.

"Are you certain you're not inventing these?" Sukata asked for the third time.

"Look them up in that library when we get back."

"I will do that."

Kellian humour, Kendall decided. It was growing easier to work out Sukata. Not chatty, but a lot like Nina Lippon, who was the quiet, smart one of the Lippon brood. She wasn't shy, she wasn't particularly stuck-up, but she liked to listen more than talk. The thing was *all* the Kellian were like that. Maybe talking hurt them: their voices all sounded damaged in some way, thin and weak. Captain Faille had said the first Kellian hadn't been able to speak at all.

"Do you see the wolf's nose?"

"Possibly."

"Look the way it's pointing and there's a swirly clump. That's the Emperor's Clasp, the one the Emperor of Kole lost when he was trying to walk across whatever that sea is called."

"The Sanase. The Sea of Tears. It is...it is a lake, not a sea, but a large lake. The legend says the water is sweet. Have you heard the story behind that?"

Kendall didn't answer right away, because Sukata had stopped looking at the sky, had turned her head and gone extra still. Then the Kellian girl reached out and gripped Kendall's arm urgently, so Kendall managed to say: "Don't think so."

"Alar Anase, the founder of Kole, was a wandering mage. This was after the days of the Elder Mages, when the kingdoms were fractured and Eferum-Get had begun to walk the world. She was exploring north, following the rivers and trying to penetrate the deeps of the Forest of Semarrak, but was caught in a storm-flood. She managed to make it to land, but was in a very bad state, and collapsed on the stony shore."

While she spoke, Sukata had produced the long knife she kept strapped to one of her legs and was slowly shifting, moving by inches to a better position in which to spring up. All the while Kendall strained to discover what it was she was reacting to. They weren't alone in the camp, and Sukata was staring toward the tents around the central fire, where a few of the Ferumguard were working on dinner preparations.

"When Anase woke, she was in a palace," Sukata continued, rising to one knee. "Sumptuous in every aspect, the walls shimmering with colour. Servants of glass dressed her in robes of gold and conducted her to the palace's lord, who was so brilliant she could barely look upon him, and yet his eyes were dark with grief. Anase was not a reverent woman, and she–"

Sukata moved. Moved like a Kellian, the first time Kendall had seen her do so. In star and firelight Kendall couldn't even track her until she stopped, and when she stopped she had clapped one of the big cooking pots over something on the ground.

"What are–?" began one of the extremely startled Ferumguard, and broke off just as quickly as a sound like tortured metal erupted from the pot. Whatever was underneath was bouncing frantically about, wailing in ear-splitting tones. Then, just as abruptly, it fell silent.

"Is it a Night Roamer?" Kendall asked, as three more Ferumguard and a Sentene pair came hurrying up, weapons at ready. "But–" They were in a circle. Night Roamers couldn't cross circles and surely someone would have noticed if a breach had opened in the middle of camp.

"Sukata, move away," said the Kellian half of the Sentene pair, taking the girl's place in holding the pot firm.

The woman's mage partner was Captain Medan, the huge man who had stayed with them inside Rennyn's shield when the crab-thing was attacking. He unfolded his slate and said as he began writing: "What did you see?"

"Felt," Sukata replied, replacing her knife in its sheathe. "Worked magic. I noticed the signature of a casting – in Lady Rennyn's tent."

Captain Medan grimaced. "Time to do a little housecleaning, then."

Kendall thought it very good timing that Rennyn Claire returned to camp just as Captain Medan was holding up a flimsy little silk undershirt left on her bedroll. Her brows rose very high indeed, then she said: "I don't think it will fit you, Captain."

"Not my colour, anyway," Captain Medan replied, unembarrassed. As Captain Illuma followed Rennyn into the camp he nodded at the cook-pot, which was now in a circle of its own, with a rock sitting on top. "Drogan's just headed out with a message about our visitor – must have missed you. A 'chanted animal. Sukata caught it coming out of your tent, Lady Rennyn, and while I can't feel anything that's about to explode, I'm certain there's something off."

"What kind of enchanted animal?" Rennyn asked, with a flicker of interest. She took a step toward the centre of the camp, but Captain Illuma stopped her.

"To walk into a trap now would lose the advantage gained in discovering it."

For a moment Kendall thought Rennyn would object, but then she let herself be escorted to the far side of the camp, where she sat with her chin on her knees watching as her tent was dissected.

She'd been in a weird mood since dinner yesterday. Riding through the forest she'd seemed quite happy, going on about the use of symbols in Sigillic magic while eating every berry that came into her reach. But she'd come back from a walk yesterday totally withdrawn and gone straight to bed and then straight to the Hells the next morning, without saying more than two sentences the whole time. Now, while the Sentene pulled all her stuff out of the tent, she just sat and did nothing.

Kendall took her over a plate of pan bread, greasy with cheese. "You don't seem too worried."

"They're professionals." Rennyn took the plate, but put it down by her feet.

"I guess there wasn't any great horde of Night Roamers at the breach?"

"A lone and very surprised Stalker."

"All this fuss and preparation–"

"I'm sure it amuses my Wicked Uncle no end." Rennyn lifted her head at that, and gazed out into the dark forest. Searching.

"You think he's out there?" Kendall asked, realising just why half the Sentene had left the camp again.

"Not at this moment."

"Eat your dinner."

That won a brief glance, but no other response. Kendall squinched her eyes in frustration, and was annoyed at herself for caring. If Rennyn didn't want to eat, let her starve. If she had circles under her eyes once again, then – but with a half-dozen Sentene playing with her tent, probably she had no choice about staying awake. Sukata brought two more plates and they ate their own meals and watched their teacher brood.

Finally Captain Illuma and Captain Medan came over and displayed a half-grown and very skinny grey cat, supposedly disenchanted, and a small lump of damp brown fur, apparently far from it.

"Underneath one corner of the bedroll," Captain Medan said. "The power signature isn't large, but it's a very elegant piece of casting."

It looked like a half-eaten mouse to Kendall. She knew by now that a 'signature' was the detectable trace of magic from a spell or enchantment, and was disappointed to not feel anything at all from the lump. She was still too weak a mage.

Rennyn, on the other hand, tilted her head to one side, narrowed her eyes, then said: "Some kind of message?"

"We believe that it would cause a sleeper to dream along a set pattern," Captain Illuma said.

"Ah. Tailor-made nightmares."

"Or possibly an attempt to influence your waking behaviour. Magister Eldian will continue to attempt to divine its exact content."

"What are you going to do with the cat?"

Captain Medan hoisted the scrawny grey animal doubtfully. "Give it dinner?"

That brought the hint of a smile to Rennyn's lips, but it was the last real response Kendall saw out of her that night. It was like she'd decided she didn't want to be with them any more, was moving away from them even while she sat among them. Like she was already gone.

TWENTY-ONE

S eb."

"Ren!" Her brother turned from his desk, then checked and frowned at her. "When did you last sleep?"

Rennyn sat on the bed, dropping her bag to the floor and unclasping Solace's focus from her wrist. "I swear, everyone treats me like I'm three years old. You probably sleep less than I do."

"But I'm only casting small magics." He didn't press the objection, and certainly knew her well enough to know that the things most likely to keep her from sleep weren't avoidable. Glancing past her at the door, at the signal she was giving by leaving it open, he changed the subject. "Why did you take Kendall and Sukata with you?"

"Mainly to distract myself. Though I was curious about the potential you saw in Kendall."

"I was right, wasn't I?"

"She'd make quite a mage if she was interested. She'll probably still become competent enough. Sukata–" She paused, then continued carefully: "Sukata might turn into something special. She has a passion for it." Rennyn put Solace's focus on the floor, as far from furniture as she could manage, and felt the faintest tremble as it failed to break through stone. She walked around the room, checking the tight lines of sigils which ran along the walls and above the door. "The wards are good. How's the research going?"

Shrugging, he indicated more than a dozen books lined along the shelf above the desk. "There's still a couple of background things I want to mark, but I've found something similar enough for you to work with. Are you – are we going ahead?"

"I'll mark out the room today, put up divinations. I'll rest before activating tomorrow."

"Here?"

"For a while, perhaps. Do you want to come set up some divinations for me?"

Seb nodded briskly and fidgeted with his cuff, where a pin was threaded, a match for the one which she regularly wore. They exchanged glances, then both looked at the door. This was a conversation they'd rehearsed in part long ago, and she wondered if it sounded as artificial as it felt. Giving it up, they went out into the main hall of the Sentene barracks, where Captain Illuma was waiting, talking to a handful of the mages under her command. Since her walk in the forest, Faille had not assigned himself to play bodyguard, keeping busy with other duties. Rennyn was pretending she was glad of that.

"Will you permit observers, my Lady?" Captain Illuma asked.

Rennyn nodded, unsurprised. "You might find the construction of a few of the divinations interesting."

"To look into the Eferum from this world," said Captain Medan. "You have us all quite excited."

"Hardly interesting visually. But I'm hoping to take a few useful readings."

The Hall of Summoning was a square, grandly columned room in the Old Palace, very large. Guards had been set on it weeks ago, posted outside both ornate doors in anticipation of waves of Eferum-Get, though they'd only had curious courtiers to deal with.

Rennyn had deliberately stayed away from the room until now, and was surprised by it. The vaulted ceiling was a glorious, graceful meld of curves, and the tall windows of smoky glass kept it glowing with soft light without being open to outside eyes. A beautiful and calming place, unexpectedly soothing.

It was also very bare. Nothing but walls, columns, ceiling and the empty expanse of floor. Milky-white stone with a dark square between the columns: a dusky marble version of a slate, waiting to be covered with sigils. She gazed at the large central expanse, trying to estimate how much of it might be filled by a focus created by the Grand Summoning.

"This attunement stage is simply a further progression of what I did at Surclere," Rennyn explained, carefully creating the circle of sigils where she would tomorrow place the focus. "It's primarily related to the container rather than the focus itself."

"Why is this vessel necessary at all?" asked a sunburned woman she'd not spoken to before. There was a fading scrape on one side of the woman's face: remnant of battle or perhaps the explosion of Darasum House.

"Physically handling the younger focuses, or even having them bound in wire as a pendant, would interfere with the attunement. The vessel attempts to simulate the Eferum, to prepare for the final alignment between the old and the new." She glanced at the reflection of filtered sunlight on the floor. "We'll write out all the divinations before we power them, since they won't take kindly to people walking among them once they're activated."

"She is right before us." Lieutenant Danress had come in late, freckled face solemn. "On the far side of the veil, but right before us."

Not particularly wanting to think about such things, Rennyn pushed on. Working with Seb, she prepared a series of divinations, answering the occasional question about the Sigillic construction, but for the most part ignoring her audience. Not completely, for she knew very well that Captain Illuma's attention was on her, not on the interesting magic she was preparing.

Rennyn was painfully aware of the damage she had wrought by allowing her guard to drop with the Kellian. After her behaviour the last few days, there would be none among them unaware that she was dreading tomorrow. And they were puzzled and concerned and worried *for* her. She mattered to them. She'd tried to convince herself that they were simply being superlative bodyguards, but that day in the forest she'd looked into Faille's eyes and seen that he hated that she wouldn't trust him. Tomorrow would always have been bad, but–

How would she deal with their reaction? She should have kept her distance, alienated them from the start as she'd initially thought to do. But it had proven too difficult to offer them the cold discourtesies served to them by an ungrateful kingdom. Now their instinct toward her was strongly protective, and they would feel so betrayed.

Walking about in an oppressive cloud of misery had been distracting everyone around her, and she suppressed it as best she could, allowing herself to be drawn into the complexities of setting the divinations, patiently explaining how each operated as she activated them. Concentrating on work was better than thinking about tomorrow. Seb was useful, preening a little as the Sentene mages realised they'd underestimated his knowledge, and handily distracting them often enough that she was sure none could have noticed when she pricked her finger and pressed a tiny droplet of blood on one corner of the black marble. She and Seb would be coming back here tonight, and that would be the beginning of the end.

CR&SO

Kendall didn't think much of being returned to the Arkathan to sit doing nothing, so just after lunch the next day she used a half-forgotten promise of a book as an excuse to go see Sebastian. The Sentene barracks were a lot busier than usual, with everyone gathering for a big meeting later that afternoon, and Kendall bet Sebastian Claire would know just what was going to be said. The challenge would be convincing him to tell her.

After settling her approach while she was escorted to Sebastian's room, Kendall was thrown off stride when Rennyn, not her brother, answered the knock at the door. Sebastian was noticeably absent.

"Uh, my Lady?" asked the Ferumguard escort, a stocky, fair man. "Your brother is–?"

"Gone," Rennyn answered, shortly. "He's out of this now."

"Gone–?" the man repeated, then took a look at Rennyn's flat, black gaze, saluted confusedly and departed to tell those in charge.

Kendall, not so easily cowed, asked: "Gone where?"

Between yesterday and today Rennyn Claire had found enough sleep to ease the haggard lines which had marked her face. Her eyes were focused and determined, but lacking any warmth. "Did you want something?"

"To go to the meeting," Kendall said, worried to the point of being truthful. "I want to know what it is you're going to tell them." And she wanted to know what in the Hells had happened to Sebastian Claire that his sister looked so empty. For a moment all those suspicions of ambition and plot resurfaced, but this only prompted Rennyn's expression to lighten marginally.

"You need to learn to hide your thoughts, Kendall. No, I haven't done away with my brother. Of everything I do, keeping him alive is the most important to me. As for this meeting, it's not exactly–" She paused. "Go get Sukata. You can both watch the attunement, and if you should follow me back to the meeting, I doubt there'll be objections."

Not entirely happy to be given what she asked for, Kendall went and found Sukata, diligently studying in their dormitory.

"So why would Rennyn particularly want you to be at this meeting today?"

"Lady Rennyn has asked for me?"

"I don't think she means to be nice," Kendall said, disliking the way Sukata sat up straighter, eyes widening with pleasure. As they started back to the Sentene barracks, she grit her teeth and asked: "What do you think she's going to tell everyone?"

"Nothing we will like." Sukata's grey eyes were steady. "Mother has been studying the accounts of the Grand Summoning, attempting to discover further details of Prince Tiandel's actions. Lady Rennyn has so steadfastly refused to discuss the final attunement that our best guess is that it involves Blood magic."

"Blood magic? That means killing people, doesn't it?"

"Despite her attempts to disguise it, we've seen how strongly Lady Rennyn reacts whenever certain matters are discussed. The topic of sacrifice is particularly upsetting to her."

"You seriously think she's going to ask people to let her kill them?"

"It would explain a great deal. But it is a guess, no more."

Kendall stared at the girl, who was walking with an almost eager, very upright step. "You'd volunteer. Wouldn't you?"

"Yes." Sukata was serenely certain. "Now, will you tell me something?"

"What?"

"Why is it so important to you to not admire Lady Rennyn?"

Kendall felt her face go hot. "Because she lies. And she decides things for people without asking first."

"Those are details."

"They're damn important ones."

Sukata gave Kendall a pensive glance, but didn't comment. They found Rennyn still in Sebastian's room, standing at the window, but she just nodded and led them to the main hall of the barracks where Lady Weston was waiting with her Senior Captains and a small selection of Hand Magisters.

"You have sent your brother away, Lady Montjuste-Surclere?" Lady Weston asked.

"We're moving into the most dangerous period," Rennyn said, even curter than before. "Shall we go?"

They went. Everyone including Lady Weston had learned that there was no point arguing with Rennyn when she went all brief and crisp. Exit Sebastian Claire, without so much as saying goodbye.

Grumpily, Kendall focused on her first excursion into the palace proper. She made herself enjoy it. Massive halls, tapestries, fancy pictures, golden candlesticks and mage glows fitted everywhere. It was worth looking at. Just as good were the goggling courtiers, who would stop and stare quite openly. Rennyn was worth watching, too; the many times great-granddaughter of the Black Queen, sweeping through the Halls as if they were deserted. Everything she did said hard and clear: "I want to get this over with."

They went to a chilly pale room with a black square in the centre, covered in glowing sigils. Rennyn removed the active spells one-by-one, politely informing the Grand Magister of the result of each divination, but going on to the next before anyone could try and discuss them with her. Kendall had no particular interest in a bunch of numbers representing the strength and speed of the storm raging in the Hells. The way Rennyn avoided looking at anyone except the Grand Magister was much more fascinating.

Was she really going to ask them to let her kill some of them? Would anyone actually volunteer? What if she needed to kill dozens of people? How many before it became too many? How many to make Rennyn as big a monster as the Black Queen?

With a glance Rennyn cleaned all trace of the divinations from the floor, leaving only the big central circle of chalk figures. Into this she carefully lowered the Black Queen's focus. Nothing spectacular happened. Rennyn made the sigils glow, but the focus just sat there. Getting closer Kendall could see that it had filled with a murky blackness, though the focus was still visible, shining like a star in the night sky.

"This simulates the Eferum?" Lady Weston asked.

"As much as anything can." Rennyn picked the globe up. "The next time I take it into the Eferum, the link will complete as the compression of the greater focus begins. That's what we need to talk about now."

"Ah." The Grand Magister looked relieved, as if she'd been biting back demands for answers all day. "An explanation past due, I think. Shall we return to the Houses?"

As Rennyn had predicted, no-one objected when Sukata and Kendall followed them back to the Sentene barracks. The main hall of the barracks stretched about a third of the length of the building, and rose two levels to a dim ceiling. It was overlooked by walkways circling the next level up, and had a single long table down the centre with plenty of space on either side. This was filled with a sea of black uniforms, made brilliant by the Montjuste phoenix, and sprinkled with senior representatives of the Hand and the Ferumguard as well. Tyrland's defenders.

While Rennyn sat at the end of the table, Kendall tucked herself and Sukata away in the near corner. They were close to where Sebastian's room sat empty, and had a good view of the audience, but could only see Rennyn in profile. She was turning the Black Queen's focus slowly in her hands, examining it.

"This thing has a range," she said, before everyone had quite settled in. The words brought an instant hush, and every eye in the room focused on the dark-haired woman. "When my family were using it to push her back at the beginning of the Summoning the range was small, because none of the power of the full Grand

Summoning was behind it. When this is complete, it will reach beyond the kingdom, the continent."

She looked up, her expression more resigned than anything else. "That range is a very important thing. Because sixty years ago was the first time a Kellian was within reach."

Kendall felt Sukata flinch. Whatever they'd been expecting her to say, the Kellian hadn't anticipated an accusation.

"While Solace is in the Eferum, her link to the Kellian is severed," Rennyn went on, her voice pitched a little louder so she could be heard over the ripple of disbelief running through the room. "But for the final day before she returns, the attunement will be complete, and will act like a door between worlds. Solace will be able to project her will into this world. As my family believe she did sixty years ago, when my great-grandfather was murdered."

The human Senior Captain, Lamprey, was first to manage to speak, his hand on the arm of a Kellian woman as if to hold back her anger instead of his own. "You – you are suggesting that one of the Kellian killed him?"

"Solace killed him. But, yes, I am saying that the weapon she used was a Kellian." The words were flat, precise. Rennyn hadn't wanted to tell them this, but she was quite certain of what she was saying.

Noise rippled through the room again, but Sukata's mother quelled it with a brief gesture. "We are not the original Ten, Lady Rennyn," she said, very carefully. "We have more human than golem ancestry, and are by no means lacking in will. Why would your family believe that Queen Solace is able to control us?"

Rennyn had been staring across the room – to the place Captain Faille was standing – but she turned her head at this, then said: "Kneel."

Captain Illuma knelt. Without hesitation. Lively astonishment crossed her face – the most human expression Kendall had ever seen on a Kellian – then she stood up again, every inch of her radiating shock.

"The Kellian were made to be inherited," Rennyn Claire said, as the entire room took a single, outraged breath. "Though Solace's control over you will be considerably more profound than mine."

Kendall reached out blindly to take Sukata's hand, and had it immediately crushed. The Kellian girl's face was frozen with horror, staring at Rennyn as if she were a nightmare made flesh. Which, to the Kellian, she must be.

"And you've waited till *now* to tell us this?" asked – shouted – Captain Lamprey.

"You would have preferred this was known earlier?"

"Of course!"

"Wait." Lady Weston, pale but unwavering, moved to the forefront. "See the consequences, Elias."

"The *consequences?*!" Captain Lamprey's dark skin had gone a purple shade, but he stopped shouting and swallowed harshly as the Kellian woman he was with took one of his hands between both of hers.

"Debates in Council," she said, gazing steadily at Lady Weston and not anywhere near Rennyn. The Kellian had all turned their faces from her. As if it hurt to keep looking.

"The question of exile or imprisonment," the woman continued. "Imprisonment. The question of execution, for safety's sake. It is exactly what we will face now, but with so little time left it does not have the chance to reach the same fever-pitch it would have after a full month. And it means we were there at Darasum House."

This calm recitation of exactly why it mightn't have been a good thing to know earlier did a small amount to ease the anger in the room. But even the Kellian woman who had spoken so reasonably could do no more than glance at Rennyn before her eyes flinched away. Sukata was shaking.

"I am presuming that if there is a way to prevent this you will inform us," Lady Weston said, turning to Rennyn.

"There is none." Rennyn's face was impassive. "The Kellian are a spell construct. Symbolic magic, which has not altered in form for all that it is perpetuating itself in a rather unique way. To be Kellian is to be–" She paused. "To be at the command of the Montjuste-Surcleres. You cannot be one without the other."

She stood, and lifted the focus in both hands. "When this is complete, the range will be far beyond the distance you could have travelled in a month. I cannot be entirely certain what will happen when Solace's will replaces your own. The original Kellian were extensions of Solace. She could see through their eyes, experience everything they experienced. I don't know if she will be able to access your memories. But I cannot work with you any longer."

She turned away, pausing only when Lady Weston caught her elbow long enough to murmur something in her ear. With a nod she moved on, back toward Sebastian's room, walking past Kendall and Sukata as if they weren't there, but close enough for Kendall to see that she was white to the lips.

Sukata's grip tightened on Kendall's hand, so hard now it felt like the bones were grinding together, but she noticed Kendall flinch and released her.

"Let's go somewhere else," Kendall said, and Sukata immediately turned and fled through the nearest door, leading Kendall out into the passage and then up a stairwell to the second floor. They paused to look down into the hall, where the Sentene had started to slowly move, like people who had fallen hard and weren't quite sure what was broken, then Sukata headed through a door into a bright living room with two other doors: a Senior Captain's quarters. The windows up here were bigger than the lower level, and there was a huge vase of daisies on the dining table. The faint trace of sigils chalked on the floor marked the space as belonging to a mage.

Sukata opened one of the doors, and led the way into a bedroom decorated with draperies of white linen, with a big painting of a very blue lake on one wall. It was sunny, neat and totally Sukata's, a place which was really hers, which said 'Sukata' everywhere you looked. At any other time Kendall would have had to be jealous.

"She changed what she was going to say," Sukata said, as she stopped in the dead centre of the room, rigidly upright. "To be Kellian is to *belong* to the Montjuste-Surcleres. We're property. She *inherited* us."

The thin voice cracked on the final two words. Kendall grimaced, searching for anything useful to say. How do you comfort someone when the thing they faced was something you found completely horrible?

"The Queen gives you orders too. And if you don't do them you could end up in prison, or executed."

"Then we at least have the choice of imprisonment, of execution. That – that was no choice at all."

"I don't think she's very likely to want to give you any orders," Kendall tried, tentatively.

"She made my mother *kneel*, Kendall!"

"What would you rather she had told her to do?" Kendall asked practically. "Given that she was trying to warn you that you've got a bigger problem than her out there."

Sukata was too fair to deny the point, but only succeeded in replacing angry horror with gloom. "Permanent slavery. We thought ourselves so...above, but we will never be anything but tools."

"What if they all die? All the Montjuste-Surcleres. Would you be tools still?" When Sukata just turned restively, Kendall added: "Do you think that's why she sent her brother away?"

The purely offended look she had in response was answer enough.

"I'd hate it," Kendall said bluntly. "Hate it, hate it, hate it to death. I'd want to kill her. I can't stand it when anyone tries to do what they think is for my good, instead of letting me do for myself." She paused, searching for inspiration. "You saw that Captain Medan brought that cat back with him, did you? Made a pet of it, and it likes him enough to have not run off on the trip. Is it a tool? This compulsion it was under was the same thing, wasn't it? Yours is just permanently there, waiting for an order. Could you cast one of those? Could your mother?"

"We would not," Sukata said firmly.

"Lady Weston put something like that on Rennyn when she first met her. Something to force her to tell the truth. She got really annoyed. The thing is – any mage who's good enough can make anyone else into a tool. There's laws about it and all, isn't there? About whether you're responsible for things you do under magical influence. You're stuck under a permanent one, which is really awful, but I don't see how it makes you not people, any more than the cat isn't still a cat."

Sukata felt as dangerous as she had outside Falk, like she could tear someone's arm off, but then her shoulders slumped, and she sighed softly. "I suppose we are both. Property. People. Thank you, Kendall. I don't think I can feel any better about this, but I won't let it destroy me."

"No bones broken." Kendall shook her head. "Will you be all right here? I need to go do something."

"What?"

"Get her some dinner. Best I can make out, she hasn't eaten since yesterday."

Sukata went still, then she lifted her chin. "I'll come with you."

"Sure?"

"Very."

TWENTY-TWO

A tap at the door set Rennyn to hastily wiping her face, and she looked back as it opened to reveal Kendall and Sukata carrying a plate, pitcher and glass. They didn't say anything, just put the meal on the desk and left, one with her chin set mule-stubborn and the other with eyes wide with dismay and determination.

Rennyn stared at the door as it closed, then managed a shaky smile. "You made some good friends, Seb."

The idea of eating repelled her, but she forced down a few bites, and drank half a glass of sweet barley water. It did help, but when she pushed herself to open the first of the books Seb had collected for her, the pages were a blur, meaningless.

She'd known this day was coming, had known she would take the brunt of it. When she'd found herself having to work closely with the Kellian earlier than planned, she'd tried to armour herself against them, to maintain a distance so it wouldn't hurt quite so much when they looked at her as they had today. And then refused to look at her.

She doubted they would try and kill her or Seb. They were a resilient and practical and very proud people, but not unjust. They would recover from the initial shock, and prepare themselves for the horror of Solace's control. Rennyn would do everything she could to ensure it wasn't permanent. Then – well, she was sure they would treat her with every courtesy, and try not to flinch too obviously whenever she spoke.

The best move would be to leave Tyrland afterwards. It made sense, was the kinder option for everyone involved. There was the property in Kole, and the holdings and investments there. Tyrland was her home, but it would not be comfortable staying to play nightmare of the Kellian.

She wished Faille had been closer, so she could have better seen his reaction. He had not spoken, had not turned away, had not moved at all. But she knew he would loathe the thought of being subject to the Montjuste-Surcleres. She kept hearing his voice, asking her about trust.

Even in their horror they had not withdrawn their trust – they believed she would stop Solace where they could not. And since she wouldn't be able to do that sitting around paralysed by things she couldn't change, Rennyn put aside the day's losses and moved on to future battles, focusing on reading through the marked places of the books. There was little time left, and she was increasingly worried about interference from her Wicked Uncle. Using creatures of this world as cat's-paws completely bypassed the strongest of their defences.

"My Lady."

Not quite able to suppress a start, Rennyn turned to discover Faille standing in the doorway. It was fortunate she hadn't eaten more, because her stomach turned to a knot at the sight of him: as correct as ever, but his eyes so dark.

"What has been decided?" she asked, managing to control the concern in her voice.

"The Council debates a call for execution. It will not stand, but it delays the announcement of the more likely decision."

"Imprisonment?" she guessed.

He nodded. "We are confined to barracks tonight, and likely the dungeons tomorrow. They will need to be reinforced."

Not strong enough to hold Kellian. Probably, they would have to chain them. All of them, even Sukata.

"I would like to test the limits of your control," he said.

Rennyn blinked. But he meant it, was waiting for her to give him an order, braced for the ordeal. He actually expected her to do it.

"There are no limits to my control," she said. "I'm not going to torture you to prove a thing I already know."

"Can you control our thoughts? Our feelings?" The vertical lines on either side of his mouth deepened, but then he said: "I wish to experience this so that I know its scope, so that my people can prepare for it. I do not doubt that it is as you describe."

"A fear faced?"

He nodded, the jerkiness of the motion betraying how true her words were. "It may not be as complete as Queen Solace's, but it will give me a basis for comparison."

"Sit down."

Such a commonplace phrase to produce such distress. His eyes did no more than widen as he moved to sit tidily on the bed, but the set of his shoulders after was that of a man who had taken a crippling blow.

"Stay there."

She turned back to her book because she was angry, and saw no reason to make him deal with that. After their walk in the forest she'd promised herself that she would never give Faille an order. Broken already.

It also seemed important to hide that she was glad. Grateful for forbearance. That he could set aside the mountainous bar she had revealed to come and speak with her without open revulsion, to deal with the issue rather than despise her for her inheritance. That he was even able to look at her.

And it was impossible, of course, to concentrate on anything with him sitting behind her being incredibly upset. She tidied the desk, allowing him a lengthy opportunity to take his basis for comparison, then turned and said, "Enough."

He half-rose, but sat back down again, eyes hooded. "I could as well be telling someone else's body to move."

"In a way, you are," she said, not avoiding harsh truths since he wanted to confront this. "As to controlling feelings: no. The spell isn't structured for it. The original Kellian were Solace's fingers. Literally. She used part of one of her fingers in the casting, as that was the symbolism she desired. Fingers do not have emotions: they are an extension of one's self. She wanted guards who would never betray her, no more than a hand would betray a wrist. Thoughts – that's more difficult to define, but though I expect I could cause you to behave as if the sky was green, I doubt I could make you believe it."

He took a long breath, weighing this. "How will Solace's control differ from yours?"

"I can give verbal commands which control your actions. Tiandel left extensive observations of his experiences with the original Ten – the only thing which allowed me to risk speaking to any of you at all, to know that only a direct, intentional order must be obeyed. Solace – Solace is a part of the spell which makes you Kellian which has been absent." She watched his long, dagger-tipped fingers curl in his lap. "When Solace left this world, the original Kellian had memories of what they had experienced, but little impulse to act. Your human ancestry isn't likely to make any great difference: your mind will probably not be destroyed, but at the very least she will suppress your will. You may be aware while this is happening, but your body will not be your own. I don't know how it will...damage you."

"We might become as the Ten once were?"

"Possibly. If she has control of you for an extended period of time. A kind of death."

"Preferable, I should think." He was recovering, the harshness fading from his face as he rapidly turned over options. "And there is no shield, no way to block her access to us?"

"Nothing viable. You can't even go into the Eferum, if that was feasible for sixty people, since she will exist in both worlds."

Faille went still, eyes narrowing. "Sarana has been in the Eferum."

"I know."

Another blow. He closed his eyes, but opened them again immediately, thinking it over. "Could Solace erase memory?"

"That I don't know. Perhaps. Or she could be under a command not to reveal her experience. I don't think it would be possible for Solace to have...withheld herself from Captain Illuma, or that Captain Illuma would have been unaware of her presence. It is possible that Solace was simply out of range – the physics of the Eferum are not something I can fully predict. In any case, I would already be dead if she'd been under orders to kill me."

Before he could respond there was a dull vibration and the bed shuddered. Faille stood up in a blur, but it wasn't an attack.

"The latest expansion," Rennyn said, slipping past him. The corner of the bed was caught in the field of effect from the focus she'd set near the far wall. Faille lifted it out with one hand, setting it at an angle, then stood looking down at the focus.

"Which of you can command us?" he asked, his voice very thin. She couldn't tell if he was keeping back anger or deepening dismay, only that he was very upset and very near.

"The current head of the family. Within this world." She wished she still owned the arrogance of her early teens, when she'd believed herself capable of anything, but the more she'd learned of magic, the more she understood what she could never do. "I'm sorry," she said, touching his shoulder. "I don't know any way to make this different. I would change it if I could."

"I know that," he said. Then he glanced down to where her hand remained resting against him.

Rennyn felt muscle tense, and her face grew hot as Faille gave her a very searching look. She was astonished at herself, but suddenly and fiercely determined to not step away or drop her gaze, though it was one of the most difficult things she'd ever done. It was the wrong time. He was so distressed, and she knew very well she could be totally misreading that small exchange in the wood, and this was something she should not do, but she just couldn't stand that she might never see him again. She felt like she'd staked herself out in the sun, and if his surprise turned to anger or disgust, a new-found part of her would shrivel completely. But the worst time was the only time, this moment between lies and the end.

Faille lifted one hand, catching strands of hair up until he curled his fingers around the nape of her neck, still searching her eyes for reaction. The flood of relief and uncertainty made her heart thump so painfully she thought for an instant she might faint, and she tightened her hand on the heavy cloth of his uniform, wondering what her face looked like and if it was possible for her heart to race so fast it stumbled.

Whatever her expression, he found his answer. And kissed her. Not tentatively. Not lightly. This was certainly the worst night of his life and his response was one of a man at an emotional extreme, faster and more violent than she could have anticipated.

As she caught her breath and tried to respond, his other hand swept down to the small of her back, pressing her against him, and then she was against the door, gasping as she was lifted up so she was closer to his height, bare skin tingling as her shirt came free. There was no space left between them.

She was fumbling distractedly at the heavy undercoat he wore when he finally broke free of her mouth, long enough to cast a dissatisfied glance at Seb's bed. Rejecting it, he picked her up. The door was a minor obstruction, then out into the hall, a right turn to the stair where she'd once seen him sitting, and up to the next level of the barracks. Another door, a dark room and then one made vivid by moonlight. Rennyn had no idea if anyone had seen them: he'd kissed her the entire way.

But he paused when they reached his bed, and set her carefully on her feet again. The window was wide and unshuttered and the high, full moon set him burning: eyes white disks, hair cold flame, fingers tipped with diamond. He was watching her face, and though it was nearly impossible for her to make out his expression, she thought he was stepping back from the urgency of his first response, giving her a chance to change her mind.

She was vaguely aware of fear. Partly of doing anything which would make him stop, of embarrassing herself. A little of a thing she'd never done. But most of all of hurting him more. She hadn't expected any of the Kellian to want anything to do with her, after she'd told them the truth. Faille, most of all, she'd expected to hate her. She'd been trying to come to terms with that ever since she'd realised that she'd started to more than trust him, and still could not quite believe that he had come to talk with her once he knew that the Kellian could not leave behind their origins. Reaching out had been an impulse, and perhaps she wouldn't have done it if she'd thought the implications through. This threw aside common caution, and in its way was the most selfish thing she'd ever done.

She brushed a finger along the vertical line to the right of his mouth, barely visible against opalescent flesh. She was close enough to feel the heat of him through her shirt, and the quiver which ran the length of his body when she touched him. She should never have come near him.

CRID

Rennyn lay watching Faille dress. The first time she'd seen him wearing anything other than a variation of his uniform, he was buttoning a charcoal grey shirt above loose leggings. Preparing himself for the dungeons. He looked thinner without the layers of uniform, ropey muscle stretched over a long frame, lean and spare.

She felt so greedy, and painfully protective. Possessive. Ironic given how very much she didn't want to consider herself anyone's owner, how much she objected to the idea of inheriting people. A different kind of possession, she supposed. They hadn't spoken at all, not since she'd touched him. She hadn't dared, didn't want to complicate the night with any possibility of commanding him, though she was sure more than a few would suggest or suspect exactly that. It had also seemed more natural, letting actions speak for them, pushing aside the shock of the day's revelations. He'd been so hungry for her, the totality of his response overwhelming.

He noticed she was awake and crossed to sit on the side of the bed. Rennyn looked up at him, wondering what she could possibly say, and in the pause he reached down and traced the tip of a lock of her hair coiling on the sheet. There was a black band about his wrist, and she recognised her hair ribbon, the ends neatly tucked under tightly wound loops. That made her want to cry, but she settled for gripping his hand, the calluses of a swordsman hard against her skin.

"I don't know your first name."

"Illidian."

She smiled at the absurdity of herself who had never asked, and he curled his fingers through hers, then bent and kissed her. Saying goodbye. He didn't need to tell her anything else, not what it would mean if she didn't succeed, not what he hoped they might do after. They couldn't speak of that yet, so he just kissed her. And left.

For a long time Rennyn stayed where she was, keeping her thoughts on the previous night instead of the future. Eventually she rose, found her clothes neatly folded on a chair, and wandered around exploring. Three rooms, the bedroom very sparse and clear, but the other two devoted to books. Philosophy, history, science, memoirs, travel journals, plays, poetry, fictions. An extensive selection of the better works on magic, and a larger one focusing on Eferum-Get. The books covered every wall except one, which held more than twenty swords, all different lengths and edges. A small shelf by a window seat wasn't ordered by subject, but instead held a disparate collection of books, covers worn from frequent handling. It was like seeing inside his mind.

None of them was anything she had read, not one. She only knew magic and the mission of her family. It was the whole of her life. What would it be like, after? She'd never dared to make real plans, and her mind recoiled from dreaming of what she and Illidian Faille might do together. The chance that she would be killed was too large. The chance that he would be wasn't much lower. Even if they survived, her inheritance would always stand between them.

And that only if he forgave her for the things she hadn't yet told him.

TWENTY-THREE

The marshes west of Asentyr started as freshwater and ended salty. The last breach point was well toward the centre, where the water was brackish and black and the reeds thick. Most of it was hardly more than knee-deep, but below was sucking mud, and anyone wading risked sticking themselves firmly in place. Long Sentene coats were quickly abandoned, and movement was either awkwardly accomplished in flat-bottomed boats, or involved getting very dirty. Power-hungry levitations were carefully rationed, for all the Sentene mages felt they would need their full strength.

There were no conveniently large areas of dry land where a traditional circle could be constructed, let alone a camp, and the Sentene had been working for weeks on the technical problem this presented. Rennyn was faintly astonished by their solution. Not that they had sunk pylons and constructed a platform, but that it was so large. Enough for dozens of people to move about freely. There were a scattering of smaller artificial islands surrounding it, an archipelago of wood doubled in size again by the boats used to travel across the swamp. Like ocean-going ships, the main platform had wards built into the boundary. Wards were more energy-intensive than the circles placed around fixed locations, but they were quicker to establish so long as you had the power to feed them. The platform was safe for sleeping, and difficult to attack.

It was also extremely crowded. Determined and anxious people, busy preparing spells and weapons, discussing strategies, resting, eating, stretching. They still managed to leave a clear space around Rennyn. Intellectually, they might understand that she had not created these circumstances. That didn't make them any less angry with her: for concealing what she knew, for not warning them. For being the owner of their friends.

It didn't help that she'd made it clear, during the uncomfortable meeting yesterday, that the question of how she would reach the throne room, how she would survive the day between the attunement and Solace's arrival, was something she still wasn't going to discuss. Her position hadn't changed: the easiest way to protect herself was to be difficult to find. Travelling with an escort was like painting a target on her back.

"Counting the hours?"

Captain Medan. He'd become designated babysitter, perhaps because Lieutenant Danress no longer seemed able to talk to her.

As he settled his bulk against the wooden railing, Rennyn shrugged. "I'm surprised how close this is to the incursion point." They would be able stage much of their attack directly from the platform.

"Very complex calculation based on the previous breaches," he said, then met her sideways glance. "Or luck. One of those."

"It never hurts to have a little luck."

"Just don't rely on it." Captain Medan bent down and studied her face. "And sleep more, for pity's sake. You make me tired just to look at you."

"It's hard to sleep when you know you have to," she said, lying. Every time she closed her eyes she saw Illidian Faille chained to a wall. "I'll go in a few hours, anyway. Has there been any sign of observers?"

"We've scared everything down to the guppies out of the area. If there's going to be an attack here, it will come out of the Eferum, not from this side."

She nodded, unsurprised. "If it's equal to the Asentyr incursion, will you be able to handle it?"

"Ah–" He shrugged. "I wouldn't care to try an Azrenel that wasn't handily leashed. You made Asentyr easy for us. But we're better prepared this time."

Rennyn lifted her eyes and looked at him until he sighed. "We'll be able to handle that many, yes," he said in a slightly less booming voice. "But the Kellian are the backbone of the Sentene for a reason. Speed and instinct. The Ferumguard have the same training, and they'll do us proud, but a lot more people will die tonight, if we face even half the numbers."

The sun was sinking, and birds and insects began to clatter and call, revealing just how much life still remained in the marsh. Captain Medan watched a heron fly overhead, and when he spoke again his voice was stifled. "Will it hurt them, do you think?"

"I can only guess. Like a slow suffocation, perhaps. Or drowning. I can't be sure."

"I'd appreciate it if you got some rest, then. Even a couple of hours." His hands gripped the railing like he wanted to wring someone's throat. "She means the world to me. Dessaile. My partner. If you fail, she drowns."

This wasn't news, but to make him feel better Rennyn returned to the flat, covered boat which was her personal bed and lay down, curling around Solace's focus. The heavy wards on the boat stung at her senses and made her brain itch, but she fell asleep despite them for all she really didn't want to, and had the same dream as she'd had last night. Illidian, kissing her, touching her. His weight on her. Looking up at him with growing doubt as he pinned her hands. She couldn't see his face, couldn't make out his expression. Didn't know whose will moved him. Illidian's? Solace's? Or her own.

It was just barely still light when she woke, gasping. She felt sick, her head pounding, and she was keenly aware that Illidian was not nearby, was not watching over her. Chained to a wall, waiting for his mind to be taken away, his body to be made puppet.

Rennyn couldn't continue to allow her self-command to fray at the seams. It would have been easier if she could have had Seb with her. She would at least have been spared the constant, nagging worry that he'd been found and killed. Lying with Solace's focus on her stomach, she began a series of mental exercises. She had to set this aside. Illidian. Seb. Sukata and Kendall. People glaring at her and depending on her at the same time. Fear of failing. Fear, even, of succeeding. She had a task. She would carry it out as she had been trained to do. When it was done, she could spend as much time being upset as she wanted. Or wouldn't care either way.

When dusk had moved to moonlight, she forced down a little dry food and cast a number of preparatory spells before emerging. She had asked that the small platform closest to the breach point be left free, and she levitated across to it now to wordlessly begin marking out her circle.

"Good luck."

Rennyn looked over at Lieutenant Danress, sitting in one of the many small boats. Her face was pallid in the magelights.

"You too."

Enough said. Enough waiting. Rennyn stepped into the Eferum, bracing herself against the pull of the Summoning, and lit up her surroundings with an outpouring of power. Enough to disrupt any ambush.

The wave was already swelling: she'd almost left it too late. Rennyn let loose another barrage, aiming it directly at the approaching surge of power, and then busied herself with the final attunement. She kept herself methodical with the discipline of life-long training, and concentrated only on completion as the surge of the Grand Summoning swelled. Then, the focus hanging heavy from her wrist, she looked up to see a horde even larger than the first, heading toward the rapidly forming breach. An attempt to eliminate the Sentene mages once and for all.

Rennyn emptied the remaining prepared spells directly into the centre of them, then stepped back into the world as the remnants tumbled through the breach.

Her shield was active, but she still ducked as something flew close to her head. Needing to get her bearings, she levitated up, trying to make sense of a tangle of fighting beneath moon- and mage-light. There were fewer Eferum-Get moving than she'd expected, dominated by a group of hopping things, all legs and long jaws. Spindly, grinning foxes.

Heat washed over the area from a barrage of spells, but the foxes shrugged off the flames, no more than briefly stunned. A shielding aura? They moved extremely quickly, leaping high into the air, bounding about like over-excited foals. She saw one come down on the shoulders of a nearby woman, overbearing her so she fell. White teeth flashed into red, but the thing leapt away before those nearest could react.

These were the kind of Eferum-Get which the Kellian had been most valuable in countering. The Ferumguard, using a combination of swords and pistols, were just too slow. Frowning, Rennyn dropped to the large platform, since she'd agreed during yesterday's meeting to be properly guarded while the battle went on. She allowed herself to be surrounded while she tried to puzzle out a solution. Magic directly used was often resisted – it was far more effective to create fire or throw stones, and these things seemed resistant to conjured fire. Nor would the technique the Sentene had used back at the Arkathan work here: the creatures were rarely in one place long enough to be hit by missiles. Besides, she had already seen a mage fall to musket-shot gone astray. She watched one of the things leap up, soaring well above everyone's head, and then closed her eyes.

Trying to move things you couldn't see was far from easy. Not looking at all helped a little, but it still took far more energy than she liked. There was a faint murmur from those surrounding her as glistening black columns rose from the water around them, thickening as they grew. Mud, glutinous and stinking.

Tendrils began to extend from each column, curling and twisting like the new growth of plants, reaching out to each other, lacing together, sending out new feelers, linking and interlinking until there was a net, a ceiling, a web of the stuff.

Three of the leaping foxes were stuck immediately. Rennyn allowed the mud to encase them as they struggled, and saw that the rest were intelligent enough to start trying to avoid the new obstacle. That limited their movement enough for the Sentene to more effectively counter them. Already, most of the Eferum-Get were gone. But not killed, Rennyn realised. The foxes had kept the Sentene busy, while the rest of the creatures had run. A deliberate delay.

Mud was heavy, so Rennyn let it funnel back beneath the much-churned water, and then went and sat down while the Sentene did efficient things. She didn't know the name of the woman whose throat had been torn out, but she recognised a body taken out of the water as one of the Ferumguard who had travelled to Surclere with her. Lieutenant Danress was injured: a bite to her arm which she was trying to bind herself. Illidian would be less than pleased.

Illidian. Had the Black Queen set the Kellian to fighting their way from their prison? Killing people? Rennyn looked down at the sphere in her lap, smoky black with a shining spot of white at its core. The power rolling off it was tangible, grown strong enough that any mage would sense the focus nearby. Only an echo of what Solace would bring to this world.

Captain Medan squatted down beside her. "We're going to have to hunt them through this."

"Eferum-Get acting under orders."

"Yes. The idea of them using tactics isn't a pretty one. Feints and ambushes. Not what we usually have to deal with, and hunting through this stuff will be painful, especially when half of us have been instructed to return to the city for its defence. We may find it more useful to head to the nearest settlements and wait for them to show up, rather than expose ourselves in small tracking parties. Now, can I talk some sense into you?"

"Can I have something to eat?"

He sighed deeply, but went and fetched her a bowl of thick soup, barely warm but filling. She drank it down and handed him the bowl, then said: "It will take me about two hours to reach Asentyr."

"Two–?" His surprise was understandable. The journey into the marsh had been slow and tedious. Eight hours of working the boats through shallow channels.

"Captain, if I hadn't been throwing so much power about today, I could probably levitate all the way there. I'll use something a little more efficient though. I want to get inside the city's circle as quickly as possible."

"You said, yesterday, that you think this uncle is capable of passing the circle."

"He's an outstanding mage, just lacking the strength of a focus. Teleporting a short distance would be well within his abilities, and totally bypass the circle's protections, though not the alarm I added. Now that he's in this world, he would also be able to create gates into the Eferum, and travel there and back at will. And he's definitely capable of placing people under injunction, and could use them to access Asentyr, though the duration of the spell would be limited. But the city's circle is still the first line of real protection, and I need to be inside it. When I reach Asentyr I will hide myself and wait until there's only an hour or two left, and then I'll head to the Hall of Summoning."

Captain Medan rubbed at his black-stubbled chin, made wary by the sudden flow of information. "I get the feeling you're about to say something I won't like."

"In a way. I want you to do something for me. You know the flag that sits on top of the tower at the centre of the Halls of Magic?"

"I may have noticed something of the sort."

"If the Kellian escape, lower it."

Rennyn watched the muscles bunch in his jaw, but then he nodded. "Very well."

"Solace's obvious move is to take control of the Hall of Summoning. Unless her son brings another army of Eferum-Get into the city's circle, the Kellian are the ideal tool. All that talk yesterday, the defences Lady Weston plans, do you think it could stand against them?"

"That would depend on how much warning we had. And—" His voice dropped. "And whether we were willing to kill them."

Rennyn stood. It was time she started moving. "One thing I am at least sure of, Captain." The thing she clung to, whenever she thought about this plan. "They'd prefer death to the alternative."

TWENTY-FOUR

There was nothing worse than waiting. Kendall supposed she should be glad she was in the Arkathan rather than the dungeons, but the hours still grated by. At least she had the dormitory room to herself. All but a handful of the Arkathan students had been sent back to their homes until the Black Queen had been dealt with.

Earlier that day a squad of Sentene had returned from the marshes. Kendall had managed to find Lieutenant Danress, who had a bandage down one arm, but she didn't know anything much. Rennyn had left them. If everything had gone to plan, she was somewhere in the city. The Sentene were refining the defences in the Hall of Summoning, and would sit there hoping she showed up before the Black Queen did. Typical Rennyn.

Sick of doing nothing, Kendall decided to go over to the Sentene barracks. The palace was at highest security and nobody was supposed to be moving about right now, but the most they could do was send her away again.

All the security meant too many guards. They were even patrolling the barracks, for all that it was practically empty. Kendall made it to the garden between the Arkathan and the Sentene barracks without any problem, but then was stuck watching one of the Ferumguard pacing back and forth, tensely alert. He didn't even have the decency to stick to a predictable pattern. The windows on the ground floor were too narrow to squeeze through, and it didn't look easy to climb the side of the building. One day she'd be able to levitate up there, which was a nice thought, but useless right now.

Stymied, Kendall was wondering if she could bluff her way past when she heard voices, and the patrolling guardsman went to investigate. Not slow to take advantage, she nipped inside and hurried along inconveniently bright halls to Sebastian's room. There were too many magelights in the palace, and every one of them had been left uncovered this night.

The wards itched at her as she shut the door, but that only made her pleased she was able to tell they were active. Kendall had made Sukata try and explain the difference between wards and circles, but mostly because she had wanted to distract the Kellian girl, who had gone all mute and hunched after they'd found Rennyn crying. Kendall hadn't much liked that herself.

The bed had been pushed to one side. Odd. Kendall checked under it curiously, but found nothing unusual. Otherwise, the room was tidy, the bed made, the desk clean, with no sign of the meal they'd delivered. Except for the lines of sigils around the walls, it looked like any other room. Dissatisfied, Kendall took down one of the books above the desk and flipped through it. Healing magic, which Rennyn had said she didn't do. Maybe she'd decided to learn. With nothing better to do, Kendall started on another book, and found that it was full of pictures of what people looked like with all their skin gone.

This was definitely distracting, and Kendall was busy turning the pages when the room grew gloomy. Dark lines on the walls grew darker, then twisted across and out, as if the shadows were stretching out fingers to grab her. Kendall was a breath from diving under the bed when the darkness fell apart to reveal Rennyn.

"What in the Hells was that supposed to be?"

The black-haired woman gave her a brief, unsurprised glance. "Teleportation using Symbolic magic. From shadow to shadow basically. Conditional and expensive, but very useful."

If Rennyn said it was expensive, it probably meant most people couldn't begin to cast it. What did it matter? Kendall took a couple of deep breaths and switched to the far more important matter of Rennyn being here, now.

"Are you heading to the Hall of Summoning?"

"Not quite yet." For once Rennyn looked like she'd slept, though the circles under her eyes seemed to have become etched in place. She sat down on the bed, holding the bulky focus on her lap.

"Why hasn't anything happened?" Kendall asked, frustrated by Rennyn's calm. "There haven't been any attacks. Everyone's just sitting about. Even the Kellian–"

"Are just sitting about?"

"Lieutenant Danress told me that they stopped moving. Since before midnight yesterday. They don't move, and don't react if anyone talks to them. They drink a little water sometimes, and that's it."

"No orders," Rennyn said, curtly enough that Kendall knew she didn't like to think about it either, no matter how cool she was acting. "She's conserving her resources. Although they're formidable, the Kellian are tremendously outnumbered. Since the aim is to stop me, it's logical to wait until I'm easily located, which I will be once I go to the Hall of Summoning. After that, I doubt Solace will be too concerned with how many of their lives she spends trying to overcome the Sentene's preparations."

"You've been hiding all day?"

"Sleeping in a warded room. I can't hide the focus completely, since it's too powerful a thing, but wards make it difficult to track. Presuming my Wicked Uncle is even bothering to try."

"So you're safe until you leave this room?"

"No ward is guaranteed safety." Rennyn turned the focus over in her lap, the chain clinking softly. "They just make attacks and divinations harder. There is no ward which cannot be overcome, no spell which cannot be countered, no defence which can't be breached. Strength can be overcome by imagination. Imagination can be defeated by strength."

"Still giving lessons?"

"Still–"

"What in the Hells is that?!"

Power. Power of the kind Kendall had only felt at the dome around Falk, monumental, beyond the scale of people. Rennyn stood up, obviously startled, and took a step to the window.

"Is it the Black Queen come early?"

"No." Rennyn was gazing out over the city, searching. "My Wicked Uncle is making his move. Strength and imagination combined."

"I thought he was supposed to be weak!" Kendall protested, as Rennyn started drawing power of her own.

"Was." A shield began to shimmer around Rennyn, but she looked more resigned than alarmed.

"It's coming!" Kendall gasped, as the bloom of power roared into something larger. Far away, all the way down by the river, a wave was flowing toward them.

"Sit down."

"What?"

Rennyn reached out and put a hand on Kendall's shoulder, pressing until she sat down on the bed. And then the power reached them and everything went black.

CR℘

"Wake up."

A man's voice. As Kendall fought her way through groggy layers of darkness, a cold finger moved away from her temple. Upside-down. She was hanging upside-down. Someone was carrying her over their shoulder.

She stiffened, lifting her head, then tried to go limp again. Whoever was carrying her didn't slow down, but a man laughed, and then a hand gripped Kendall painfully by the hair and lifted her head.

"Little fledgling mage," the person said, in a pleased, purring voice. "Have you by chance seen my nephew?"

"Wha–?" Kendall managed.

"What kind of answer is that?" the man chided, letting go. "Well, the question will keep. Hold her there."

Kendall was upended, her arms trapped behind her back, but this gave her a better look at the room she'd been carried into. The Hall of Summoning. There were bodies scattered on the black and white floor. Sentene mages, Hand members, palace guards with their swords and pistols fallen from their hands. Unable to hold back a gasp of dismay, Kendall jerked forward, but the person who had been carrying her didn't move an inch, and her arms twisted painfully. Kendall looked back.

"Sukata."

The Kellian girl didn't react, wasn't even looking at her. Her face was impassive in a way that made Kendall realise that Kellian really were far more expressive than she'd given them credit for. This girl, this thing with Sukata's face and eyes of glass, was no more a person than a doll.

The only people upright were a handful of Kellian, Kendall, and a man with black hair and black eyes, dressed very finely in dark blue. He had more angles to his face, was better looking, but was, no matter what Rennyn had said, very much like Sebastian Claire. There was a weird shimmer in the air above him, a hint of violet light. Hanging from his wrist was the Black Queen's focus.

They had lost. The shock of it made Kendall dizzy. This was the Black Queen's demon son. He had the only thing which could stop her return. Rennyn had lost.

"Put her over there."

Kendall twisted in Sukata's hold as Sukata's mother moved forward from the Hall's entrance and lowered a still figure to the floor at one edge of the central black square. Rennyn. She lay without moving, her hair making black swirls on the marble.

"Is she dead?"

"No more than you are, fledgling." The demon prince walked over to stand above Rennyn and nudged her with one foot. With a sharp sideways glance he said: "Put one of the restraints on her, then clean this place up."

Captain Illuma, eyes as empty as her daughter's, drew something out of a black bag. A barbed and twisting thing, like a mix between a bramble and a worm. She dropped it on the back of Rennyn's hand, where it writhed for a moment, then slid around her wrist. Rennyn twitched as the spiked bracelet pierced her skin, sighed, but then lay still again.

Asleep. She was just asleep as Kendall had been. Perhaps they all were. There was no sign of any injuries, no blood. Everyone had just fallen to the ground in a scatter of swords and slates.

"Wake up!" Kendall yelled immediately, careless of consequences. "Wake up! Wake up!"

The demon prince laughed. "Noisy fledgling. Would you like me to give you a reason to scream? It wouldn't stir them."

"Don't talk to me, monster!" Kendall cried, caught between panic and fury. "You're a horror! You're a wrong thing! Just – go away!"

The demon only looked entertained. "Spirit, if a little lacking in common sense," he said. He seemed an oddly smiling and cheerful sort for a monster, though there was a taste to his words she didn't like. "Now, what was it I wanted – oh, yes, my distant nephew. Tell me, fledgling, where is he?"

"Why would I know that?"

"Don't be obtuse. That was his bed you were lying on. You were with his sister. My little cousin's best little friend, isn't that so?"

How did he know? But the last question had not been addressed to Kendall. She felt the faintest movement behind her. Sukata had nodded. The demon prince smiled, cheerfully smug.

"I don't know," Kendall spat, grateful for ignorance. "She sent him away, somewhere safe, somewhere only she knows. Somewhere monsters like you can't get him."

"How lacking in confidence. Really, I overestimated her. What a disappointment she must be to you."

This was unanswerable, and Kendall made a searching study of Rennyn's still body. It could be possible to wake her. Would she be able to do it?

More Kellian began arriving then, carrying people. Kendall's eyes widened at the sight of Captain Faille with Princess Sera across an arm and Prince Justin over his shoulder. He put them both down to Kendall's right, where Captain Illuma had been clearing away unconscious Sentene. Another Kellian set a woman down beside them, one who resembled Sera enough for Kendall to guess that this was Tyrland's Queen.

As the demon prince walked over to inspect the new arrivals, Kendall twisted experimentally in Sukata's hold, but the Kellian girl was far too strong and not the least inattentive. Kendall didn't bother to try appealing to Sukata, to try and break her free of the control. There was no feel of the person she knew in this silent creature holding her, and definitely no sense that any words would reach her. Talking to a wall would achieve as much.

While the demon son of the Black Queen bent over Princess Sera, Kendall decided the only thing left to her was Thought magic. Pebble skipping. It was useless for attacking or escaping, but she figured that she could try and pull that horrid spiky thing from Rennyn's wrist. Even if it didn't come off, the movement might wake her.

Taking a deep breath, Kendall focused, determined to pull as strongly as possible. And Rennyn's wrist moved. Not much, as if someone had plucked at the skin. That was it. Totally, utterly, completely useless.

The demon prince just laughed again, not the leastways bothered. "You don't listen well," he said. "Watch."

He reached down and touched Princess Sera's temple, murmuring softly. The girl immediately stirred, and sat up, blinking. It took a count of three as the princess looked around at the strange man standing above her, at all the people lying in heaps, and her brother and grandmother on the floor. Then she screamed.

It pierced the skull. The whole huge room was filled with it, rising with each hiccupping breath the girl took. Rigidly upright, she did nothing but scream, till her face was scarlet and she looked fit to pitch over. But the demon prince had made his point. Not one of the fallen so much as twitched. Even the Kellian didn't glance her way.

"What a sad lack of dignity," the demon said, about the time Sera was starting to go maroon. "This is the quality of Tyrland's false kings, is it?"

Amazingly, that was enough. Sera jittered to a stop, gazed up at the demon in outrage, and then threw herself on her brother's body, shaking him urgently. Skin mottled and hair all-abouts, she looked just a baby, no match for anyone.

"Put restraints on those two," the demon prince said, and Captain Illuma left off lining the Sentene along the wall and produced two more of the thorny things.

Princess Sera gasped as the first of the things wrapped around her grandmother's wrist, and shook her brother with increasing desperation, then stood and tried to pull him away from Captain Illuma. "No!" she cried. "Leave him alone!"

Captain Illuma didn't even seem to notice, just dropped the worm on Prince Justin's free wrist and turned back to moving people off the black central square, removing their weapons and lining them up against the walls. The demon prince looked critically around the room as more Kellian arrived carrying people. Kendall recognised two members of the Hand, ones who had been in the infirmary.

They were sorting out the mages. Not killing anyone, just moving them all together and putting one of the thorny worm things on the wrist of every mage. A restraint. It must be something to stop them using magic.

"Wake up," the demon prince said, bending over Prince Justin, and then repeating the motion for the Queen. "Can't have the guests of honour sleeping through the royal progress."

Queen Astranelle was the same dainty, pretty type as her granddaughter, but didn't show any sign of blubbing despite waking up with a demon standing above her. She picked herself up off the ground with the minimum of fuss, looked around her and said, "The worst result?"

"I suppose that would depend on your point of view," the demon prince said, in the same conversational tone he'd used with Kendall.

Prince Justin, struggling as his sister latched her arms around his neck, managed to get to his feet. "You – you're–"

"Helecho Montjuste-Surclere," said the demon, nodding as if they'd been introduced at a party. "Be quiet now."

A group of Kellian came in carrying more people. The only one Kendall recognised was Lady Weston, but they all looked important. A few were given horrid bracelets, and then the demon walked from one to the next, telling them to wake. But he wasn't interested in talking, completely ignoring their outrage and distress and the Queen's murmur of explanation. With a glance at Captain Faille he said: "Tear the throat out of the next one who speaks."

Even the most hysterical of the newcomers instantly choked into silence. Kendall didn't blame them: Captain Faille was always scary, and was far worse now that he wasn't a person anymore. Unconcerned, the demon turned all his attention back to Rennyn, like a wolf who had decided to stop circling and go in for the kill.

It must be nearly time. Kendall tried escaping Sukata's grip again, but it was pointless. Still, most of the Kellian had left, so they were really only dealing with the demon, Sukata, her mother and Captain Faille. There were ten captives standing now, and while the Kellian were strong they weren't carrying any weapons. Could they possibly give Rennyn the chance she needed?

"Lift her."

Captain Illuma hoisted Rennyn up by the armpits, which didn't wake her any more than Kendall's efforts. The demon prince reached out and gripped Rennyn's chin, his mouth widening in a gloating smile.

"Wake up, cousin."

Rennyn blinked, and tried to stand straighter, but was hampered both by Captain Illuma and the demon's hold on her chin. Kendall could tell the demon wanted her to be upset, and was glad Rennyn didn't give him any satisfaction. She turned her eyes left and right, taking in the piles of people, and the Queen and her small group of nobles clustered nervously under Captain Faille's watchful eye. For a long moment she looked at Captain Faille, then finally the demon.

"I suppose it really was too much to hope I'd never have to deal with you again."

"So pleased to disappoint," he said, letting her go. Captain Illuma stepped back as well, and Rennyn lifted her wrist to look at the thorny thing. There wasn't any blood where the spikes had pierced the skin, and the flesh around it was blanched white.

"Don't play with it – its defences are very amusing," the demon said. "And you don't have a chance of overwhelming it without this." Eyes glittering, he held up the necklace which carried Rennyn's focus.

But Rennyn barely glanced at it, surveying the room again. "She means to rule, not ruin."

The demon looked just a little nettled. Not, Kendall thought, because of what Rennyn was saying, but because she wasn't acting particularly frightened of him. "Ruin? An odd notion. A Queen overcomes treasonous attacks to return to her kingdom. That is what is happening here."

"And the incursions, the Azrenel particularly, would have benefited her rule how?"

"Azrenel are not at my beck and call," the demon said, shrugging.

Rennyn glanced at him, assessing him in a way which left Kendall unexpectedly hopeful. Rennyn hadn't given up. She might have lost the power of her focus, and have that thing on her wrist, but she was looking for weaknesses, a way to turn this around. If she could grab the Queen's focus at the right moment—

"Where did you get the power for that casting?" she asked next. "Even with some immunity to the perils of the Eferum, that was beyond any focus you could have summoned in so short a time. At least with much of the localised Efera being caught up in the Grand Summoning."

"Borrowed power," the demon said, and recovered his smile. "A tiny fraction of what is coming."

"You used the city's main circle to transmit it?"

The smile broadened. "Yes, and yes the sleep doesn't extend outside the main circle. But, dear cousin, if you're counting on rescue I hope whoever is playing hero can overcome these." He cocked his head toward Captain Illuma and finally had the satisfaction of disrupting Rennyn's calm assessment of her surroundings.

"The Kellian are weak to magic," she said, narrowing her eyes. "I wouldn't rely on them overmuch."

Pleased, the demon stepped closer to Rennyn. "Is it your brother you're waiting on? I'm told you've put him somewhere safe. Does he come dashing in at the last moment to save the day?" His hand darted out to tangle in Rennyn's hair, stopping her move to step back. "Aren't you worried? Time's running out."

"Did you start out as a monster?" Rennyn asked, sounding more annoyed than anything. "Or do you work at it?"

"I knew I was going to enjoy you," the demon said. He tightened his grip on her hair, pulling her head back. "Where were we, cousin? Do you remember?"

His head lowered, and he bit her. Bit her neck. Kendall wasn't sure if she only imagined the sound it made, or the faint swallowing noise which followed, but she couldn't mistake the pain and disgust which flashed across Rennyn's face. Princess Sera made a sympathetic whimpering sound, quickly stifled. Kendall didn't blame her. The air felt thick with dark magic. This was a true monster, a Night Roamer, a blood-drinker, and none of them were enough to stop him.

Not that this would keep Rennyn from trying. Lacking magic, she simply curled one of her hands into a fist and hit him in the stomach. It was hard enough to hurt him, and she managed to wrench herself away, leaving a long hank of her hair tangled in his fingers. Blood streamed from her throat, from the ragged tear his teeth had left, but she didn't have a chance to do more than take a step back before the demon said: "Hold her," and Captain Illuma obediently got in the way.

"Did that make you feel better?" the demon asked, only a little out of breath. He was all excited and pleased, eyes shining and mouth bloody, though beneath it there was a hint of puzzled surprise.

"Not much," Rennyn said shortly.

The demon chuckled and looked around, then went and fetched a silky scarf from one of the conscious captives, laughing again when she flinched away from him. Rennyn only stood, stiffly upright with her arms held behind her, as the demon wiped his face, then tied the scarf around her neck. Her shirt was slick and wet, and Kendall felt the twitch of magic as the demon cast something to stop her from bleeding so much.

Then he balled up one fist and slammed it into Rennyn's stomach just as she had hit him, except with a monster's strength, so that she was smashed back against Captain Illuma and then crumpled and hung, gagging, in the Kellian woman's hold.

Her hair fell across her face, but Kendall didn't miss the way her eyes flicked at the nearest door. She *was* waiting for someone, just as the demon had said. Sebastian? Or could there be more Montjuste-Surcleres, and the story about them being the last just a lie?

And it was too late. A snatched breath and a stirring among the captives told Kendall she wasn't the only one in the room who felt it. She realised it had been growing for a while, swelling, and now was made obvious by the way the Black Queen's focus swung on its chain, pointing toward the middle of the room like it thought that way was down. The demon glanced at his wrist, irritated, interrupted in his play. But then he smiled, and shrugged, and said:

"Time to meet your Queen."

TWENTY-FIVE

I t happened far too quickly. The demon walked around the edge of the room's big central square so that he was opposite Rennyn, putting the Black Queen's focus well out of her reach. Kendall made one last attempt to wriggle free of Sukata's grasp and the other captives exchanged urgent, impotent glances as the heaviness turned suffocating, and all the mage glows dimmed.

The whole room shuddered, and she heard panes of glass crack. All the edges went off the sounds, drowned out by a thrumming which filled the air, crushing Kendall's ears, her chest, her bones. The whole of the heaviness over Falk was squashing down into this one space.

The black square became a pool, a pit and all the room was tipping into it. Kendall found herself tilting forward, but was held upright by Sukata. She could hear more glass breaking, but it was far away, outside this heavy, dark world–

Light. Bright, painful, stabbing into the eyes. Kendall flinched from it, and found that she was sweating, shaking, but no longer crushed. She took an overwhelmed breath and stared at the crystal sun which had taken over the room.

For some reason she'd thought that Queen Solace's new focus would be black like Rennyn's, but this was clear and bright like those that ordinary mages wore. It was just – big. Twice the height of a man, floating in the centre of the room, shining brighter than any of the mage glows. The air still throbbed with power, but it was more contained and less painful.

The huge focus rose slowly toward the big vaulted ceiling of the room, and there on the floor was the White Lady again, just as Kendall had seen her in Falk. Feet neatly together, hair spread out in a great fan to the tips of her fingers, beautiful dress shimmering. But this one's eyes were open.

The woman sat up, moving very slowly. She wasn't more than average height, but it felt like the floor quaked from her weight, leaving Kendall dizzy, small and scared spitless. Lieutenant Danress had been right about the pointlessness of attacking the Black Queen direct. There was so much power in the room, swirling around and through everyone like a live thing, as obedient to the Black Queen's will as the Kellian. Casting a spell, drawing a weapon, making any kind of attack would be suicide. Only the Kellian might have the speed to succeed, and they were on the wrong side.

"Your Majesty," said the demon prince, and bowed extra-deep, before offering her his hand.

The Black Queen stood up, her long fall of waving white hair swinging to her knees. She didn't seem awkward getting up off the floor, wasn't in a hurry, acted totally in control as she gazed round at them all. The smaller focus detached itself from the demon's wrist and moved to hover at her shoulder like a glass courtier. Tyrland's new Queen.

Kendall became a little tangled over whether it was right to call her the new queen or the old queen. Either way, the haughty, disgusted look she suddenly fixed on Queen Astranelle, like she was some bug crawled from under a rock, left no doubt over how she felt about anyone else holding the title.

"You descend from the Pretender?" Her voice was strong and commanding, and colder than the Hells.

"I am a successor of King Eliathas, yes." Queen Astranelle stood steady, not moving even when Princess Sera was unable to hold back a hiccupping sob, burrowing her face into Prince Justin's side.

The Black Queen's lip curled, surveying the small royal family. "You claim a right to this land?"

The menace in her words hung in the air, a sword ready to fall at the wrong answer. Tyrland could not have two queens. But Queen Astranelle wasn't about to swear fealty to the Black Queen, no matter the consequences.

"I have accepted a duty to this kingdom," she said, with quiet pride. "I will not turn my back on it."

Other than that she wasn't a friend of the Kellian, Kendall didn't know much about Queen Astranelle, but she had to like her for standing there so calm. Chin up in the face of death. She liked Lady Weston even more for stepping to the Queen's side, a show of support from a mage who couldn't even cast.

The Black Queen's eyes narrowed, but then she glanced away, and Captain Faille moved, faster than fast. In a breath he was standing before Rennyn and one of his hands rose and fell, and left a line across her shirt. A choked gasp broke from Rennyn's lips, and she moved like she wanted to clutch her side, but couldn't because Captain Illuma still held her arms. He'd cut her open. Those nails were every bit as much a weapon as a sword.

As everyone stared in confusion, Captain Faille reached out his long, pointed fingers and actually stuck them into Rennyn's side, which made her turn very pale and writhe rather. Blood was streaming down from the cut, a bit below her ribs on her left side, but it didn't look like the wound was too deep. When he drew back his hand he was holding a familiar black sphere. Rennyn's focus.

"Did you imagine such a simple ruse would overcome me?" the Queen asked, sounding genuinely curious.

Rennyn didn't answer immediately, watching Captain Faille hand the blood-slick focus to the demon prince. The demon held up the necklace with its identical black stone, then dropped the necklace on the floor and pocketed the real focus. Only then did Rennyn turned her attention back to the Black Queen to say, "May I ask you a question?"

"Traitor's child, do you hope to postpone your death or hasten it?" But behind the Black Queen's dry words Kendall glimpsed suddenly sharpened attention. Captured and bleeding, her focus taken from her and facing a mage as powerful as the gods, Rennyn Claire still managed to act like *she* was the one in charge. Did she have a plan, or was this just Surclere arrogance?

"Are you able to withdraw from the Kellian?" Rennyn asked, completely ignoring the Black Queen's comment. "Your presence is killing them as people."

This brought scorn. "The golems will not fail their purpose."

"I suppose not," Rennyn said, with a distant note in her voice. "But that wasn't quite the point, was it?"

Captain Faille backhanded Rennyn across the face. Again, the suddenness of the move made all the captives flinch, and Kendall sobbed beneath her breath. Even though she knew that it must be at the Black Queen's orders, it still *felt* like Captain Faille had turned on them. It was one thing to think him a scary man, but it was purely horrid to have him act like it.

"Who do you think you are talking to?" the Black Queen asked, picking out each word.

Rennyn didn't immediately respond, but then she straightened, looking unhappily at Captain Faille. She had this trick of ignoring the Black Queen — of both queens, really — which almost made it so they didn't matter, for all their power. The mark of Captain Faille's hand stood out white, with a thin red line at the centre, and already one eye was starting to swell. Yet she lifted her head as high as before, not quailing in the least.

Rennyn had to be bluffing. Ignoring the Black Queen to keep her attention fixed and wary. But her skin was grey from the effort of staying upright, the whole of her front slick with blood now starting to pool around her feet. Even if she didn't provoke the Black Queen into killing her, she couldn't last much longer.

A flicker of movement at the door betrayed her into another glance, but it was only the Kellian again, carrying more people. She stared at them, then closed her eyes, looking deadly tired.

"Still hoping for rescue, cousin?" asked the demon prince. "Perhaps your brother found a...wiser course of action."

"You shouldn't judge Seb by your own standards," Rennyn said.

"Enough of this," said the Black Queen, and Kendall quailed because she knew this meant that Rennyn was about to die and then probably the rest of them.

But Rennyn nodded. "Yes," she murmured, as if she were sorry or glad. "Enough."

Kendall didn't see her do anything, and the thorny bracelet meant there was no way Rennyn could cast, but suddenly all the Kellian started glowing. Not gold or white like they did in strong sun and moonlight, but with an angry ripple of dark rainbow tints which heralded a gust of power so strong it set Kendall's teeth to aching. Sigils began writing themselves up each of the columns and across the ceiling, and the Black Queen staggered as if a crushing weight had been set on her shoulders.

"Three hundred years," Rennyn said, stepping away from a frozen Captain Illuma to stand shakily unsupported. The floor washed black, as if someone had poured a bucket of ink across it. "We had time to plan for many contingencies."

Kendall realised Sukata's hold had also relaxed, and pulled free as something stung at her arms. The Kellian girl didn't even notice, standing paralysed as tiny little lightning-bolts played over her skin. The air smelt of storms. Beneath their feet the blackness kept spreading out from the central square to cover the floors and climb up the walls, dousing the mage glows as it went. Even the Black Queen's focus dimmed, and below it they could see pinpricks of lights clustered together in the dark, rapidly growing smaller and then fading away.

"What is it?" Kendall whispered, awed, as a round shape came into sight. Most of it was black, but there was a long band along one side which was blue and green and brown and there was a kind of halo around the whole thing. It shone like a jewel suspended in the floor below them, slowly growing smaller.

"All the world," said Rennyn unsteadily. "And more. How beautiful." She had her own faint halo, and her hair was moving gently though there wasn't any wind.

The Black Queen was having almost as much trouble staying on her feet as Rennyn, shuddering like she was holding up a mountain, power pouring off her in an ever-increasing wave. "Kill her!" she hissed urgently at the demon.

"Useless spite," Rennyn murmured, glancing up. If she'd seemed calm before, now she acted like someone who'd finally reached the top of a hill and had no further to go.

"Quickly!"

None of the Kellian moved: they were statues beneath purple lightning crawling about so you could hear it fizzing on their skin.

But the demon prince hadn't been effected by the spell. With an odd smile he started forward.

"Don't even–!" shouted one of the wakened prisoners, and leapt to intercept the smaller man. But the prince caught him and with a sound of tearing cloth threw him straight at Rennyn. They both went down with a horrible thud.

"Ren!"

Sebastian came running out of nowhere. He stumbled to a stop by his sister as the nobleman scrambled awkwardly off her, slipping in the pooling blood. Rennyn didn't move.

"The late-come hero," commented the demon prince, who actually seemed to be enjoying himself, not showing any concern for his mother. He reached casually down and scooped up one of the abandoned Sentene weapons, then threw it at Sebastian.

Kendall reacted without thinking, pushing with all her might. The sword twisted in mid-air, jerking off in a completely unexpected direction. The demon laughed, and with a gesture lifted a dozen swords from near the sleeping guards, all of their points lining up at Rennyn and Sebastian.

And then the Black Queen's focus exploded.

CREAD

Kendall fell over before the blast of power, curling into a ball as the side of her face and arm were stung by glassy wasps. Her ears rang and echoed before settling back to normal, and she lifted her head warily. She couldn't tell how long it had been and all the light had gone out of the room so that there was only a bit of brightness through the doors and windows; no good to see by.

A faint crunching of crystal, eerie and directionless, made her heart jump. Where was the demon? But nothing leaped on her, so she shifted and found she was lying on someone's legs. Sukata. Sitting up, she pulled at the girl, who didn't resist or react. Kendall wasn't even sure she was breathing.

Light flared, and Kendall looked hastily around for the demon. Nowhere. The only people moving were the small clutch of wakened prisoners, dusting off shards or picking them from their skin as they climbed to their feet. All of the sleeping guards stayed where they were, still under the spell. None of the Kellian were standing.

The light was a mage glow conjured by Sebastian, but his attention was all for his sister, not for little matters like monsters. He pulled off his jacket and wadded it against Rennyn's side. The nobleman who had been thrown at her made a pad for her head out of his own jacket, but then picked up a pistol and stood.

"It can't have gone far," he said, with an urgent glance from the centre of the room to Queen Astranelle. "Your Majesty—"

The Queen, bleeding from a cut above her eye, cut him off with a gesture. "The thought does you credit, Tassin, but none of us are equipped to fight that creature," she said and looked at Lady Weston, who nodded in agreement. They both ignored the centre of the room, where bits of white hair and dress poked from beneath of a pile of crystal.

Queen Astranelle turned to Sebastian. "Child, can you break this sleep spell?"

But Sebastian didn't even seem to hear her, eyes only for Rennyn, who didn't respond when he called her name and didn't react when he tried to straighten her.

Before the Queen could speak again there was a sound at the west door. A Kellian blurred into the room, slowing from top speed to a frozen full stop as she looked around the room. Out of uniform, Kendall barely recognised her as Lieutenant Faral, and didn't know if it was the right reaction when the nobleman called Tassin raised his pistol at sight of her.

Lieutenant Faral saw it, and there was a faint flicker behind her eyes as Kendall thought about just how dangerous Kellian could be. But then two other Kellian followed her blurring entrance, and she sounded as proper and correct as ever when she said: "My Lady, there are fires in the city."

"Fires?" Lady Weston looked briefly puzzled, then said: "Of course. A city asleep where it stands. There are bound to have been injuries and accidents. Muster what you can and bring in the fire crews from outside the main circle. But set a small force to locating Helecho Montjuste-Surclere."

"Yes, My Lady." Lieutenant Faral saluted, and added a tidy little bow in the Queen's direction before sending the other two Kellian speeding back out of the room. She made a second, more thorough survey of the room, lingering for a moment on Kendall, who had propped Sukata on her lap in an effort to try and work out if she was alive. And then Rennyn, all bloody and broken.

Swiftly, she crossed to the two Claires and knelt on the other side from Sebastian. Taking hold of both his wrists, she said: "Stop panicking."

This at least made Sebastian look at her, though his eyes were so full of impending loss that Kendall wasn't sure he understood what she'd said.

"Your sister needs a healing mage, Sebastian," Lieutenant Faral said, thin voice very clear and steady. "And quickly. You need to wake one up." She let go of his wrists and pressed lightly on the bloody coat. "I'll look after Lady Rennyn. You help Lady Weston with a healer."

Sebastian stared at her, then nodded jerkily. "Yes. Of course." He took a deep breath and pulled himself together, turning to Lady Weston.

With that settled, Kendall shifted her attention back to Sukata, who wasn't burned and felt properly warm and alive, but didn't wake even when Kendall pinched the skin on the back of her hand. Her chest did seem to be moving, but it wasn't something as simple as sleep, or surely she'd react a little. Kendall stared from Captain Faille's body to Rennyn. This was what she'd been hiding? The price of killing the Black Queen?

Lieutenant Faral had finished checking over Rennyn's injuries, and stopped to smooth strands of hair off her face. The movement was very tender, like a mother with a new baby, not revealing any anger underneath. But probably she didn't know what Rennyn had done. Used the Kellian to win.

Painfully unhappy, Kendall focused on picking bits of crystal out of Sukata and her own skin. Everyone in the room had been peppered, but most of the pieces were small and at least no-one seemed to have been hit in the eye.

It didn't take long for Sebastian to find a way to wake people up, though he could only do it one by one. But once he'd woken a couple of mages who didn't have bracelets, and shown them what to do, things really started moving. The room grew confusing and Kendall lost sight of Sebastian until he showed up trailing a tall, thin woman with a long neck who took over Rennyn, freezing Lieutenant Faral out with a cold stare.

"Let me look after her now," said a deep voice, and Kendall looked up at Captain Medan.

"She won't wake," Kendall explained, closing her fingers tighter around Sukata.

"I know." Captain Medan looked calm, but Kendall could see he was upset underneath. "But she's not going to get better lying here on the floor."

That was hard to argue with, so Kendall let her fingers relax. The big Sentene mage lifted Sukata easily, nodded, then carried her away.

Kendall almost followed them, but then she saw Sebastian walking after Lady Weston and changed direction. She needed to hear what he knew, needed to know if using the Kellian was what he and Rennyn had planned all along.

"Lediage Sorathar is the Queen's own healer," Lady Weston was saying, leading Sebastian deeper into the palace. "Your sister could not be in better hands."

"I'd still rather stay with her," Sebastian said, but in the resigned tone of someone who knows he's lost an argument.

"Soon enough. You know very well this explanation cannot wait."

The Queen had lost patience with the Claires carrying out their plans without telling her anything, Kendall bet. From a room ahead Kendall heard Princess Sera's voice in very definite, determined tones. It sounded like she didn't intend to miss the explanations either. Kendall shook her head. She mightn't like the princess, but no-one could say she didn't bounce back quick from being scared half out of her mind. Or that she didn't know how to get her way.

The room was some kind of sitting-room, all brocaded chairs and glittery ornaments. Princess Sera, having won her argument, was enthroned on a couch all to herself being fussed over by a lady in a long white apron. Prince Justin was picking some more crystal out of his hand. The Queen's dress was blood-specked, but she looked a lot tidier and more regal now. Two of the nobles who'd been in the room, the man called Tassin and a sleepy-looking woman, shared another couch and even though this made it a lot of people, Kendall abruptly realised that it was probably far less than usual for an audience with the Queen. They were all still wearing the horrid bracelets, and there weren't any guards or servants other than the nurse. Most of those who had been woken couldn't be spared from trying to fix the mess caused by an entire city sleeping all at once. Fires. People who'd been standing at the tops of flights of stairs. Holding babies. People on horses or driving carts. Had the animals fallen asleep as well? Would birds have just dropped out of the sky? Kendall hadn't even begun to think through the implications.

"Have there been any sightings of the one called Helecho?" the Queen asked Lady Weston, making a sweeping gesture to sit down. Sebastian bowed first, and Kendall bobbed a belated curtsey, remembering that she was from a village and this was Tyrland's Queen. The only one.

"Not yet, Your Majesty," Lady Weston said, her movements stiff as she sat down. "The indicator Lady Rennyn placed on the city's circle was reacting to him in the Hall, but it hasn't been sighted since Queen Solace's focus shattered. Most likely he teleported."

"What level of threat does he pose?"

Lady Weston hesitated, then looked at Sebastian. "He was able to command the Kellian when Rennyn could not, Sebastian."

"Solace probably ordered them to obey him while the distortion kept her from giving them more than general commands." Sebastian was acting more like himself, but he didn't manage to sound so detached when he added: "But he'd be heir after me. If Ren and I die, he'll inherit control."

Inherit. The word made them less somehow. Kendall saw the two nobles exchange glances, and wished she could tell what the

Queen was thinking. What if she decided it would be simplest to get rid of the Kellian?

"Regardless, an Eferum-Get of that calibre who is also a mage is a considerable threat, Your Majesty," Lady Weston said. "Unique. A creature who can bypass the circles, who can command other Eferum-Get. If he chose, he could raise an army of the creatures, could kill with impunity."

"But he didn't." This was Prince Justin, strained but unflagging. "He could have killed us easily, and he didn't. He didn't even seem that interested in stopping whatever it was you did which killed his mother."

"Perhaps he wanted to be free of her," Sebastian said, with the faintest of shrugs. "Ren thought he might be under an injunction. Once Solace was dead, he just – left."

"Once she was dead," the Queen repeated. "And that has been your intention all along? Despite this performance with Queen Solace's focus?"

"That was – oh, not just a distraction, but a backup plan as well." If Sebastian had noticed the Queen's flat tone he pretended not to.

"For what, exactly?" Lady Weston asked. "I saw it, felt it, but I have little idea of what actually happened. It almost seemed that the Kellian were casting."

"Almost." Sebastian looked down, and noticed for the first time that his trousers were soaked with blood where he'd been kneeling. He went perfectly white, and jerked in his seat, but then began speaking rapidly: "The Kellian, the originals, were part of Queen Solace. She sacrificed a piece of one of her fingers making them, and they were true extensions of her will until she went away. The Kellian descendents aren't quite the same, but the spell which makes them Kellian means they had no barriers against Solace. Her will overrode them totally.

"When our great-grandfather was killed, and our family guessed at who was responsible, my great-grandmother realised that the Kellian's weakness to Solace might be true in reverse. They can't protect against her at all, but she can't stop being linked to them either. That was something new. For years, centuries, we've been trying to find a way to stop the cycle of the Grand Summoning's return. Mostly we tried to find ways to move in the Eferum, to be able to reach her before the Summoning began so we could kill her before the power levels became too dangerous. But we've never succeeded, and when we realised the possibilities of the Kellian descendents, we hit upon a different approach.

"They're not quite Montjuste-Surcleres. Ren did wonder if they counted as a kind of cousin, but Lieutenant Faral couldn't pick up the attuned focus, so I guess the spell excludes them in some way. But they are – were – part of Queen Solace, and gave us access to her, the opportunity to cast a spell which ordinarily she would see and spot easily. Symbolic magic, strengthening the ties between Solace and us through the Kellian. Ren's the direct heir and so her blood made the strongest link. She marked Solace with it – the expression of Solace at Falk – and ever since then we've marked every Kellian we met with a drop of mine or Ren's blood. And then cast a small start to a very large spell." He glanced at his knees again, but only for a moment. "I missed four, ones who were never called to the city, but we'd attached a link to the rest, a tiny casting so we could use them to make *Solace* cast a spell. So that's what happened. We prepared the room that night after Ren put up all those divinations, and set the trigger of both spells there. Then it only needed the Kellian and Queen Solace to be in the Hall of Summoning, and one of us to trigger it. After that, her own magic would end it, whether she killed us or not." He stopped and took a deep breath, looking a lot like he wanted to cry.

"So, you held the trigger?" Prince Justin asked, looking puzzled. "Where were you? How did you escape the sleep spell?"

"No. I would only have needed to trigger the spell if Ren couldn't. I was in the Eferum."

"But why?" managed Lady Weston, in a tone which said 'impossible!'. "More to the point, how? The risk of being discovered–"

"Small," Sebastian said. "In the Eferum, it's your thoughts and feelings which make you exist. Ren made me sleep – more than sleep – before she put me in there. Unless I was conscious, thinking and feeling, I didn't fully exist there."

Going to the Hells asleep. Even the Queen looked disbelieving. But still angry. The Claires had lied to her, had meant all along for the Grand Summoning to be completed. Had done things their way without telling anyone.

"How many Kellian were needed to trigger this spell?" Prince Justin asked abruptly.

"Two," Sebastian said. "Well, one, but with just one Queen Solace would have been able to cast in the early stage of the spell."

"But there were three Kellian here, the entire time. Yet your sister stood there baiting the Black Queen."

Sebastian looked down at his knees again. "It would have killed them," he explained, his voice hardly loud enough to hear. "Channelling power like that, it's not true casting. And for that spell, the amount of Efera involved would be – like a flood ripping away the banks of a river. Three Kellian would have been destroyed. Even – how many were there? Eight?"

"Nine," Lady Weston murmured.

"How deadly is a ninth of a lightning bolt? There was no way to test how much they could bear. The most we could do was arrange for as many Kellian to be present as possible, but this sleep spell took control out of Ren's hands. With so few in the room when the Grand Summoning completed, Ren wouldn't have – Ren would have held the trigger till she had no choice."

Sebastian's voice broke on the last word and he jerked to his feet. "I'm sorry we didn't tell you, but we couldn't," he said, the words so fast they fell over each other. "Any hint that we wanted the Kellian present was too much to risk. It's what we had to do, we had to stop her, and that was the only way we could find. I – please, can I go back? She could be – I want to be there."

The Queen still looked less than happy, but maybe she was softened by the tears running down Sebastian's face. "Very well," she said. "Go."

g oing was one thing, seeing another. Rennyn had been taken to a bedroom not too far from the Hall of Summoning, but the healer had woken assistants to crowd every corner, all murmuring and bustling and fetching things in and out. Sebastian hadn't been allowed more than a glimpse, and they'd ended up sitting on an ugly couch listening to snatches of conversation from the next room. They would, Kendall supposed, at least *hear* if Rennyn died.

"Sukata was there."

So he'd noticed. "Mm."

Sebastian picked at his trousers above the drying patches of blood. He'd ignored suggestions he go change, just kept worrying at the cloth. There was probably some way to magic it clean, but Kendall doubted he was in any state to cast.

"Tell me what happened."

That took a while. Kendall wasn't sure how much he listened, attention only partially on her, straightening at every change of tone in the next room. Finally she said: "What was she trying to cast? All that did was make the Black Queen beat her up."

"Probably just a distraction." Sebastian shrugged. "The trigger wasn't linked to her casting."

"Was the focus on her necklace always a fake?"

"No. I researched that concealment for her. Nothing to do with the Black Queen." Sebastian hunched his shoulders. "She just, she was worried our Great-Uncle would...do things to her."

The way the demon had touched her made it pretty clear what he wanted. Rennyn had hated that he'd bitten her. It was the most upset Kendall had ever seen her, outside when she'd told the Kellian she owned them.

"If she dies, the Kellian will belong to you."

"I'd inherit the ability to control them. That's all." Frowning at the words, Sebastian worried his trousers again. "Did they hate her for it?"

"Not...hate."

"She's dreaded telling them for years, even before we knew them. Perhaps after all it would have been better if we'd been able to stay hidden till we had to prepare the Hall of Summoning. Easier to mark them over a month, of course, but it was cruel that they grew to trust us."

"But that helped," Kendall protested. "They hated the idea of it, and what the Black Queen would do to them, but at least they knew what kind of person Rennyn was. Is."

Sebastian gave her a dark look, then said: "The kind of person who makes decisions for other people? Who takes their choices away from them?"

Kendall fought a flush which left her hot all over. "Well, she does."

"I know. You think she never asked herself if she was doing the right thing? Hells, she wasn't even sure it was right to kill Solace."

Soft-hearted. Not liking what she was doing, but accepting she had to. What would have happened if the two Claires had simply packed their bags and left Tyrland rather than take on the Black Queen?

"I never thanked her."

"You went with her. She liked that." Sebastian leaned back, eyelids sagging. "She liked you for not trusting her." He sighed deeply and fell asleep, head tipped awkwardly back. Days enchanted in the Eferum didn't add up to much rest.

Kendall sat listening to the noises from the other room. The attendants clucked like hens, voices rising and falling with each new excitement, making it hard to tell real disaster from stupid fussing. Occasionally the healer's voice could be heard, never hurried, not loud enough to make out any words.

"Lord Montjuste-Surclere."

The couch heaved under Kendall, and she realised she'd been leaning on Sebastian's shoulder. Muzzily she sat up, rubbing at her eyes. The tall healer was standing in front of them.

"How is she?" Sebastian asked, his voice small and tight.

"We have stabilised her," the healer said, choosing her words with a judicious air. "Ordinarily I would give her a fair chance of recovery."

"But?"

"There are two areas of concern. This wound on her throat – I'm told it is an Eferum-Get bite?" Without waiting for Sebastian to respond, she swept on. "There is some property to the wound I cannot unravel. Perhaps a mild toxin which is resisting removal. That may have an impact on her recovery. There is a more immediate issue which I would appreciate your help with."

"Anything."

"Your sister appears to have been physically worn down before being injured, and then has suffered major blood loss. Replacing the blood has exacerbated the exhaustion. The major injuries – bruised organs, and badly broken ribs piercing one of her lungs – have been caulded and she is no longer bleeding internally. It is very important that she lie still and rest as much as possible. And she will not."

"Ren's awake?"

"Not lucid. We removed the creature on her wrist, of course, and immediately she began to resist our enchantments. We even resorted to drugging her, a thing I would not ordinarily approve with a subject in such a depressed physical state, and this held her barely longer than the casting. She is counteracting everything."

"Ren's *casting in her sleep?*"

The way Sebastian leapt to his feet, almost shouting, told Kendall just how bad a thing this was. Even the graceful healer looked disconcerted.

"Thus far we have seen no effects outside her continued waking," she reassured him. "But I must ask you to try and calm her. She is killing herself. If she can see you, hear your voice, she may cease to fight against our castings."

"Maybe she thinks it's the demon's spell," Kendall said pragmatically, then pulled a face and followed Sebastian as he ran into the next room.

The bed made Rennyn look small. Nor was she moving about, but lay neatly tucked up and totally still. Kendall could feel the itch of magic, but could not tell what was the healer's work and what was Rennyn.

"Is she casting?"

Sebastian leaned close over his sister. "I think so."

"That's bad because she might melt the room, or something?"

"Yes. A Thought mage should never cast except with absolute deliberation. You can't get drunk, or smoke that Haze Weed. Fevers are best avoided, though I haven't heard of sleep-casting before."

"Stay with her," said the healer. "Talk to her. Even in sleep she will hear you and be reassured. Above all, keep her still."

As the healer left the room, Sebastian obediently picked up one of Rennyn's hands and began murmuring to her. Kendall edged around the side of the bed for a closer look. One side of Rennyn's face was a single, huge bruise with a scratch through the centre. Her cheeks were sunken and her bones stood out beneath the skin.

"She doesn't look like she's been healed at all. What does 'caulded' mean?"

"Holding wounds or bones together. You can't just fix a person with magic. Well, some healers have managed it, but more have killed their patients trying. Even if this one was arrogant enough to try, Ren's too weak to stand it."

"Patch her up and wait, huh?"

Sebastian looked up, then felt around in his pockets and produced a square of crumpled, inky cloth. He was just the sort who would carry a kerchief. Kendall ignored it, wiping at her face.

Rennyn shifted on the bed. Kendall watched her, then peered closer to see beads of sweat on her face, though there was no flush to the skin. "She's waking up."

Sebastian had already noticed, squeezing Rennyn's hand as if that would help. "Can you hear me, Ren? It's me. It's over. We're safe. You can rest, it's all over."

Rennyn's head turned toward his voice, her eyes opening to dark slits.

"Ren!" Sebastian said gladly.

But there was no recognition in Rennyn's swollen face. Instead of being calmed by his words, she continued to turn her head, then tried to sit up, barely managing to raise her head.

"What's she looking for?"

"Ren? You're safe." Sebastian tried to stop his sister from moving. "Lie back. It's over."

This didn't help at all. Even though she didn't have the strength to lift herself, and trying obviously hurt a lot, Rennyn kept struggling to move. Kendall looked about for the one of the healers.

"Did she just say something?"

Sebastian leaned over his sister, but when he lifted his head he just looked puzzled. "Liddan? Is that a place, a person?"

Kendall shook her head. "Something undone that's worrying her? If she knows you're alive, and that the Black Queen is dead, is there anything she needs to do?"

"Our – Solace's second son," Sebastian said reluctantly. "Not in our original plans, of course, but I don't think we can leave him out there. We're going to have to deal with him."

"His name's not Liddan."

"No. But there isn't anything else." He tugged the blanket back toward Rennyn's chin. "She was looking forward to that so much. To not *having* to study, to letting herself indulge useless whims. To travel and read novels and sleep in every day. To not have this huge duty sitting over her. She doesn't want to be responsible for anything ever again, won't even admit to worrying about the political consequences for the Kellian."

"Are they going to be all right? Sukata and the others who were there?"

He bit his lip. "They should be, since they survived the end of the casting. But we had no way to test it, no way to be sure if there would be any side-effects."

"And none of them are called Liddan either," Kendall said, adding doubtfully: "Captain Faille's first name is a bit like that. Lieutenant Danress told me it once."

"Really?" Sebastian blinked, then looked worriedly back at his sister as she shifted and then caught her breath. Broken ribs.

"Stay with her, will you?" Sebastian said, and strode abruptly out of the room. Startled, Kendall could hear him speaking to someone outside, and then one of the healer's assistants came in, already chalking on his slate, and brushed Kendall aside so he could cast some more spells.

"Even the pain suppressors are being countered," the assistant said, clicking his tongue. Then he noticed that Sebastian hadn't followed him back into the room, and looked scandalised. Kendall pretended not to notice, and eventually the assistant finished his spells and went off, no doubt to say nasty things about heartless boys.

Rennyn was so still Kendall went back to the bed to check her. She felt almost as tired as Rennyn looked, and it made it worse that she had to lean close to be sure the woman was even breathing. But the bruises didn't make her any less the person who'd shown up at Kendall's door in Falk and told a pack of lies to get Kendall to do what she wanted.

"Why should I thank you?" Kendall asked softly. "It was all what you wanted. Saved my life to spare your own feelings. Dragged me about the country to distract yourself. None of it was about me."

There was no response, of course. Kendall picked up one limp hand tentatively, then put it down again. It felt like the kittens the Lippon cat had had too early, cold little bundles of skin and bone too weak to live.

"A hair's-breath from death, and you're still trying to get your way. Bossy to the end." Kendall wiped at her face again impatiently. "Don't you understand? You mixed yourself up in everyone's lives. Made yourself important to them. It's not fair if you just go and die after all that."

Probably it was a good thing that everyone showed up then. Everyone in the form of Lieutenant Danress and three other Sentene mages, most of them battered around the edges. A tiny, grey-haired lady followed them in, Sebastian tagging at her elbow, with two of the healer's assistants trailing them all, fussing away.

"If you would just wait until Magister Sorathar returns," burbled one of the assistants. "I am sure she will–"

"–agree that familiar surroundings will soothe Lady Rennyn," said the old lady, who looked like she was enjoying herself. "Even the smallest factor could make the difference to her survival."

"But to move her–"

"A delicate business, I agree," said the old lady cheerfully. "We'd best get it over with quickly."

While she'd been speaking, the Sentene had opened out a canvas stretcher, and used the sheet from the bed to transfer Rennyn. She'd been put into some kind of half-tied robe, giving a clear view of bruises and bandaging all down her front, but Sebastian was quick to cover her properly with a blanket. They were out the door before the assistants had done more than flap a few times and send someone running for their mistress.

The old lady giggled like a girl as soon as they were safely out in the corridor. "This is the first time I've had to resort to kidnapping a patient. Sorathar will be livid."

"Thank you for helping, Magister Arandal," Sebastian said. "I didn't mean to make trouble for you."

"Not at all. Sorathar does consider the upper nobility her due, but the Lady Rennyn was originally my patient. The Surclere title makes little difference."

Sebastian gave the old healer a sharp look, but didn't act surprised. "They figured that out, did they?"

"Ah, you knew, then?"

"Of course. Tiandel wasn't the sort who'd give up all his titles. He had it set that he'd come back to resume Surclere once Solace was dealt with, but of course that never happened. Ren was hoping that the King's copy of the arrangement had been lost. Being a

Duchess doesn't suit her plan to do absolutely nothing responsible or resembling work."

Duchess of Surclere. Fitting another name to Rennyn's place in the world didn't put any colour back in her cheeks. Having some title wasn't going to fix her.

The first thing Kendall saw when they reached the Halls of Magic was Lieutenant Faral. The Kellian woman had surely been told at least part of Sebastian's explanation, but whether she was upset about it was impossible to guess. She just nodded and led the way into the infirmary. A lot of the beds were in use. The Sentene and Ferumguard had taken too many casualties the past week. Even though it was nearly dawn, most of them were awake, and watched through the open doors of the small rooms as Rennyn was carried past. Kendall thought she saw Sukata, but they passed on to a room where only three of the beds had occupants, and settled Rennyn in the last. Everyone stepped back as if expecting her to suddenly be better, except the old healer, who began chalking on her slate.

"Are you certain about this Keste?" Lieutenant Danress asked, looking doubtfully at the bed next to Rennyn's. Captain Faille lay there, as grim in sleep as waking.

"Illidian told us early on that we could not depend on his evaluation of Lady Rennyn," Lieutenant Faral said. "We were sorry for him. But glad it proved not such a hopeless case after all."

Lieutenant Danress looked about as disbelieving as Kendall felt. Rennyn and Captain Faille? When? They'd never so much as given each other a warm glance.

Not bothered by the general air of disbelief, Lieutenant Faral adjusted the blanket covering Rennyn. "Magister, do you not think it wiser to lift this casting? By fighting it she is doing worse damage to herself than anything she could manage moving about."

The old lady must have agreed, because she finished writing up her slate, put some power into it, and immediately Rennyn began to shift about.

"I've removed the sleep and some of the pain suppressants, though I dare not lift them all," said the healer. "A delicate matter, because she is obviously resisting anything cast on her. She may dispel the caulding as well, putting her lung at risk of another collapse. We can hope that even a partial consciousness will keep her from casting."

Almost as if she'd heard, Rennyn shifted again. Her glazed and feverish gaze swept the ceiling, and she began the futile struggle to sit up.

"Ren?" Sebastian caught her shoulder, then touched the unbruised side of her face, turning her head a little toward him. "They're alive. They survived it." He stepped aside so she could see past him to Captain Faille, still but breathing. "They're just sleeping."

Rennyn didn't respond, and Kendall couldn't tell if she'd even understood, but she did seem to be looking at Captain Faille. She closed her eyes, and everyone held their breath, then let it out when she didn't shift again.

"She wanted to know if they were alive," Sebastian said, and shook his head. "That's all."

The old lady healer laughed. "Well, she's had her way. Now let's leave her to rest, a thing I'm sure all of us need. It's over. Go to bed, the lot of you."

Dismissed, they shuffled off, the healer giving Sebastian an extra prodding when he looked like he wanted to stay.

Over. Done with. Finished. Just pieces to be picked up and tidied away. Kendall thought about just what those words meant as she went back to the room where she'd seen Sukata. Dawn was creeping through the window, giving the figures in the beds a milky sheen. She listened to them breathe, slow, deep and reassuring.

"At some point during all that, did you happen to save my life?"

Kendall glanced over her shoulder at Sebastian. "You notice a lot more than you make out."

He shrugged. "I saw the movement, but I wasn't giving it a lot of attention. Thank you. Not only would I have hated to die right at the end, but if he'd killed both of us, our Great-Uncle would have control of the Kellian. His own private army."

"I don't think he was particularly keen on killing you," Kendall gave Sukata one last glance then started out for the Arkathan. "Or not Rennyn, anyway. He wasn't trying very hard."

"I guess not." She'd made Sebastian worried, and he shifted subjects probably so he didn't have to think about what the demon had planned to do to his sister. "Are you going to stay?"

"The Arkathan's not my idea of worthwhile."

"No. With Rennyn. You're her student now, remember?"

"That wasn't real."

"Since when?"

"It was just something for her to do so she didn't have to think about how bad she felt."

"So you're saying you didn't learn anything?"

Kendall gave him an exasperated look. "No."

"Don't have anything more to learn from her?"

"Don't be stupid."

"Then you're staying," he said as if it was settled, and added helpfully, "You can still pretend you don't like her," then laughed at the expression on her face.

"You're just as full of yourself as she is."

"Probably." Sebastian was inexplicably pleased.

Hunching her shoulders, Kendall looked up at the jagged wreckage in the middle of the Arkathan and then headed through the nearest door. "Do you believe Rennyn likes Captain Faille?"

"Who knows? The most she ever said about him to me was that he was dangerously intelligent. And I would have thought any kind of relationship with a Kellian was out of the question, that our inheritance of control would make us completely intolerable. But Lieutenant Faral wasn't even surprised when I asked. None of the Sentene mages knew, but it looks like all the Kellian did. She said they were glad. Glad. Faral acted like she still was, didn't she?"

"I guess. What she told them gave them the horrors, and I don't see any chance that that'll change, but they didn't blame it on Rennyn. Maybe they won't want to have much to do with her, but do you think it likely they'd hate her for saving them?"

"No." Sebastian breathed the word, then shook his head to banish whatever thought lay behind it. As they reached the dormitory he looked around as if he hadn't realised where they were walking.

"Goodnight," Kendall said pointedly

He smiled. "I don't think I have a hope of sleeping. But I'll leave you to try. Thank you again. And, Kendall—"

"What?"

"It's not that Ren needs students, or probably even wants them, but she likes you and so there's a place for you if you want to be taught. All you have to do is decide whether you want that."

A place for her. Kendall thought about it for a long time after, and decided that Sebastian was definitely as annoying as his sister.

TWENTY-SEVEN

T he wrongness of the empty bed filtered through layers of cloth and wool. Looking at it brought Rennyn a tidal surge of panic, slow and overwhelming. It should not be empty.

A touch on her shoulder broke into the suffocating waves, and she managed to turn her head, then let out her breath. Illidian.

"Hello," she said, or tried to. The tiny croaking noise she managed was lost in the dry cough that followed it, and then the pain which overwhelmed everything. The itching of her throat was overwhelmed by the need to not breathe, to prevent the agony of coughing. Her chest stabbed at her, her face ached alarmingly and the rest of her made muffled suggestions that all was not well.

A glass was pressed to her lips, and Illidian's hand curled behind her head, lifting her enough so that she could swallow. Honey water. The itching faded, but the pain blocked everything out, and she closed her eyes again.

The light had changed when she next looked. All shadows and glowlight instead of sunshine. This time she was facing the right direction, and could see Illidian. Long form balanced on a small chair, he was reading a book held loosely in one hand. He was here, with her.

The instinct which served him so unerringly brought his eyes to hers, and in that intent, searching look she found an echo of her own questions. But drawing a breath brought back a memory of dire consequences and she stopped any words. Illidian immediately turned and picked up a glass. Diluted apple juice this time, which she could feel all the way down her throat to a hollow stomach. Swallowing it made her realise her weakness. Without Illidian's help she wouldn't even be able to lift her head.

He propped two pillows behind her, moving her with infinite care while she catalogued the failings of her body. She was still a roiling mass of hurt, but there was a casting which turned a thousand alarms into a little list she could review without flinching. Other spells seemed to be holding bits of her in place. Bruises everywhere.

"I dreamed that I'd killed you," she said, her voice small and worn, but working this time.

"No."

Even more uncommunicative than usual. She gazed up at this man who had so unexpectedly become central to her world, who she had used as a weapon, who had every reason to want to be as far from her as possible. It had astonished her beyond words when he'd been able to step across the chasm of her control, but that divide would always be at his back, dragging him away. And that even before the final lies, before she'd nearly killed him.

He was watching her steadily, but she could not see the distance she had dreaded.

"Are you angry?"

"For the deception?" His gaze shifted from her face, and she felt a moment's terror, but then he curled his hands through hers and leaned over her, pressing his cheek against the undamaged side of her face. As close to an embrace as he could manage without hurting her. "I am not such a fool." The words, breathed into her ear, were accompanied by a tremor which ran through both their hands.

Rennyn closed her eyes. She hadn't pushed him beyond endurance. The tangle of lies were so much what she suspected he would despise, yet he did not hate her for them.

But his hands. She managed to tilt her head to look at them as he straightened, the fingers long and tapering and blunted. He'd trimmed the nails. Both hands.

"For always?"

"I don't know."

She curled her fingers further around his, unable to completely hide her distress. He might have chosen to be here with her, but he

241

was fantastically upset. None of the Kellian trimmed both of their hands: it would be a denial of their selves.

Exhaustion was blurring thought. She had let his hands drop without realising it, and when she tried to lift her head further she couldn't manage it and realised he'd moved, that she'd been asleep again. Not so long this time, for it was still dark and he was sitting holding her nearest hand between both of his, face meditative.

"I don't think I'm going to like being kitten-weak," she said.

"No."

The certainty of his agreement made her laugh, and laughing made the world turn black with dancing white spots. She stopped.

"We are all adjusting," he said. The words were quiet, but the lines on either side of his mouth had deepened during her small episode, and his grip on her hand had briefly tightened to steel. Illidian wasn't going to enjoy her recovery either.

"Seb?" she asked, when she could. Her voice worked better this time.

"Uninjured. Sleeping."

A small part of her relaxed, enough that she could ask: "My Wicked Uncle?"

"No trace."

He was less than pleased about that. She wondered incuriously how much time had passed, and drank some more of the juice Illidian had ready, feeling markedly better for it.

"Are the Kellian confined to barracks again?"

"No. At the moment there is too much which needs doing."

The words were full of the knowledge that while the Kellian were spared imprisonment because of their usefulness, the Sentene uniform would no longer deflect attention now that the people of Tyrland had been given a demonstration of how dangerous they could be. Their future would not be simple.

He rubbed the ball of his thumb around the palm of her hand, soothing. "The Court officials have tentatively scheduled your annunciation as Duchess of Surclere. Two months from now."

"Bah."

"You had not intended to make the arrangement known?"

The neutrality of the question made her remember Lady Weston on the subject of Kellian offering their opinion. Rennyn had no doubt about the depth of what was between herself and Illidian Faille, for all that there would always be barriers to overcome. And Illidian changed everything. All those plans to have no plans, to please only herself, to not be weighed down by any more grand responsibilities.

"I have always enjoyed visiting Surclere," she said slowly.

"I saw that."

"We walked through the field where the Kellian were created."

His eyes narrowed. "It is not a lack of connection with Surclere which makes you reluctant."

A neat side-step of the importance of Surclere to his people. It was home to her family, but the birthplace of the Kellian race. And loving Illidian meant no longer pretending she was not involved in the issues surrounding the Kellian.

"A voice on the Council." She considered the tedium involved, then said in weary half-sentences: "Hardly likely discovered those records just tonight. Known of Tiandel's arrangement for weeks, but held off until saw whether Seb or I survived? Suppose the Queen considers it a means control me. Seen enough of me to know would take an oath seriously."

"You don't want to give it."

She tried to shrug, which didn't really work, and she blinked hard at all the different parts of her which protested. "To someone who treats those who protect her with such bare tolerance? No, I don't want to swear an oath to her."

"But you are going to."

He read her so well. "I think I'm talking myself into it. Because I want Surclere. Because I—" She flushed and that made her dizzy. "Because I want you. Because it would be useful. Would you rather I didn't?"

"I see the value in it." He didn't sound entirely convinced, and diverted her attention by touching a hand to her forehead. "It's not something for now. Go to sleep. I will be here when you wake."

"I know," she said, and marvelled at the certainty of her words, along with the thread of fear which underlay them. "I don't think I can stand you not to be," she admitted. "Not yet. I never imagined being so consumed by anyone. Can – can we be this?"

He was slow to answer, finally saying: "There is no value pretending that I won't struggle with what you can do. But I have a sense of rightness with you which has nothing to do with your heritage." His fingers brushed her forehead again. "We already are this. I will not run from it."

He was going to make her cry. But a particularly tiresome possibility had occurred to her. "Can we get married? Soon?" She wished she was strong enough to do anything, to be able to hold him as she wanted. To lift her head.

"When would you like to hold the ceremony?" he asked, obligingly.

"Tomorrow."

"Perhaps better when you are capable of standing through the vows."

Kellian laughed with their eyes. She was fascinated that she could see how obviously happy she'd made him, for all his expression barely changed. He touched the side of her face that didn't hurt, and she could feel that quiver in him again. He could not have told her more clearly that he wanted her.

"Prince Justin seems an inoffensive sort of creature," she said, wishing the thought hadn't occurred to her.

Illidian didn't even blink at the apparent change of subject. "I've heard no harm of him."

"Nor I. Still, I'd like to limit the amount of time people have to realise how convenient it would be if I married him."

It hadn't occurred to Illidian. He froze, then turned slightly away from her, taking a breath. She could see the veins stand out in his throat. Illidian's opinion of the Queen obviously matched Rennyn's own: a pragmatic woman.

But he recovered with the next breath, saying matter-of-factly, "When you are able to stay awake through the ceremony, then," while his hands closed possessively over hers again.

Rennyn curled her fingers through his, reassured. Forewarned, he would arrange everything. Not perhaps the most romantic setting, but she preferred it to facing the threat Prince Justin posed.

Since Illidian still wanted her, she'd be damned if she'd let political expediency get in the way.

So a marriage. And playing teacher to Seb and Kendall and Sukata. Hunting her Wicked Uncle and defending the Kellian and fixing up Surclere. So much to do, with little room for the sloth she'd long planned.

"I would have been bored, anyway," she murmured, and slept.

www.ingramcontent.com/pod-product-compliance
Lightning Source LLC
Chambersburg PA
CBHW071147170626
46809CB00002B/805